Acknowledgments

This novel wouldn't be possible without the many amazing people in my life. To my partner, Kael, thank you for supporting my dreams and listening to me ramble at all hours of the day. Thank you for always believing in me and never brushing off my ideas. This novel has been at the forefront of our lives for the last few months, and it wouldn't have happened without you. To my girls, I hope I make you proud. To my friends that have turned into family, Maggie and Iris, you not only loved these characters, but you also understood them. Additionally, thank you for your help in bringing Callum and Scarlett to life in the best ways. To my sister, Faith, thank you for always providing your input, even though you don't like anything dark or twisty, you made an exception for me. And to my mom, thank you for knowing that this was my path and for encouraging it endlessly. Thank you to the rest of my family, friends, and those who were always there to support and uplift me. To my beta readers, graphic designer, and editor, Julia, none of this would've been possible without you all.

Copyright © 2025 by Cassy Vincent

All rights reserved. No part of this publication may be reproduced, stored or transmitted in any form or by any means, electronic, mechanical, photocopying, recording, scanning, or otherwise without written permission from the publisher. It is illegal to copy this book, post it to a website, or distribute it by any other means without permission.

This novel is entirely a work of fiction. The names, characters and incidents portrayed in it are the work of the author's imagination. Any resemblance to actual persons, living or dead, events or localities is entirely coincidental.

Designations used by companies to distinguish their products are often claimed as trademarks. All brand names and product names used in this book and on its cover are trade names, service marks, trademarks and registered trademarks of their respective owners. The publishers and the book are not associated with any product or vendor mentioned in this book. None of the companies referenced within the book have endorsed the book.

First edition: October 2025

978-1-0696723-0-8(Paperback)

978-1-0696723-1-5(EBook)

I crave the darkness in you, for it is where I feel the most alive.

   -RIYA BHOKAR

Trigger Warnings

Dear Reader,

This novel contains mature and potentially distressing content that may be triggering. Themes include:

- Violence and physical assault
- Graphic sexual content, including emotionally intense scenes
- Substance use
- Emotional manipulation and psychological distress
- Mentions of past sexual trauma
- Sexual assault
- Possession
- Stalking
- Death
- Praise kink
- Bondage
- References to sex work and exploitation

Your mental health matters. If any of these themes are difficult for you, please proceed with caution.

That said, if you're into morally grey men, dangerous secrets, and the kind of tension that burns slow then scorches, you're in the right place.

Don't say I didn't warn you. Buckle up.

Cass. XO

Table of Contents

Prologue
1- Avoidance
2- Sweet Science
3- Debt
4- Sparring
5- Clean Up
6- Trash
7- Looking Back at Me
8- Untouchable
9- Fighting Demons
10- The Boxer
11- Holding my Breath
12- Liability
13- Bloody Knuckles
14- The Bomb
15- Fire
16- Lift. Your. Fucking. Hips
17- Burning
18- Forgotten Roses
19- Clarity
20- Bliss
21- Challenge Accepted
22- Watching From the Shadows
23- Explosion
24- Protection
25- Sympathy
26- Ricochet
27- Selling Your Soul
28- Silent Gestures
29- Protection
30- Emotional Confessions
31- Times are Changing
32- Things Left Unsaid
33- Signed, Sealed, Delivered
34- Secrets
35- Beneath the Surface
36- Familiar Fries

37- Glove Boxes
38- Trauma
39- What Money Can't Buy
40- That Night
41- Garbage Day
42- Strength in Tears
43- Confrontational Fathers
44- Better Left Unsaid
45- Panic
46- Eternity
47- Betrayal
48- Lake House
49- Becoming the Fire
50- Grenade
51- Quietly Suffocating
52- Keep Your Enemies Closer
Epilogue
About the Author

Scan the QR code to listen to the playlist that was there every step of the way, enjoy!

For Granny.
The strongest fighter I know.

Prologue

Four Years Earlier

Scarlett

When I was around four years old, I would always ask my dad to check under the bed and in my closet for monsters before I went to sleep. We'd laugh as he'd lift the covers off the ground and say, "none under here honey." As I grew up, I realized that the monsters that would scare me most are already in my life, disguised as people that I should trust.

I've always been a homebody, so a house party on a Thursday night is the last place I want to be seen. My best friend, Sophia, basically dragged me out of the house to come. And on top of that, I'm wearing too much eyeliner. The burgundy colour she put on my eyelids helps to make my green eyes pop. Sophia is naturally bossy. After all, she's the daughter of a lawyer and the captain of a cheerleading squad.

I make my way into the marble lined kitchen to get a drink. The heavy bass drums out of the speakers and runs through my body. There are so many people here, and I don't know most of them. We only started classes at Langford University a couple of weeks ago, and the transition from our small local high school to an ivy league university has been tough. I'm completing my undergrad in psychology—I doubt I'll see any of my classmates here. Even if I do, I'm not very social.

Of course, Sophia brings me here and leaves me to fend for myself. *I need to find her.* I push through the crowd and see her standing by the pool outside. Her hot pink bikini pokes through her translucent white cover up, showing off her long, tan legs.

"Sophia!" I yell.

She tilts her head back with a drink in her hand and laughs, clearly flirting with the captain of the football team. I chuckle to myself—*of course she is.*

"Dammit Sophia, you told me we could leave after an hour, it's been almost two." I'm glad one of us is enjoying ourselves.

"Chill out, Scarlett." She laughs and takes another sip of her drink.

I sigh and sit on a wet pool chair. My ass gets slightly damp—now I'm both cold and miserable. I lean back against the chair's cheap plastic and close my eyes. The music gets louder. *I'll give her fifteen minutes, then we're gone.*

All I can smell around me is alcohol—it feels like poison seeping into my skin. I cross my legs and try to relax for a few minutes.

I scan the area to see if I know anyone. Someone catches my eye. He leans against the pool shed and stares directly at me. His icy blue eyes pull me in. I get lost in them and am unable to look away. He's not just looking *at* me, he's studying me. I continue to watch him. He takes a swig of his drink—it's controlled and precise. I notice his dark hair and chiseled jaw.

When we break eye contact, my gaze instinctively drifts down his body. His broad shoulders are concealed by an expensive looking, plain black t-shirt. His dark green shorts accentuate his muscular legs. *Damn, that's a man if I've ever seen one.*

I look away, breaking the invisible bond between us. I hastily take a sip of my drink.

~~~~~~

I wake up, my head is pounding. The air is hot. My hair sticks to my face. I don't see anything around me that I recognize. I lie on a bed, the walls around me are a deep red. I pat my body down—thank God, my clothes are still on. As I sit up, my ears ring. There's a faint light in the corner of the room, and I spot a closed door. Tears roll down my cheeks. I pick my phone up from the floor then lunge for the door handle. My legs ache. *I don't remember coming here, where am I?*

I open the door, and I hear the same loud music from earlier. I'm still at the party... *I need to find Sophia.* I unlock my phone and call her. My hands shake and tears continue to flood my face as the panic settles in. *Come on, please pick up.* No answer.

I hesitate as I walk down the stairs, slowly finding my bearings. My feet feel unsteady, and my legs aren't responding as quickly when I move them.

There aren't as many people here now, and I don't recognize most of who is left standing in the kitchen. It's three thirty in the morning. The last thing I remember is sitting by the pool—it was just after eleven then.

Cold sweat covers my back and my chest heaves. I cover my mouth to muffle a cry.

Don't make a scene.

I finally spot Sophia sitting on the couch. She has a drink in her hand and looks exhausted.

Did she notice that I was gone? No, that doesn't matter... we just need to leave.

As I approach her, the motion makes my stomach swirl. I think I might puke.

Sophia looks up at me.

"Scarlett, what's wrong? Are you okay?"

She stands and steps toward me, grabbing my arm.

"Sophia, we have to go now."

She blinks slowly, taking in my words. Clearly, she's tipsy.

"Where have you been?"

"Soph, I–" I stutter, not sure what I'm saying. Tears start to flow down my cheeks again. "I think someone- I, um, I think someone put something into my drink." I look at the floor and hope no one else hears me.

Sophia immediately sobers up and fear flashes in her eyes.

"Okay, let's go, now."

She grabs her purse off the couch and doesn't let go of my arm. Holding my hand, she leads us out of the house.

Once we step outside, Sophia hugs me tight. I gasp, finally catching my breath as cold air hits my lungs. Sophia unlocks her car, helps me into the passenger seat, then steps around to the driver's side. Once she's in her car she locks the doors then faces me, her eyes squinting as she holds back tears.

"Scar, I'm so sorry," she says, "Who do you think it was? Who were you with last? This is so fucked. Were you hurt? Do you remember anything?" I don't respond. I don't have any answers.

"Soph, you can't drive." I point out as she starts the car.

"I know, I just want to warm you up, you're freezing." She pulls out her phone. "I'm calling Stirling."

Stirling isn't a good friend of mine, but if Sophia trusts him, then I will too.

"I need you to come get us." Her voice is stern. "No, not your driver Stirling, *you*." Her eyes are full of so much left unsaid. "Okay, yeah I'll send you my location, but hurry up." She ends the call.

We spend the next fifteen minutes trying to recall what happened.

All we can piece together is that Sophia last saw me by the pool. I was sipping the only drink I had all night, and then I told her I was moving inside. She told me that one of the girls in the house saw me go upstairs, and Sophia said she looked for me but couldn't find me. She called me three times.

"I shouldn't have stopped looking for you." She stares out the window. I hate that she feels guilty. Finally, Stirling pulls up in his blacked-out sports car.

"Please, don't do that Soph, you didn't know." I say as we walk toward his car.

"Get in." She motions with her head toward the back seat.

I slide in and curl against the door.

Sophia gets into the front and slams the door harder than necessary.

"My house."

The ride is quiet. Stirling doesn't push conversation—I'm sure he can sense the tension. I lean my head against the window's cool glass and suppress another cry as the engine hums. Outside, the streetlights flash past. I squeeze my fingers together and don't say a word.

This night feels surreal.

Every inch of my body aches. As tears finally fall, humiliation washes over me, and my eyes burn. Through the window, the night blurs.

I wonder if I'll ever feel whole again.

Avoidance

Scarlett

I step into Dad's auto repair shop and get hit with the smell of motor oil and hot metal, it's pure bliss. These scents, along with the taste of Sour Patch Kids, can instantly cure my anxiety better than deep breathing ever could.

I see my dad, Jake Voss, bent over and elbow deep in the hood of a beat-up Camaro.

"Hey, Kiddo." He emerges from the front of the car with grease on his cheek and a smile on his face.

I walk across to the old fridge in the corner and pull out a grape Crush.

"Hey, Daddio."

"I didn't think I'd see you this early," he says as he dives back into the car's engine.

I lean against its fender and watch him pull at the engine's wiring harness.

Dad is the hardest working man I know. He's the type of guy that would give you the shirt off his back, a shoulder to cry on, and an ear to listen. When I was a kid, he never missed any of my dance recitals and he taught me how to ride a bike—that's always an important one for some reason. No one ever asks who taught me the real things in life. Who handled the sex talk? Who was there when you were failing math because you talked too much? Those are the really important ones... but the answer is still him. It's always him.

"I always say hi when I get home from school," I respond.

"Yeah, but I thought you were going to the gym tonight?" He faces me, confused.

"Not tonight, I went this morning instead."

He scowls, his greying eyebrows almost touch. "You don't usually go in the morning."

There's no point in hiding anything from him because he figures everything out sooner or later.

"I couldn't sleep, and Ricco is always there in the morning, so I knew he'd be around."

Dad snorts.

"How is Rocky doing?" God, I can never tell Ricco that Dad still calls him that. He would love it too much.

"Do not call him that."

"What, it's funny."

I chuckle and roll my eyes, shifting my weight off the car. "It was funny when you said it eight years ago, Dad."

It still is funny, but I don't tell him that. I walk across the garage and toward the house.

"I'm going inside to start some research for a paper. Anything planned for dinner?" It's Wednesday, so I'm thinking leftovers.

"Leftovers?" He adjusts a bolt with his wrench.

"Sounds good." I make my way to the door. "Need anything before I head upstairs?"

He resurfaces. "Yeah, call your mom, Scar."

I shrug and take a sip of my pop. I don't answer.

"She just wants to hear your voice."

Vanessa Voss—the beautiful and chaotic spitfire that is my mother.

"Yeah, okay Dad." I open the door and make my way through to the kitchen.

Of course, Mom probably told him that I haven't been over to visit lately. I'll never understand how he still loves her after all they've been through. Mom left us for the luxurious life of take-out dinners and a clear schedule. She picks up shifts at The Yacht Club Steakhouse whenever she wants. As I've transitioned from an angry teen to a mature(ish) adult, I've tried to understand why she left, but I still can't wrap my head around it. I pull a chair out from under the kitchen table and grab my phone from my back pocket. I scroll to find my conversation with Mom. I don't feel like talking to her right now, but I'll do it for Dad.

    Scarlett: Hey Mom, it's me. The daughter you are SO proud of but don't talk to.

Delete.

    Scarlett: Hey Mom. What's up?

Send.

I stand and make my way to my room. Our house is nothing fancy, but it's home. Its stone base compliments the natural wood tones that outline the windows. It doesn't look like the typical big city house, but here in Millhaven, it feels right. Besides the gym, it's the only place where I truly feel like myself.

While most people resort to journals or therapists, I box and listen to a playlist that could drown out just about anything. Putting my gloves on brings me a sense of calm, followed by a rush of control I don't feel anywhere else.

I'm never fully angry, just near my limit. I carry around so many different versions of myself and I'm not sure which one fits best. I'm the quiet girl, daddy's girl, the girl who doesn't call her mom back. I'm the boxer who looks out of place, a star student, a psych major. There is a saying that people who study psychology want to help others. Maybe we're just desperate to understand ourselves? I definitely am.

I step into my room and switch the light on. Flopping into my desk chair, I pull out my laptop. I have two papers due next week, so I push down all my distracting feelings and save them for another day. My brain is sort of like a filing cabinet of emotions—I don't open it unless I have to. And if I can't quiet my mind on my own, I throw some punches at the gym until the noise dies down.

The rest of the evening plays out like a typical Wednesday night. We eat leftovers, Dad tells me about the car in the shop, he asks me about school, then tells me how proud he is of me.

I make my way upstairs to shower and get ready for bed, undecided if I want to go to the gym in the morning to get a few rounds in before class, or if I want to wait until the afternoon. I pack my bag anyways, just in case. As I climb into bed, I check my phone and see that Sophia texted me.

>**Sophia:** Still good to come to the senior party with me at the end of the month?
>
>**Scarlett**: Yeah!
>
>**Sophia**: You need to wear those new jeans and that black top that make guys forget how to speak.
>
>**Scarlett:** You're insane.
>
>**Sophia:** And you love me anyways.
>
>**Scarlett:** Unfortunately <3
>
>**Scarlett:** Goodnight xoxo

Ever since that night from first year, Sophia always checks in multiple times before a party, in case I change my mind. I have other friends, but we don't see each other much, and I'm content with life this way. Over the last four years, a lot has changed, and I've grown apart from many friends that used to feel like home. While I stayed in Millhaven, most of my other high school friends moved on to universities out of town. It's hard to maintain friendships with people when I've always got so much on the go. We're all busy and don't stay in touch often, but we know we can rely on each other. It's the kind of friendships where we could go months without talking but can pick right up where we left off. I also don't make new friends easily and there aren't many people I can relate to in my program. I think about Sophia and smile. I'm glad to have a friend like her.

    I turn my phone on 'do not disturb' and place it on the nightstand. I lie in the darkness that fills my room. The world silences around me but my mind never does. There's always something just beneath my surface— memories I haven't dealt with, questions I haven't asked, or a hope for change that may never come.

    A shift is coming. I don't know what it is yet, but I can feel it, just out of reach.

Sweet Science

Scarlett

8:23 a.m.

I squint my eyes to see the bold red numbers on my bedside clock. *Shit.* I slept in.

"Ugh." I roll over and climb out of bed. I stumble across the hall into the bathroom and pull my hair half up, not bothering to brush it. I've always had Dad's hair, light brown and coarse, Mom has long, beautiful blonde hair. While it's not all natural, its honey colour shines through no matter how much she tries to cover it. As I finish getting ready, I try not to think about her. The house feels emptier without her, like it's faded over time, but I know that's a void that I can never fill.

I rush downstairs to see Dad before I take off for the day. He's in the kitchen reading the paper with a mug of black coffee in his grease-stained hand.

"Morning, Dad." I bend down and give him a kiss on the cheek before pouring a coffee for myself.

"Morning, you must've slept in. I wasn't sure if you were going to the gym?" He looks to me and scrunches his face.

"I was going to get up and go before class, but I must have missed my alarm. I'll go tonight." I plop a piece of bread in the toaster and force it up before it has a chance to pop out.

"Sorry, I'm in a rush! Love you, Daddio." I grab my coffee and head toward the door.

"Love you, Kiddo." He takes another sip and goes back to his reading.

I walk out to my 2003 BMW X3 in our driveway and scramble to find the keys in my bag. This car has seen me through all my good and bad days. She's not new or subtle, but she runs smooth and smells like motor oil and coconut. She likely has more of Dad's fingerprints on her than mine, but she's still in good hands.

I veer into my usual spot close to campus and grab my coffee and bag before I make my way to class. I hurry toward the health science building— I have two lectures there today. The crisp fall breeze is strong enough to push my hair away from my neck but not cool enough to give me a chill.

Everyone rushes by in a hurry. It's still early in the school year, and a lot of students are still figuring out where to go. Something about all the new people gets me curious. Why are they here? What's their story? We all have one to tell.

Langford University is beautiful at this time of the year. The older stone buildings covered in vine look like they belong in a storybook, but only on the sunny days. On rainy days, each building seems dreary, dark, and mysterious.

Some of the students here also have the same cold feel to them.

I knew before I came here that a lot of rich kids attended Langford, but until I started, I didn't have a clue just how many there *actually* were. I'm nothing like them. Without my scholarship, I wouldn't be here, and I have to work my ass off to keep it. My grades have to be top notch, and after four years of ass-kissing, it's become more difficult to keep up. I've earned enough respect from my professors to know that using flattery to get ahead won't work. Besides, I've had too much noise in my own head to care. Maybe it's harder to fit in when you know you don't belong.

I sit in the middle of the lecture hall in my Early Development psych class. It's late in the afternoon. I tap my pen against a notebook, not because I'm bored, but because the professor has already given away his theory.

Professor Shane Elliot paces in front of the board.

"So, let's build off Bowlby's attachment theory and explore how early caregiver relationships might influence adult romantic attachments, particularly in the context of emotion regulation."

He looks around and everyone avoids eye contact. No one rushes to answer. The room is silent.

I raise my hand. "Anxious or avoidant attachment styles don't just show up, they're survival strategies. If comfort wasn't reliable as a child, then intimacy as an adult can feel like a threat, not a reward. It's neurological and not necessarily behavioural."

Professor Elliot leans against the podium and crosses his arms. "Exactly, well said Scarlett." He pauses and scans the room, then looks down at his watch. "And that's the end of the lesson. Make sure to do your readings and be prepared to discuss them next week."

Everyone files out of class. I'm not in a hurry to fight the crowds, so I take my time. Over the last four years, I've learned a lot and caught on to the ebb and flow of the school.

"Scarlett." I look up to Professor Elliot in front of me. "I just wanted to say, your insight there was sharp. You've got a gift for cutting through the noise."

I shrug and softly smile. "It's something that comes naturally to me I guess."

He nods. "Keep speaking up. You're perceptive."

Professor Elliot turns and walks away. I watch him, my cheeks still red from his compliment. Finally, I snap out of it and pack my bag to head over to the library. Once I get there, most of the tables are full. This always happens at the beginning of every school year. Give it a few weeks and I'm sure everyone will be less invested in their studies.

I see an open spot at one of the large study tables. I know they are usually reserved for seminars, but there's no one here right now. I place my bag down on the light wood table and pull out the matching chair. Everything about Langford screams money—from the polished oak tables and chairs in the library, to the cast iron light posts outside.

Time slips away. I sit in the library an hour longer than I planned to. As I'm about to pack up my things, I notice someone walking in. It's not unusual for that to happen, *in the library*, but something about him makes the air shift.

I can tell that this man doesn't belong in a place that smells like old paper and lemon cleaner. He wears dark clothes, his face is unreadable. When he walks in, he doesn't scan the room, almost like he already knows what's coming next.

My eyes can't help but linger on him. For a second, sounds seem muffled, and it takes a moment to snap back to reality. I shake my head and ground myself, returning to the chatter of the library.

I make my way back to the car and head toward the gym. I can't help but think about the man from the library. I know I've seen him many times before. *Am I just noticing him now, or has he always been around this much?* He was definitely at that party four years ago, staring at me from beside the pool shed, but something about him has changed. He used to look like every other guy at school, unfazed and full of life. Now he looks aged, not in years but in the way he carries himself. It's like he's been fighting battles and keeping secrets that have slowly carved away pieces of him—ones that will never return.

I get lost in my usual pump-up music that ranges from Beyoncé to The White Stripes. When I arrive at the gym, I'm greeted by the smell of sweat and broken dreams.

I open my locker and place my runners and gloves on the bench behind it. Before I shut the rusty door, I pause to look at the pictures hanging inside. There's one of Dad and me in the garage. Another of us from a camping trip. Below them are two snapshots of me and Sophia, mid laugh, frozen in what was probably something stupid that we thought was hilarious. The pictures remind me of the times when Dad tried so hard to fill the broken pieces that Mom left shattered.

I stare at his face for a moment longer. *He's aged so much since then.* Within the first few years after she left, we spent more time together than ever before. Instead of pulling away and closing each other off, we leaned on one another. We didn't talk about the family stuff much, but he always kept me busy. We went camping whenever we could. Even though Dad wasn't much of a fire starter, we always got to the s'mores by the end of every trip. If he had too much work to get done after being away from the shop for the weekend, he'd ask for my help. He never wanted me left alone, and part of me thinks he didn't want to be alone either.

I tie my shoes and slip my mouth guard into the top of my sports bra. I climb through the ropes that surround the ring. The canvas is rough under my shoes. Ricco stands in the corner, his arms crossed as he chews on a toothpick. He's sizing me up for a fight, not a lesson.

"You're late."

"Oh, you still love me." I tighten my glove.

"I love discipline and your left hook."

I smirk at him and roll my shoulders. "Flattery will get you nowhere old man."

He snorts. "Let's see if your punches can show up on time then." He steps toward me. I pop my mouth guard in and we touch gloves.

He's going to make me work for it.

The sting of my sweat burns my eyes and pools inside of my gloves. Ricco doesn't care, it never stops him.

"Keep that right arm up, Scar." He isn't even winded, and I call him an old man.

I grit my teeth as I try to reset my stance. My legs burn but I stay sharp. This is the only place where my thoughts don't crowd me.

Ricco ducks left then catches me with a body shot. I stumble back and almost lose my balance.

"You okay?" He comes in closer to me.

I nod and keep my jaw tight. "Keep going."

His eyes narrow before he strikes me again.

By the time we're done, my arms shake. As I remove my gloves, Ricco doesn't say much, he just taps my shoulder as he walks past me, out of the ring. I grab my water and sit on the edge. Silence settles in.

Today's session wasn't perfect, but it was progress, and that's good enough for now.

Debt

Callum

They say that legacy is an honour, but no one talks about what it's like to carry the burden of a name that you didn't ask for. Mine is a brand, burned into my skin.

I walk down the halls at Langford University to my Strategic Management class. I can't wait to finish this year. After I graduate with my business degree, I'm expected to work for my grandfather's tech company—another jail they can contain me in.

No one makes eye contact with me as I walk down the hall. Even if they wanted to, they know better. I've never felt the need to be liked but I've always known what it's like to be wanted. There's a difference—one's about control and the other is irrelevant.

My phone vibrates in the front pocket of my jeans.

"Yeah?" I answer.

"There's been a situation. We need you here."

I already know what's happened.

"I'm on my way."

I turn and walk toward my Jag instead. I don't care about grades, I care about understanding the game. The numbers, the power, the psychology behind the power—that's the only reason I'm here. Half of these kids are just learning how to play business, but I'm learning how to use it... how to control it.

The door unlocks as I pull the handle open to my car. It's the latest gift from my gracious father after I handled another one of The Society's problems. I grab a cigarette and press it between my lips. I hate smoking. Although I could quit anytime I want, today is not the day. I roll my window down and let the breeze roll over me as I flee from the parking lot.

Pebbles crush under the weight of my car as I slowly enter the driveway. I'm already frustrated before I enter the mansion.

As I stand at the dark red door, dread washes over me. This house was once so beautiful. Now, it's a place of secrets and sin.

I tread into the lounge upstairs, the tension is palpable. Deluca, one of the Highers, sits in a chair while everyone else stands. He looks annoyed.

"We've got a problem, Mercer," his words hold urgency. "A girl is in bad shape. One of the pledges got out of hand and she overdosed."

I sigh. They either want me to deal with the pledge, deal with the girl, or both.

"What do you need me to do?" A knot tightens in my stomach as I wait for the response.

"I need your help with the girl, we can talk about the rest after." He nods toward the back of the house and sips on his drink.

Of course, I'm the clean-up crew.

"She's in the back room."

I don't waste any time. I want to deal with this as quickly as possible and get out of here.

I open the door to the back room and see an unconscious girl. Her skin is pale against the dark wood floor. Her lips are blue. Women are discarded like objects in The Society. Only certain women are untouchable, and even then, I've seen boundaries tested.

As I get approach, I realize it's Emily Black. She was in a couple of my first and second year business classes. I've seen her at a few parties recently, and she was always quiet and shy. She doesn't deserve this—they never do.

I crouch to feel her neck. There's no pulse.

"Who did this?" I look back to a couple of the pledges, Josh and Kyle, who stand behind me in the doorway.

No answer.

"Get her the hell out of here. We don't need a scene. Her body can't be found."

Josh and Kyle move into action. One of them brings in a clear tarp, while the other brings tape and bleach.

"Take her to the basement." I search her for any personal belongings. Then, Kyle wraps her up and Josh throws her over his shoulder, like she doesn't weigh anything.

The estate used to be a funeral parlour. In other words, it was part of a front and The Society only allow the wealthy and powerful to step foot inside. Now, there's a crematory in the basement for when things like this happen.

My jaw tightens as they take her downstairs. I head toward the parlour. This wasn't an accident. It's a sign that things are slipping and order isn't being followed. I won't stand for it.

I barge through the door and see Deluca, still sitting in the chair.

"Who was it?" My tone is flat and cold.

He doesn't say anything but his eyes flash to Jasper, a second-year pledge.

"It's just a fucking game, Callum. She knew what she was getting into. No need to do anything stupid." His words are loud and sloppy.

"Shut. The. Fuck. Up." The room is dead quiet. All eyes are on me.

Jasper opens his mouth to speak but I beat him to it.

"You don't talk about women like that, you don't talk about The Society like that, and you sure as hell never let things get this far."

Just looking at him fills me with rage. This is why Deluca called me.

I grab Jasper's collar with my hands and shove him. He stumbles and falls against the floor. Before he can move, I pin myself on top of him. My right fist meets his jaw, and I hit him in the face, again and again. I lift him up off the ground, just enough to slam him back down.

"Get your shit together. You want to play this game, you play it right. You don't make it personal, and you don't get sloppy."

I push myself off him and kick him in the ribs as I stand. I straighten my ironed shirt. No one moves. Jasper coughs and gasps for air. He doesn't look at me, but I stare straight into his eyes.

I have zero sympathy for him.

"Next time you forget your place, it will be worse. You won't get a second chance."

"Everyone out." Deluca drawls, unimpressed. "Callum, come have a drink." He motions at me with his glass.

I walk slowly over to the bar and pour myself some scotch. I take a few steps toward the bookshelf and lean against it, facing Deluca.

"He needed that," Deluca says, lifting his eyebrow.

I don't need a pat on the back. I chug my drink and put the glass down on the shelf.

"I'll go deal with the body."

I look up at him and wonder what made him so controlled, but I already know the answer—legacy, family, and expectations. Matthew Deluca has been in The Society for over ten years. He knows about earning respect and keeping order within The Society. He's an investment banker by day, and a cold-blooded monster by night.

I nod and hasten down the spiral staircase to the main floor. Thick red curtains fight to block light out as I head toward the back of the house, down another set of stairs. Guilt tries to creep in, but I force myself to block it out.

I turn the lights on and flick a switch to heat the oven. Emily's still body lies on a cold metal table. The sound of the furnace heating up hums in the background.

I need to do this. I check the temperature.

I open the door and slide the wheeled table in. The steel table scratches against the walls of the machine as I close the door.

My eyes are drawn to her through the small panel of glass, not able to look away as the fire clicks on. I stare at the flame and try not to think about my actions, because I know if I do, they will consume me. *This isn't justice, this is a crime.* My jaw tightens.

Heat surrounds me, but I don't flinch. It's muscle memory by now: load the body, turn the dial, walk away. But this time I can't leave.

There's no grief, just the hollow pain in my chest that's been there for years. This is the cost of silence, and the price of legacy. I accepted that debt a long time ago.

Minutes turn to hours. I stay until the fire finishes what I started. When there's nothing left, I finally walk away. I turn off the machine, head up the stairs, and flick off the lights.

Just another day.

Sparring

Scarlett

It's just after six in the morning and I've finally made it to the gym before the busy time. By seven, I know it will be packed.

I love the smell of metal and lemon cleaner. Before everyone gets in and ruins it with the stench of sweat and blood. I pull my wraps on as I climb into the ring. Ricco adjusts the pads on his hands.

"You're late," he says without looking at me.

"Oh stop, I'm early."

He grunts and steps into place. I know he's not a morning person, even after owning a gym that opens at five for the last twenty years.

"Let's see what you've got. Clock's ticking Scar."

I square up and start bouncing on the balls of my feet. My first jab hits his pad—it's sharp and clean. Ricco shifts and lines up for the next shot.

"Again."

I move through combinations as he calls them out. Sweat runs down my forehead and a warmth surrounds my muscles. I can't stop the clutter of thoughts from flooding my head. The decision of what to do after I graduate next year has been weighing on me. My mind clears a little bit more with every hit.

"Is this ballet, kid?" I know he's pushing me whenever he throws kid in there. "Hit like it matters."

"It always matters." I fire back without thinking. He drops his hands for a moment.

"Then show it." He lifts the pads back into position. I exhale and wipe my forehead with the back of my hand. We go again. Failure isn't an option. I strike at Ricco, my fists controlled but quick. Every punch I throw has purpose.

After a few more solid rounds, Ricco steps back.

"That's better. You're still in your head, but it's better," he says.

"You're so comforting." I roll my eyes.

"I'm not your therapist, Scarlett. I'm here to make sure you don't break." He grabs my shoulder and squeezes it. I smile at him. He's gotten me through more hard times than he'll ever know.

"Get out of here, you're going to be late for class," he chuckles.

I glance at the clock over the change room door. *Shit.* I jump through the ring ropes, head toward my locker, and grab my clothes to get ready for class.

"Same time tomorrow?" I yell over my shoulder at Ricco as I run out of the gym.

"I'll be here." He nods his head toward me.

I unlock the car and throw my bag in the back seat. As I slip behind the wheel and drive to school, my phone rings. I lift it to see who's calling.

Mom.

I don't have the energy for this. I decline the call. Two minutes later, my phone rings again.

Mom.

She's not giving up this morning. I might as well answer and say that I'm heading into class—an exit strategy.

"Hi Mom." My voice is flat.

"Hi baby. Oh Scarlett." I roll my eyes. "I miss you so much. When are you coming over?" Her questions are always so dramatic.

"I'm not sure right now, things are busy with school."

"You can only use that excuse so many times Scarlett." Her tone changes. "I live eight minutes from the school you know."

"I know Mom, I will try to pop by next week. I'm just pulling in. I'll talk to you later."

"Don't be a stranger, sweetheart. I'm your *mother*." I'm sure she meant the extra emphasis on the last word.

"I know Mom, bye, talk to you later."

"I love you so much honey."

"You too." I end the call and throw my phone on the passenger seat.

"Ugh!" There are no close spots and I'll have to book it across the parking lot.

Mom's voice triggered an anxiety I thought I wouldn't deal with today. I rush across campus as the weight in my chest turns into a dull ache. A mother is supposed to provide comfort, not agony. As I pick up speed, I fight the growing heaviness between my ribs.

I hope Professor Bugley didn't lock the door again, I can't afford to miss any more of this class. I quickly glide through the crowds in the hall, books in one arm and my laptop bag over the other. Just then, I slam into something hard, and my books hit the floor with a loud bang. *Him.* In shock, I feel a firm hand anchor my arm.

"Watch where you're going next time." His tone is low and annoyed. My gaze traces up his broad chest, from the expensive fabric of his jacket to the sharp lines of his jaw. *Callum Mercer.* His fingers dig into me as his hand remains wrapped around my arm, not hard enough to bruise, but strong enough to feel it. Sparks shoot through my skin like lightning.

He doesn't move.

"Sorry." I stare into his eyes as he lets go of my arm. Although his hand is no longer there, the area burns like he's left his mark on me. I bend over and pick up my books. He doesn't try and help. Instead, he just stands there and watches me struggle, like he's never helped anyone a day in his life. He doesn't say anything as I walk past, clutching my books tight.

"Dick," I whisper.

As I continue down the hall, I look back. He stands there and watches me, his face is flat and emotionless, like I'm his prey and he's prepared to hunt.

What the hell just happened.

I finally get to class and find an empty seat near the back. Professor Bugley faces the board and points at a graph on the screen. *Thank God she didn't notice me coming in late.* I open my laptop with shaky fingers and sigh. My cheeks burn, still flushed from my interaction with Callum.

Hours turn into minutes. Before I know it, class finishes, and I can't get out fast enough. I pace through the halls, hurry to my car, and throw my bag in the passenger seat.

It's only two in the afternoon and I'm exhausted. My bed is calling me—and so is Dad's lasagna from last night.

As I slowly back out of the parking spot, my eyes flicker to the rear-view mirror. A tall, distant figure steps into frame. My foot hovers over the brake. *Callum.*

His face is unreadable, and he clearly doesn't see me, but he has that same quiet intensity about him. He moves with precision, like he belongs in every room he walks into but despises his own presence.

He approaches his sleek black Jaguar XF and glances up as I slowly drive by. For a split second, our eyes lock.

I blink and my heart pounds against my ribs. Callum disappears into the driver's seat of his car, hiding behind the black tinted glass. There's a mysteriousness about him that I'm drawn to, something I've never noticed until now.

My fingers tingle against the steering wheel as I drive off. *What was it about this glance that keeps me thinking about him?* Although he only looked at me for a second, it feels like he's been watching me for much longer.

There's a part of me that itches to crack him open, and to figure out what makes his brain tick.

Clean Up

Callum

The smell of bleach lives on my hands no matter how many times I wash them. It's been a couple of weeks since the "accident" with Emily. I still can't believe they're calling it that. It was an overdose, or the wrong mix of drugs, or both. By the look I saw on Jasper's face, I know that what happened to Emily was a result of power and recklessness combined. The Society eats its own, and I cleaned up their mess like the good Mercer boy who chooses this burden.

I look up from my notebook, around at the classroom. We've done this case study twice now—either some of these students are stupid, or they just don't give a shit.

There's no protocol to follow when someone dies at the hands of The Society, but there is a rhythm to the silence after. Over time, I've learned to fall into it.

I scan the room and survey my peers. Half of the students aren't paying attention—they're playing on their phones or almost asleep. The other half are almost too engaged, they are the ones with high hopes that will be crushed the moment they step into their careers. Most of them have no clue that twice a week they sit in the same room as a killer, someone who hates the act but loves the release. Outside of school, they all go through life sipping expensive coffees and driving fancy cars because all they care about is fitting in and spending money. I've earned everything I have. I've put my time in with The Society.

It all started with selling drugs at parties—we all start that way. From there, I quickly became the drug runner and dealt with money, earning their trust.

My father always knew this was my path. He paved the way—I started the same way he did in The Society. He only had to put in a couple of years of grunt work before he climbed his way to the top and became our silent leader.

It wasn't long before my tasks turned from selling drugs to annihilating people with my fists. Not only does The Society supply drugs, they use them to sedate women and film as they violate them. They use masks and secret rooms so their identities are never revealed. You'd be surprised to know what kind of sick fucks love that.

I refuse to be a part of that horror—it's one thing they know they can't push onto me. They tried once, and the pledge who thought he had that kind of power over me has since relocated, six feet under.

"The most dangerous leaders are those who are born into power but are never taught to respect it."

Professor Blakeson catches my attention with his lecture.

"Legacy can be a weapon."

I'm intrigued, I look over at him.

I know that my family's legacy is ingrained in everything I do. Maybe his words are a coincidence, but they feel personal. My back shifts restlessly against the chair.

As the lecture finishes, I make my way across campus to my car. Rain starts to fall. People run to shelter to avoid the cool shower, but I'm in no rush. I sympathize with the rain. So many flee at the feel of a few drops, rejecting any chance of a down pour. Many also reject me. I smile at the comparison and slide into the driver's seat of my car.

The Mercer residence is not a home. It's not meant to feel comforting. I'm greeted by iron gates, perfectly leveled gravel, and the long stretch of manicured hedges. I feel suffocated.

This house belongs on the front of a magazine. There's not a frame that's out of place or a cushion that isn't fluffed. I pull into my spot in the six-car garage and move purposefully through the mudroom, into the kitchen. The air is still and cold, with a faint smell of aged wood and expensive cologne. I hear ice dropping into a glass before I see my perfectly put together mother. I brace myself. It's expected when she greets me like a guest and not her son.

"Hello, Callum," she cocks her head and pours herself a stiff drink. "Don't forget, the gala with the DA's office is tonight," she takes a sip. "It's for the children's hospital so I expect you to be on your best behaviour." She smiles, easing the sting of her words.

"Yes, Mother," I say as I walk toward my side of the house.

While I spend most of my nights here and the rest of my days at The Society, I wouldn't consider either of them my home. There's a roof over my head, but a home? That's just a word people use when they have someone who cares for them waiting at the door.

My room is clean but not warm. Everything has been handpicked for me, from the leather furniture and perfectly made bed, to the large desk with my grandfather's portrait above it. Apart from the books on my shelf and the punching bag hanging by the window, everything has been selected by an interior designer, to "fit the mood."

I pick up a dark navy Tom Ford suit that lies out on my bed. It's crisp with tags still on it. Mother doesn't even trust that I can pick out a nice suit and forgets that I have ten of these exact ones in my closet.

I don't hate her, she is my mother, but I hate what she stands for. For years she's been Dad's puppet, playing dress up and planning charity balls. She's traded silence for status. While the world rots under her Christian Louboutin high heels, she sits at marble tables and drinks champagne, carefree. Molded into a perfect shape that my father carved out, she's bent into The Society's rules. No spine, no voice, just a polished smile.

I don't have it in me to pretend and admire women like her. I respect women, more than most men I know—not because I was taught to, but because I've seen what happens when they're treated like property and discarded.

Father has tried to arrange marriages for me with such future generic molds. I've never allowed him and convinced him to lay off until I'm done school and begin working for my grandfather. He agrees that I should stay focused on my studies, for now.

After hitting the bag a few times and lingering in a hot shower, I change into the perfectly pressed suit. By the silence in the house, I can tell that everyone's already left.

I stride into the lavish hall. Only the most elite in our small town of Millhaven fill the massive ballroom. Glitter illuminates from a crystal bottle of champagne and bounces off the bright lights overhead. I spot my parents in the distance talking to some of the Highers. Father forces a smile toward me as I approach them.

"There he is." Father grabs my shoulder. I try not to show my discomfort.

He raises his glass toward Deluca.

"Deluca here was just telling me how proud you made us all by handling a recent... situation." He clears his throat.

"You always make us proud, Callum," Deluca says, like it's a genuine compliment and not forced in my father's presence.

"Just doing what needs to be done," I say.

Father motions for one of the waiters to bring over the tray of champagne. He grabs a glass and hands it to me. I take a large sip, probably bigger than I should.

For the rest of the night, I play the part—I nod and smile when Mother grabs my arm and introduces me to donors. I try not to show that I'm really itching to get out of here, roll my designer sleeves up, and get my hands bloody.

Trash

Scarlett

I've read the same sentence from my textbook three times, but information isn't processing like it usually does. I try again. I can't focus today. It's been one of those days where I haven't been paying attention to my feelings and they are telling me to slow down. Either that or I'm about to get really stressed. I used to lose focus a lot four years ago, after the incident at the party, I had to pull myself together. I'm sure a gym session will help.

Sophia sits across from me, smacking on gum as she reads her textbook. Deeply focused, she highlights sentences and takes notes, clearly processing things well. She flips her long curled hair over her shoulder.

"You look like you're going to scream. You good?"

I sigh. "If I read this chapter one more time, I'm going to start charging it by the minute."

Sophia laughs. "Want to take a break?" I shake my head.

"No, I'm good, I just need to–"

A shadow sweeps over the table. My stomach churns with anxiety—I can already feel who it is. I glare behind me and see Chase, my not so nice ex-boyfriend. I'm not sure why I dated him for so long. Maybe it's because he made me feel something. Or maybe I felt like settling was my only option.

"I didn't think I'd catch you in the library, Scar." His smile is accentuated by his blonde hair and dark eyes.

"Well, here I am." I smile at him but I'm sure he can tell it's forced.

"Sophia. Always a pleasure." He looks at her for a minute before his eyes land back on me.

"Cut the crap Booth, it's never a pleasure." Sophia rolls her eyes, unimpressed.

He pointedly ignores her.

"Didn't think you could go this long without texting me back." His eyes don't break contact with mine.

"Well maybe that should've been your first clue, Chase." I hold his gaze.

"I just want to talk... can't you give me a few minutes after we've spent years together?" He sighs dramatically and puffs his chest, like he's owed my time.

"We have nothing to talk about."

"So that's it... after everything?" He can try and pull at my heartstrings all he wants, but he should know better. I'm about to tell him to leave us alone, but Sophia cuts in.

"She said she has nothing to talk to *you* about."

"I didn't know you needed a bodyguard, Scarlett." He laughs immaturely and looks at Sophia with an ice-cold glare.

"Only when the trash from the past doesn't know when to leave." She pops her gum to finish her statement.

Chase looks back at me and narrows his eyes. My body stiffens. *He doesn't control me, not anymore.* I hold my chin high as he throws his hands up and stomps away. I know this isn't over, Chase never lets anything go.

After that encounter, Sophia and I decide that we're done with studying. We pack up our things and walk out of the library. I do a double take as we leave. In the corner of my eye, I see Callum, sitting at a desk by the back of the room. Why is he here now? He must have a million better places where he can study, his family practically has shares in the entire town. I can't remember seeing him at the library in all my previous years at Langford. Why does he keep showing up and why do I feel like it means something? I know it's his school too, I just find it weird that since the start of this year, we've had more interactions than ever before.

Guys like Callum Mercer don't notice girls like me. I look away so our eyes don't meet. Sophia and I walk outside. It's one of those confusing days where it looks like fall but feels like summer.

"Want to go for a drive down by the river?" Sophia asks. She can always tell when I'm fighting with my thoughts.

"You're not too busy?" Sometimes I feel like a burden to her.

"I'm never too busy for you Scar-Scar." She throws her arm around my waist and pulls me in as we walk toward our cars.

I rest my head on her shoulder. We stay like this for a minute, her presence is soothing. She pulls the keys out of her purse and unlocks her car.

"We can take mine?" She motions toward her car.

"Sure." I go around to the passenger side and slide in.

As Sophia puts the windows down, my gaze locks onto her. She has a natural kind of beauty to her that stops you in your tracks. We've known each other since we were kids. She has so much love in her soul and golden strawberry hair that matches her fiery personality. I know that she fights her own demons, but she stays positive and has always put our friendship first. I'm so thankful for that.

We're halfway to Black Lake.

"Thank you," I whisper. I don't need to say why, she just knows.

"Are you going to tell me what's going on or should I start prying?" Sophia takes her eyes off the road to look at me, only for a moment.

"I just feel like I'm not myself lately. My mom has been calling me to come over, and I have no desire to. I also don't really know if I want to do my master's next year or if I should try and get a placement. Most people have this figured out by now and I feel like a fraud for being in the same boat I was in when I started the program." Sophia listens. "And then there's Chase. What the hell was that today?"

I let out a big sigh.

"Okay. First things first. Scarlett Voss, you are one of the smartest people I know. Not just in the classroom... you understand people. You read their emotions like they're a book you're trying to learn, you have a gift." I smile faintly as she continues. "Secondly, your mom is never going to see herself in the wrong. If you don't want to see her, don't see her. Jake will support you on that too." She raised her eyebrows. "And don't even get me started on Chase. I know you can handle him yourself, but I swear to God if he doesn't leave you alone, I'll drop kick him." I chuckle.

"But I swear he's already kind of afraid of your kick ass boxing moves." She adds, removing her right hand from the wheel, making a fist at me.

"Oh god. Stop whatever this is." I ball my hands up into fists and face her. We both burst out laughing.

"I love you," I say, as I reach across the gear shift and grab her hand, squeezing it tight.

"And you know I love you." She squeezes mine back.

"So, what's new with you?" I ask her, bringing my leg up onto the leather seat.

"God, nothing. I wish something was new. You still good to come to the party with me tomorrow or do you need a night off?"

I completely forgot that I told her I would go. "Yeah, I'll go." I try not to hesitate.

"You forgot, didn't you?"

"Yes, I did. But I'll still go!"

"You bet your ass you're still going."

"Hey! Didn't you just say I didn't have to?"

"There's a difference between not feeling mentally well enough to go and you not wanting to go Scarlett." She faces me with her best scowl. She's right.

We take the long way around Black Lake. As the sun sets, the trees are full of crisp orange and yellow leaves that match the horizon. After we loop around the lake, Sophia drops me back off at school to grab my car.

My drive home is short. A sense of relief washes over me as I pull into the driveway. I walk in the front door and throw my keys on the entryway table.

"Dad?" I yell.

No answer.

"Dad?" I shout again, this time out the side door into the garage.

"Just in here, Kiddo." He is over by his work bench putting some tools away.

"How was your day honey?" His back is toward me.

"Good, I went to the gym this morning. Then I had class and Soph and I studied in the library for a bit. We went for a drive around Black Lake after that, it's such a nice day out."

Dad looks back at me. "Nice," he hesitates. "Everything good?"

I try not to brush him off too casually or else he'll keep asking.

"Oh yeah, just still trying to decide about the placement or master's."

"Ah," he turns around. "Well, you don't have to decide tonight."

I shrug. He's right.

"Dinner?" I ask. He walks over to me and puts his arm around my shoulder.

"Sounds perfect." He kisses the top of my head, reassuring me that everything will work out.

Looking Back at Me

Scarlett

I had had another full day of class.

"I'll be home late Dad, I'm just going out with Sophia," I yell into the garage as I lean on the door.

"Bye honey, I'll leave the light on."

I chuckle. "Thanks Dad. Love you!" He always leaves the porch light on when I'm out.

I shut the front door and head down the slanted driveway to Sophia's red car.

"Get in loser, we're going to a party." I snort. Sophia likes to quote her favourite movies and picks a line that best fits the situation. It's no surprise to me that she references *Mean Girls* tonight, she does at least once a week. I get into the passenger seat, the air conditioning blasts in my face, sending goosebumps down my spine.

"This isn't going to get crazy, right?" Sophia knows I don't love big parties.

She laughs, "No Scar. It'll be average. Not wild, but definitely not tame."

Typical Sophia, avoiding the question with a mediocre answer.

"Yeah, yeah, I know. I'm just not nineteen anymore, Soph. I'd rather be at home reading or doing absolutely anything else."

"I know Scarlett, but is it really too much to ask my best friend to come with me to a couple of parties a year?" She's not wrong, or at least that's what I tell myself. It's probably good for me to get out.

"No, it's not. But when I ask you to read *Heart of Darkness*, I'd appreciate it if you actually read it, considering I'm coming out with you!"

The psychological thrill and emotion that is the world adapted by Joseph Conrad is what got me into psychology—that and apparently some mommy issues.

"I'm not reading that shit Scar, I tried. Three damn times! I'm not putting myself through that again. You like some depressing shit, and I'll support that... from afar. But find a cowboy romance and I'm all ears." She smirks.

We switch from conversing to belting the lyrics to 'Any Man of Mine' by Shania Twain as we pull up to Mill Street where the party is.

About thirty people stand on the front lawn, surrounded by beer cans all over the ground.

This is definitely not a tame party.

We park the car on the road and get out.

"Okay, give me the keys." I hold my hand out. I'm used to being the DD.

Sophia shakes her head. "Not tonight, I'm on my best behavior. Loosen up. Have a couple drinks."

"Okay Soph, in all the years you've known me, when have I ever loosened up? You know I'll only have one. You might as well enjoy yourself."

We walk up onto the lawn. I see some girls from my psychology disorders class. The one girl, Claire, flirts with a football player. The girls are trying to get with the jocks, and the jocks are trying to get with everyone. It's funny—in many ways, high school parties and fourth year university parties are still the same.

The house door remains open, letting the fall breeze in. We're greeted by a game of beer pong in the front foyer.

"I was hoping to find a few friends from my constitutional law class. Want to come with?" Sophia leads us toward the back of the house.

"Sure."

She opens the sliding door, then squeezes through the crowd standing on the deck. We follow the yelling to the pool area.

"Watch out!" *Splash.* A guy does a cannonball into the pool, drenching me with water. My oversized jeans and black tube top are now soaked and heavy.

"Are you kidding me Harrison?!" Sophia yells as she tries to push the water off her cropped pink top.

"I'm going to go find a towel. I'll be back Soph." I know I won't feel comfortable sitting around in soaking wet clothes— especially around people who I barely tolerate.

Harrison Alden, also known as "the golden boy," clearly loves attention. Why else would he jump off a roof and into the pool? His perfectly cut light brown hair matches his egotistical humor. He's also friends with Chase, who I hope is not here. But if Harrison is here, Chase is likely close by—they usually come as a pack. Over the years, I've heard rumors that their guy's group is a part of some secret club. I laugh to myself, *what kind of weird club would they all be in?* While most of them come from money, they barely have two brain cells to rub together.

I walk toward the glass patio door, wondering why university students love parties so damn much. I mean sure, getting drunk with your friends can be fun. But I don't fully understand the need to be around other people who you don't trust. I guess that's the reason why I don't drink much unless I'm comfortable.

I step inside and make my way through the kitchen. There are obviously no towels around here, so I head up the stairs.

On the right, I spot a closed door and knock, not wanting to interrupt anything. I shiver in my wet clothes that cling to my skin.

"We're busy!" A hear muffled voices say from inside the room.

I continue on to the next door.

"Hello?" I yell loudly. *God, we are adults. Can people not just have sex at their own homes?*

No answer. "I'm coming in." As I open the door, a gust of wind follows. There's a patio door on the other side of the bedroom, sitting wide open. I walk into the room and spot a bed with flower sheets. They look out of place, like they belong in my grandma's house, not in a mansion on the rich side of town. I find the ensuite bathroom on the left. I head toward it, grabbing a towel from a basket on the floor, and pat myself dry.

The calm breeze draws me in. I walk over to the patio, scrunching bits of my hair dry with the towel. This house is huge. It's elegant and classy. I wouldn't expect anything less on the East side of town.

On the patio, I face a side garden. *Finally, some quiet.* I exhale and lean against the cool stone railing.

Just then, I hear someone clearing their throat and turn around.

"You're not lost, are you?" *Callum Mercer.* He sits on the thick stone railing, his back against the brick house, legs dangling over the ledge, and blows out his cigarette smoke. His eyes slowly trail up my body. I heavily blink, wishing that he'd disappear by the time I open them.

"No, I was looking for a towel." I hold it up to show him, like I need validation.

"And you found me instead." He raises his eyebrow.

I cross my arms. "Unfortunately."

He smirks. "You don't mean that."

I hate that there's an ounce of truth in his words.

"Do you hide often at your friends' parties?" My voice gets edgy now, like I need to defend myself.

He shrugs. "Just needed a break from pretending that I give a shit."

I move the towel around in my hand, forgetting that I'm still in wet clothes. "And now you're pretending to be mysterious." *Two can play this game.*

His smile is raw, almost dangerous. "I'm not pretending, Scarlett."

A chill run across my shoulders. The way Callum said my name sounded so smooth, like he was meant to say it.

"How do you know my name?"

He jumps down off the railing and stands closer to me. "I remember things that matter."

My eyes are locked with his.

"You're kind of intense."

He laughs, low and deep, almost ghostly like smoke surrounding me.

"I see you watching everyone. You study them." He steps toward me. Although there's distance between us, I somehow feel his body heat. "You do that a lot, you observe. Close enough to know everything, but far enough not to be noticed." He brings his cigarette to his lips.

"Psych major. It's a habit," I say hoping he realizes I'm not intimidated.

"No. That's survival, Scarlett." He blows the smoke out of his mouth and looks at the sky. "You've probably psychoanalyzed most people here. But I wonder how many people actually look back at you."

His words leave me speechless.

Callum steps closer. "I'll see you around."

Something presses against my hand, and my eyes shift down. He gives me his drink. "Vodka soda. Your drink of the night." Our hands touch only for a second.

He slips out through the patio door, placing his hands into his pant pockets.

My eyes follow him. *How does he know that I only have one drink?* Maybe he didn't mean it that way. *Maybe he just meant, "here's a drink, Scarlett." Or maybe I'm just over analyzing everything, like usual.*

I throw the wet towel over the railing and swish the drink in the cup.

What Callum said about wondering how many people look back at me has stuck—I can't get that line out of my head.

I swirl the liquid in the plastic like it holds the answers. Is *he* looking back at me?

Untouchable

Callum

The loud heavy music vibrates through my body as I walk through the bedroom and leave her on the balcony. I run my fingers over my hand where it touched hers. I want to look back at her, but I can't. I know if I do, it might just be the end of me. Instead, I reach for the door and hurry down the stairs.

I'm mad at myself for what I said about the drink. I want to go back and tell her, but I can't. Of course, I know that she only has one drink at a party. She's been doing that since the incident. But she can never find out that I know.

That night.

I try not to think about it. If I do, I'll blame myself. For being too late. For failing to prevent it. When it comes to The Society, I control a lot.

I push my way through the crowded house. Everyone moves as I approach them, like a calculated dance. One of the sorority girls stays in place as I try to pass. She plants herself in front of me.

"Can I help you?" I remind myself that she doesn't know what I'm capable of.

"Yeah, I was hoping you would." She takes a sip of her drink, her eyes locked onto mine.

Normally, I don't mind a casual fuck. It's been a while since I've indulged.

"Not today." I shoo her away. I can't fuck her with Scarlett on my mind.

"Callum." Harrison stands across the room with some of the pledges. "We're all going to meet in the garage." He motions for me to follow him.

As I try to get Scarlett off my mind, I spot her in the corner of my eye, coming down the stairs. I can recognize her anywhere. She scans the room, then heads toward the back door. I look down at her hand and notice she doesn't have the drink I gave her. She doesn't trust me. *Good.* She shouldn't.

She doesn't notice me as I slowly make my way toward the garage. I already know what they want to talk about, my shoulders straighten just thinking about it.

Upon entering, I shut the door behind me. I look around at some the other pledges—there must be at least fifteen of them. Some of them are good guys, but most of them aren't. These guys just love the power that comes with the title. They don't realize that The Society will grow to be their worst enemy. Most of them will resent everything they worked so hard for. They should fear what they are going to become— and fear me.

"Tonight, some of you are getting sloppy. I have seen two of you try and slip drugs into drinks with others watching you. If you do it, make sure you do it right. We can't afford a fuck up, and we can't have any extra eyes on us," Blaine remains calm. "Remember who we are. We do this for power, for control. You only get this chance once. It's a rite of passage. It's something you must earn."

Blaine Banks is the kind of guy who buys into everything The Society teaches him. He'll protect them until he's blue in the face, and he believes that stripping women of their humanity provides power—I'll never be like him.

I glance around at the first-year pledges. They must think of this as a privilege, when really, it's a suicide mission.

"No one here is untouchable. Find someone special, and don't complete the task until you are ready." He flicks his hand, motioning for everyone to leave.

I laugh to myself. His words replay in my head: find someone *special*. And then drug and rape them. Show a woman how special she is to you by asserting your dominance while she is vulnerable.

I don't need to drug and rape women for attention. Even though they shouldn't, most women already respect me without hesitation. Why do they run toward me and not from me?

I think back to the girl that was chosen for my initiation. It was the same week that Scarlett was drugged. We had consensual sex, and she was in her right state of mind to make that decision. I didn't drug her. I would never take advantage of someone, not like that. The only people I hurt are those who deserve it.

I see Harrison talking to Blaine on the other side of the garage. Harrison does whatever it takes to survive—just like I do. We've known each other since we were babies, but we grew closer in middle school.

Harrison has seen a side of me that no one else knows. I don't show that side of myself often, the vulnerable Callum. Once you show the dark world your sensitive side, you can never be the same. Darkness does everything in its power to tear you apart.

Harrison walks over to me. "Where did you disappear to?"

He hands me a cigarette.

"There's no way you were getting me up on that roof." He offers me a light.

"I heard Sophia ask one of the pledges if Chase was coming." He knows that I'm interested in Scarlett but doesn't know the full extent. Not yet. My eyes drift to the door, eager to leave.

"That douche wouldn't miss any chance to score." Harrison laughs and leans against a workbench. "I wonder if her question had anything to do with the library the other day."

My gaze snaps from the door back to him. "What happened in the library?"

"You know when we were studying? Or I guess I was, and you were not being stealth about watching Scarlett. Well, I guess the conversation that we saw wasn't very... friendly."

He waits for my reaction before he finishes. "And, it's not the first time Chase has forced conversation, from what I've heard."

I take a long haul of my cigarette then breathe out. *Stay calm.*

"What do you want to do about it?" He asks, but he already knows the answer.

"I'll handle it." I put my hand on his shoulder and squeeze. I know that Harrison would burn the whole world down with me if I asked him to, but he doesn't need to be brought into this, not now.

I flick my smoke to the ground and walk out of the garage. I hear a sweet, quiet laugh, a sound that I could recognize from anywhere but have yet to draw out of her. I smirk to myself, thinking of all the ways I want to make her scream and cry my name between her bruised lips.

My smile quickly fades. She isn't supposed to matter. So why the fuck can't I stop thinking about her.

Fighting Demons

Scarlett

I roll over and look at my alarm clock. It's six forty, twenty minutes before I'm supposed to wake up.

Some mornings are heavier than others—today is one of them. I guess my anxiety the other day was a warning that I should've listened to. I throw the covers off, get out of bed, and do the same meticulous routine that I do every morning. I stay in the shower and close my eyes, just to let the hot water wash over me for an extra few minutes.

I turn the temperature knob to cold, and I splash icy water on my face, hoping it will wake me up. Although researchers aren't fully sure if there are any scientific benefits to cold plunges or freezing showers, it sure will get me ready quickly.

When I step out of the shower, I wipe the steam off the mirror and look at myself. Some days I don't recognize the person staring back. Would I feel the same if that night didn't happen? I try not to let it consume me, even though I have so many questions left unanswered.

I get dressed, grab my gym stuff, and make my way downstairs. Dad isn't at the table reading the paper yet, so I leave him a little note telling him that I love him and to have a great day. I make a to-go coffee, grab my bag, and leave for the day.

Our house gets smaller in my rear-view mirror as I pull out of the driveway. The wooden exterior of Dad's shop adds to our home's rustic feel. I was young when Dad built it—after him and Mom bought the house over twenty years ago. The inside of the garage feels like an extension of my dad. Everything is well organized on the walls. There's a place for every tool on his work bench and small old car parts line the walls. He fell in love with it and knew that he'd be here forever. With his long work hours, he didn't want to miss a moment, so staying close to home was important to him. Every day, he still looks forward to when I pop into the shop after school and tell him how it was.

As I pull into the parking lot at Langford, I notice it's not as busy as a usual Tuesday. I guess we're far enough into the semester that people have started skipping classes and dropping out. I walk toward my Early Developmental Psych class and notice a shift in the air. It's cooler outside, and the leaves have mostly fallen off the trees. I need to bring a jacket tomorrow.

Someone brushes up against me in the hall. I flinch. *You're safe.* On days like these, where my anxiety is already heightened, my triggers seem so accentuated.

I pull some Sour Patch Kids gummies out from my bag and eat them in a colour coded way most would think is strange.

The first two lectures go by slowly. Usually, I am fully focused and engaged, but today the end of my last class can't come fast enough. I look around at the students, spread throughout the room. They smile and nod and follow along like it's just another day. I wonder if I fit into their normal.

Professor Elliot looks to me for the next answer. My eyes shift away instead of raising my hand like I usually do. I can sense his disappointment.

"Okay, that concludes today's lesson. Paper grades will be out by Friday. As always, come talk to me if you have any issues with your mark."

I shove my laptop in my bag, eager to leave the classroom and avoid conversation. My hands tremble as I do up my backpack's zipper. *You're safe.* Maybe if I repeat this enough, I'll start to believe it.

I reach for the door handle without realizing that it's already being held open. Callum's eyes land on mine as I walk by. They stare back at me like they want to understand the depth of my sadness. I don't say anything and break our eye contact.

"Thanks." I mumble, looking forward.

My heart pounds. I feel something different for a split second, something that makes me want to stay in that moment longer as I pass through the doors. I feel his bright-eyed gaze burning onto my back without having to turn around.

I get to my car and head across town to the gym. It feels like home when I get there, the smell of sweat and the lemon cleaner welcoming me back. *My safe place.*

I open my locker and stop to notice the hanging photos. I smile thinking of the good times.

I wrap my hands extra tight, like the fabric is holding me together, one stitch at a time.

Today, the bag fights back, but I don't care. I'm trying to forget, not win. Ironically, I can't remember the one thing that I've desperately wanted to—that night. Even years later, it all remains a blur.

Punch. Jab. Punch. Punch. Hook. Jab.

Slowly, I can finally control my breath again.

"What, does that bag owe you money, Scar?" Ricco yells from across the room.

I can't hold back my smile, the first real one all day.

"Wouldn't you know," I yell back. He comes over and watches me for a minute.

For once, he doesn't critique my form. "Save some of that for the real fights. You're better than this." He lightly punches my shoulder.

There's an unspoken bond between Ricco and I. He knows that I fight demons, yet never asks about them. In return, I never sulk for long. He might not know it, but he's helped me through some of my worst days.

I throw one more hard punch at the bag and laugh to myself. Somewhere under all this wreckage, I still have some fight left in me.

The Boxer

Callum

I'm not a stalker. Even though I listened to Scarlett and Sophia as they walked up the path to that party four years ago. Even though I know about her one drink limit. Even though I can't stop thinking about her. As long as I can remember, no one has piqued my interest enough to pay much attention to them. But running into Scarlett was intentional, and talking to her at the party was not a coincidence. For the first time, I've wanted to know more about someone—that alone makes Scarlett Voss dangerous.

Since last night, I haven't been able to get her off my mind. She isn't the type of girl you mold into the perfect housewife. She fights back. Although I barely know her, I'm damn proud of her for that.

I've been too busy with The Society to ever pay attention to my feelings—all I know is that they're dangerous. I can't understand why I'm so fixated on her. She's the first person I want to shelter from The Society, but nobody can find out. When I heard some of the pledges talking about drugging her at the party, it sparked something inside of me, something I've never felt before.

I often lose interest in women after a couple of nights. They provide me with a release that doesn't come with blood on my hands or pressure behind my eyes. While there's no genuine intimacy or trust in my actions, there's control. And that's what I crave the most.

The pledges know their place, just like all the other men that are pushed into The Society by their families. I hate my parents— their legacy, expectations, and everything they stand for. But being a Mercer has one benefit: people listen to you. In my case, maybe people are just afraid. I let them be. Fear gets you further than respect ever will.

I've been a part of The Society for almost four years, and my final initiation is later this year. Nothing feels worse than carrying the burdens that come with the role of a pledge. I try not to think and pull a cigarette out from inside my jacket, along with a box of matches. There's something about pulling the cedar stick along the side of the box that I love. I throw it back onto my dash and light the toxic filth that fills my lungs. I throw the match out the window and onto the sidewalk.

Right as my mind is stuck on her, my newfound obsession walks out of the arts building, without a care in the world. Her light brown hair blows in the wind, like the leaves that fall from the trees.

She talks to Sophia. I wonder if she knows that Sophia's dad is corrupt. Money in exchange for silence is all it took to guarantee District Attorney Roberts to protect his daughter. I bet she has no fucking clue.

"Love you! I'll call you later!" Scarlett yells to her sheltered friend as she throws her bag in the passenger seat and climbs into her car. I start my engine and discretely follow her across town.

We end up outside of an old gym, the kind that doesn't come with a high price tag or complimentary water. I'm not surprised that Scarlett works out, but why does she come here? There are two gyms on campus and one near her mom's house. Although, based on what I've seen, I wouldn't want Scarlett to spend a lot of time at her mom's place anyway.

She steps out of her car, carefully closing the door, and walks toward the worn building. She pulls her hair back out of her face. As she opens the door with her elbow, I feel the urge to follow her.

I get out of my car, slamming the door. My feet are heavy and quick on the pavement. She has no idea I'm following her.

When I make her mine, I need to teach her some self-awareness. She doesn't understand: this town can get you killed. The slight thought of her getting hurt makes me cringe. I approach the gym door and try not to let my anger get the best of me.

As I enter, I'm hit with the smell of sweat and humility.

This gym is large— I can blend in easily. The equipment is older, the lighting isn't great, and it feels like the kind of place you'd go to avoid others. I scan the room and notice her sitting on a bench in the back. She isn't sitting with everyone else putting their shoes on. *Why is she in the back of the gym?* She ties the laces of her tan and black sneakers.

I turn the corner to try and get a better view of her, but I try to remain hidden.

She walks up toward the boxing ring and slides in, between its ropes, like she's done this a million times. I notice the sparring gloves in her hand.

A middle-aged man comes over and greets her with a routine smile.

My eye twitches.

Who is this motherfucker?

He helps her tie the gloves, running his fingers over the calluses on hers. He's too close. He puts his own gloves on, and they put their mouth guards in. I know what's going to happen next, but I didn't expect it. Scarlett is a... boxer? *Interesting.*

I wonder if she boxes for control. There's something calculated in the way she moves, almost as if she's running her fingers along the edge of a blade just to see if it's still sharp. Boxing allows her to lose control without actually losing it, like dipping her toes in deep water. She's in a safe and controlled place with someone she obviously trusts. *I need to find out who this guy is*—an addition to my mental checklist of things to do later. The more I watch her, the more it seems like she is fighting something bigger than the man in front of her.

Maybe there's more to Scarlett Voss than I thought.

Maybe she's just trying to survive, one punch at a time.

Just like me.

Holding my Breath

Scarlett

I sit at the kitchen table, my feet barely touching the ground. The smell of bacon cooking fills the main floor. Dad sits across from me and reads the paper, sipping on his coffee. Mom flips pancakes. I can hear her humming. When I look to her, I notice her smudged mascara—a norm for her in the mornings lately. I must've asked her a question, but I can't hear myself. I watch her turn to answer me.

"Mom!" I yell.

The scene changes. I'm upstairs. Through the crack of my bedroom door, I hear screaming. I want to hear the words, but they're muffled. *They always wait until I go to bed to fight.* Ever since Mom got a new job at the steakhouse, she stays out late, and Dad hates it. When she gets home, Dad always questions her.

I slowly creep down the stairs, on my tiptoes to stop the floor from creaking. She comes around the corner as I'm almost at the bottom. Dad follows her. She parts her lips like she is going to say something to me but never does. Instead, she walks past me, up the stairs and into their room.

I wake up to silence.

Another dream. Another flashback. I open my eyes and stare at the ceiling. The room sharpens. I grab my comforter and wrap it around me. I could spend all day here, but I have things to do and I'm not going to let my emotions control me again today.

I pull my phone off my nightstand and check my notifications. Sophia wants to grab coffee before class and Dad said to have a good day in case I miss him this morning. It's enough to make me smile. I have people who love me, and today that's a good enough reason to get out of bed.

I press my palms into the bed and sit up.

"Today is going to be a good day." Maybe hearing it will help me believe it.

I try to relax in the shower. As I throw on some freshly washed jeans, I put on some Arctic Monkeys. Their music changes my mood, and I can't fight the flow that controls my body as I groove in the bathroom. I wipe the steam off the mirror—there I am. *Smile.*

Outside, the crisp fall air helps today feel like a clean slate. The drive to campus is quiet— besides the hum of the car and a playlist that Sophia sent me that's on in the background. The music matches my mood today: soft and hopeful.

I pull into the school lot, tapping the steering wheel to the beat of the song 'Talk' by Hozier. I roll into a spot, turn off the car, and put on some clear lip gloss. As I get out, my phone buzzes in my bag.

> **Sophia:** You better hurry up before I have both of our drinks. ;)

I roll my eyes and smile.

Scarlett: Keep your hands off mine. Be there in 2!

    The little coffee cart on the other side of the quad is swarming with half-awake students. I spot Sophia near the back. She has her circular black sunglasses on, looking like a glamorous movie star. Although she isn't a morning person, I know she's perfectly put together underneath them. I watch her laugh and talk with the barista as I approach. *That girl makes friends wherever she goes.*

    "Scar!" She waves and motions for me to come over. I'm just over five feet away from her, when I see her scanning me, up and down.

    "Wow, don't you look nice today."

    I snort. If anyone can get away with being blunt, it's her.

    "Gee, thanks." I roll my eyes. "I'm still groggy from a crappy night's sleep. This coffee better bring me back to life."

    Sophia hands me a coffee. I smell it before I take a sip.

    "I love the fresh smell of napalm in the morning," I say trying to impersonate Robert Duvall from *Apocalypse Now*.

    "You're a friggin' weirdo." Sophia side eyes me. We each take a few steaming sips and begin our walk down the halls to class. She glares at me.

    "Another one of the Mommy Voss dreams?"

    "Yeah, but I'm good." I reassure her with a smile. "I promise."

"Okay, well I'm headed the other way. Text me after class and we can study if you want?"

"Sure!" I yell as she disappears down the hall.

I push through two heavy doors and head down a staircase, straight to a seat near the front of the lecture hall. The classroom is filled with quiet chatter as I sit and sip my coffee. Professor Elliot walks into class, his leather satchel swings in his hand and his hair flows in tune with the speed he's going at. He looks spry with his old blazer and acts like he's perfectly on time, even though he's five minutes late.

"Morning, everyone." He sets his satchel on his desk and opens it.

"Let's see how many of you actually did the readings." He looks up at me. "Scarlett, should I call on you first, you look suspiciously alert today."

I laugh. "I'm always suspicious, Professor."

He raises an eyebrow and glances around the class before answering.

"Fair, but you are also the only one who handed their paper in two days early."

A brief flicker of pride burns in my chest. While I don't always have it together, I hate being disorganized with my schoolwork. When I can, I try to hand things in early, but it's a nonnegotiable for me to meet deadlines. It's a standard I hold myself to.

As the class discussion picks up, I'm fully engaged. Elliot occasionally paces the room, throwing questions like darts. I answer and sometimes assist in a friendly debate. *Today is a good day.*

After class, I walk across campus. The breeze is warmer than this morning. As I pass through the courtyard, I hear someone yell my name in the distance. They catch up to me as I approach the football field.

"Scarlett!" I know that tone. I dread it. It's hard to forget the voice that has humiliated me countless times. I don't turn around.

"Scar!" Chase is right behind me now. I freeze but still don't turn to face him.

He huffs, out of breath.

"Hey, I was yelling at you. Ignoring me?" He steps in front of me with a smug look.

"I thought you'd get the hint, Chase." I fold my arms over my chest. "What do you want?"

He smiles, that stupid smile that means he wants something. It used to charm me, and I can't help but wonder if that smile works on others.

"You look good, Scar."

He's trying to regain control of the conversation. I know him too well.

"Where's Naomi?" I force a smile as I mention his new girlfriend. I think about all the rumors about how he would talk to other girls, and likely more, while we were still together. I feel stupid for ignoring them.

"She's in class." He steps closer and a shiver runs down my spine.

"Goodbye Chase, this conversation is over."

I try to move around him, but he doesn't budge. He grabs my arm and pulls me back.

"Let go of me. *Now.*" His hand grips my wrist. My heart rate increases as my breaths pick up speed. He pulls me closer. I can feel his breath against my forehead. It's hot and unwanted. I slowly gaze up and quickly jerk away from him.

"Is he bothering you?" I hear a deep voice behind me. My head is locked into place, staring up at Chase.

"All good here Cal," Chase smiles, as he holds a vice grip on my wrist. I'm unable to move.

Callum's voice gets closer.

"She said no. Let her go. *Now.*" His voice is steady but harsh, it's not a warning.

Chase lets go of my wrist. I turn around, now inches from Callum's face. I hold my breath. He's just as close as Chase was but for some reason I start to relax.

Callum doesn't move and Chase is clearly intimidated by him, like there is an unspoken threat in the air. Chase puts his hands up and concedes.

"Alright," he says and backs away. Chase looks over at Callum, then back at me.

"Bye Scarlett." He smiles. *God, I hate that smile.*

Callum steps in front of me, like it's second nature. He doesn't say anything to Chase, who turns around and walks away, his light hair shines in the sun as he gets further out of view.

When Chase is about twenty feet away, Callum turns back to me.

"You alright?"

I want to say yes but the words don't come out. Instead, I just look up at him.

"You don't need to say anything, just nod so I know you're okay."

I drop my face to the ground and move my head up and down slowly. My heart pounds in his presence.

"He's gone—you don't have to hold your breath anymore."

I smile up at him.

"Thank you," I say quietly.

"Don't mention it." He shrugs and pulls a cigarette out of his jacket. I watch him bring it to his lips and light it. *Who knew smoking could be so sexy.* His eyes meet mine one last time before he walks away, leaving me speechless.

Liability

Callum

As I watch her walk away, I exhale a deep drag of smoke. Something urges me to follow her—not because I think she needs my protection, but because I want to give it to her anyways. With Chase, she's clearly harbouring feelings she isn't ready to face yet. I just need to make sure she's safe.

We're close to her car when she looks back at me.

"What, do you tail every girl who gets harassed or am I just lucky?" *Sassy.* Where's the thankful Scarlett who was just speechless a minute ago?

I smirk and look to her.

"You're not like them, Scarlett." I love watching her squirm when I say things she doesn't expect.

Her cheeks turn red.

"Like who?"

I hate that she thinks this is normal.

"Like the ones who expect to be watched. The ones who don't flinch anymore." My tone comes across cold.

She doesn't answer me. Instead, she tilts her head, like she's trying to get inside mine. *Good luck, Angel.*

"He won't touch you again," I say. It's not possessive, more territorial, laced with anger and charged with the guilt of failing to intervene earlier. I knew she could handle him—I just didn't want her to have to.

She smiles and leans on her door, as if I'm just saying something nice, not promising to protect her.

"Are you going to follow me all day now?" She looks me up and down, there's nothing subtle about it.

"If I did, you'd never know." Her lips part slightly, as if she thinks I might be serious. She tilts her head back and laughs.

"Good luck, Callum." She smiles and gets into her car.

That fucking mouth.

I don't move as she drives past, clenching my fists with the desire to touch her. I walk over to my car and open the door. I can't sit down. Instead, I slam the door harder than I mean to and lean against it, like a child throwing a tantrum. I pull my phone out of my pocket and call Harrison.

He picks up on the second ring.

"Oh, you're alive?"

"Chase Booth." I skip the pleasantries and get straight to the point.

There's a brief pause.

"What about him?"

"He touched something that's mine." I follow with a longer, heavier pause.

I don't need to see him to know that his body language has changed, like he knows what's next. "How far did he push it?"

"Far enough." I bark out. "He put his hands on her."

"Fucking hell," Harrison mutters.

I try not to let my rage take over while I recall everything that happened.

"I want him handled. I don't want him as much as breathing near her again."

"You sure you want to cross that line Callum?" He asks carefully. "You know what that means."

"I'm so far over the fucking line." My voice is quiet but final.

"You know that we can't dispose of him like that. Not unless you want push back from the Highers." He doesn't argue, he's just looking out for me.

"I'm not talking about blood." I stay calm. "I just want him reminded. Make him squirm a little."

"Enough to bruise the ego?" His tone sharpens.

I smile. "Exactly. Make it humiliating. Don't let him forget it."

"I'll get creative." There's a dark satisfaction in Harrison's voice.

I hang up without another word, my pulse racing as I think about her. My hand remains curled around the phone. I should feel control. Instead, I feel like I'm losing an unwinnable battle.

I shouldn't care—I wasn't raised to care. I was taught to push away my feelings and told that caring makes you weak and vulnerable. Growing up, I watched my mother waste away into the background while my father used people like pawns. I've promised myself that I'd be different—but not like this. Not attached. Not soft.

Then there's her. She's like a hurricane that pulls me in and breaks me down with nothing more than a look or a sassy comment. She didn't ask for my help, and she sure as hell didn't ask for me to follow her—yet I did. And I know I will continue to. My chest tightens the more I think about her.

I finally open my car door and climb into the driver's seat. *I can never lose control, not around her.* My fist hits the steering wheel.

"Fuck!"

I hate that her safety is the only thing that matters to me right now. More than The Society. More than the rules. She's unraveling me and she doesn't even know it. My knuckles grip the leather of the steering wheel so hard they start to whiten.

She was never part of the plan. I start the car and sit for a moment, in silence. I know what I need to do, I just don't like it. I check my surroundings and leave the campus parking lot.

I'm disappointed with myself, for caring about someone else's feelings. But Scarlett isn't just anyone, she's an anomaly, one that I never accounted for. *Push it down.*

"Attachment is a liability." That's what Father would always say. A low laugh builds in my chest. My parents wouldn't know the meaning of supportive if it knocked them over the fucking head. As the traffic light in front of me turns from yellow to red, I hover my hand over the gear shift and slow the car down. I'm not familiar with this side of town. The houses don't look like they belong on the front of glossy magazines, and their small square lawns are nicely cut, but don't need trucks with landscaping crews to maintain them. Life looks simpler and more honest.

I pull over to the side of the road, a few houses down from hers. The engine idles as I park underneath a streetlight. I don't want to be noticed—by her or anyone else.

There isn't much traffic on King Street—it's unnervingly silent. Scarlett's house is dark, except for a porch light and a faint glow from a window upstairs. Its curtain is slightly open—I assume that's her room. I wonder if she's thinking about me, like I can't stop thinking about her. I run my hand along my jaw and contemplate texting her. I type in her number. I don't have it saved in my phone, but I have it memorized. While some may call that psychotic, I call it endearing.

I type each word slowly.

Callum: Did you make it home?

I know she made it home. I'm looking at her car in the driveway, I'm just looking for any excuse to talk to her. I hesitate before I hit send.

My phone buzzes—that was quick.

Unknown: Who is this?

Of course, she doesn't know my number.

Callum: The campus ex-boyfriend watch committee.

Unknown: Sounds like a stalker… Callum?

Unknown: Yes, I'm fine.

I laugh.
She has no idea.
I can't help but wonder if she's actually fine or if that's just what she tells everyone. I stare at her text on the screen a bit longer, I fucking hate it. *Why won't she admit that she cares?* I don't know how to ask her again without sounding like I give a damn.
I lock the phone screen. Fine doesn't mean *okay*. Fine doesn't mean *safe*.
I don't trust myself to text her back. Instead, I turn off the headlights and readjust in my seat. I stay parked under the yellow streetlight's glow and stare at her window, hoping to get a glimpse of her.

Bloody Knuckles

Scarlett

I host a seminar in the library today. There's only six of us, so we booked a secluded room in the back. Usually, these meetings have more attendees, but as we get closer to exams, teacher's assistants host smaller sessions to get more involved with their groups. I've been a TA for different classes the last two semesters, and I love it. This term, I got to choose my group, and thankfully there are no duds— as in, the students whose parents have lots of money, but they don't really want to be here. Lately, that feels like most, but this group is eager to learn. They also ask great questions and that's always a plus.

"Okay, well if there are no more questions, we should wrap it up. We're about twenty minutes past our time." I look up at the clock. 10:20 p.m. I was at the gym earlier and had two of my own classes plus a study session before this. Busy days are what I look forward to most—there's less time to think about everything else.

"Thanks Scarlett, see you next week," Rachel, one of my peers, says on her way out. I place my laptop in its bag and grab my things. On late nights, I usually park in the garage across campus. It's not fully enclosed, but it's covered. Most importantly, I can access the garage without walking outside at night.

I text Dad as I make my way across campus and let him know that I'm leaving shortly. I open the message from Callum. He never texted back after I said I was fine. I push my phone back into the outside pocket of my bag. *Why did he text me in the first place?* That thought has crossed my mind a couple of times this week.

The halls remain lit. I only pass a few people as I walk through. Most students don't stay on campus late, usually it's just TA's, teachers, and the odd keener.

I make it to the first floor of the parking garage and take two flights of stairs up to my car. I can hear the rain from outside as I approach the third floor.

The garage is quiet, almost too quiet. As I cross the lot, a sudden loud *thud* breaks the silence.

A sharp *bang* and a cracking sound follow, coming from behind the pillars. I stop. My heart races. The noises repeat.

I stay still and debate if I should turn and run back for the stairwell or to my car, but something inside me remains curious. I know I shouldn't, but I walk toward the noises.

Callum's arms are up above his head, his palms pressing against the wall. His forehead rests against the concrete block. Blood runs down his right arm. His hands are scratched and red.

His shoulders are hunched, and his breathing is ragged. He looks like he's been in a fight, yet there's no one around. I assume he's fighting himself.

He doesn't hear me as I walk toward him.

"Callum?"

His body stiffens, like he doesn't want anyone to see him.

"Didn't know anyone was here." He removes his forehead from the cool stone but doesn't look to me.

I don't want to push him. Seeing him like this feels like I've invaded a private moment that he wanted to conceal. Still, I can't take my eyes off him.

"You should go," his deep voice cracks.

I've seen this kind of rage—I live with it. I don't pity it, I recognize it.

"I don't want to leave you alone like this."

He pushes off the wall, his face stoic and expressionless, like he's been wrestling a demon inside his head. His body looks tense and coiled. Finally, his eyes meet mine.

"You ever feel like it's all just poison inside your chest and the only way to get it out is to bleed?"

His dark eyes captivate me, staring into my soul. He's not being poetic—he's telling the truth.

"More than I'd like to admit."

Behind his rugged exterior, I want him to show me who he is. His gaze softens, breaking our eye contact as he looks into the distance. I glance up and notice some broken light bulbs.

"I thought I was the only one who parked up here." He disturbs the silence.

"I always park up here when I host my late seminars. There wasn't any parking on the main floor when I came in earlier today."

"You shouldn't park up here." It's not a suggestion.

I shrug and slowly walk toward him. He stands against a tall concrete barrier while I lean against his car, beside him. We sit in silence, but this time it's shared and not awkward.

Callum looks down at his hands, running his fingers over his bleeding knuckles.

"Sometimes, I want to drive as fast as I can through a red light." His voice is low and at first, I didn't realize he was talking to me. "Not because I want to die, just... to see what it feels like not to stop."

My throat tightens and I don't respond right away. I know that feeling. The urge to flirt with something, a*nything*, to feel alive.

"You ever do it?" I ask.

Callum lets out a hollow, humorless laugh.

"Not yet." He doesn't miss a beat. "But I think about it more than I should." Pain echoes deep in his eyes, below the surface. "Every time I push someone away, I think they're better off. Let them hate me. Makes it easier when I finally fuck it up." There's tension in this pause.

"Then don't fuck it up, Callum. Fight for what you believe in, instead of what they tell you." He clenches his jaw.

"You shouldn't worry about me," he says sharply, like he's trying to convince himself too.

"Too late." My shoulders tense. *Why did you answer, it was a hypothetical, you idiot.* We hold eye contact. Something in me flickers. *Maybe he's afraid of me just as much as I'm afraid of him?*

He pushes off the concrete barrier.

"I'm not someone you can fix, Scarlett." He examines me as if he expects me to walk away, like he doesn't know that I'm a fighter.

"Good. Because I'm not here to fix you." He softly smiles, as if the answer surprises him but he doesn't want to show it. It settles something in me.

I don't wait for a response. Instead, I leave him standing there with those final words. I can feel his eyes on me as I walk toward my car on the other side of the lot, but I don't hear him move. My pulse is tangled in his silence. When I'm almost at the car, I hear his quiet exhale, slow and controlled.

He doesn't try and stop me, but he doesn't leave either— maybe that means something.

Maybe broken doesn't mean dangerous, maybe it just makes him human.

My chest no longer feels heavy. And for the first time in a long time, I'm not walking away to protect myself— I'm just walking away to breathe.

The Bomb

Callum

I sit at the dining room table, staring at the decanter of whiskey that I haven't touched. The house is too clean and too silent, like it's staged for someone else's life. Father walks into the room like he doesn't just own the house, but he owns *me* too.

"You're late," he says and straightens his cuff links. "Don't embarrass yourself tonight. Or me."

I don't respond. I barely do anymore, arguments with him are a waste of time.

"Are you listening?" His voice drops, not loud but edgy. "You don't have to like The Society. You just have to remember that you belong to it. And that means showing up, Callum."

My jaw flexes. I want to smash something. *The decanter might feel good.*

Instead, I stand up to leave. "I'll be there," I say.

Father gives me a fake smile. "You'll do what's expected. You always do."

I leave the room and the air is heavy, not from guilt, I'm used to that, but from a legacy that's been built on lies. I walk through the house, into the garage, and open the bay that my car is in. I hear rain as the door lifts. I'm reminded of last night, in the parking garage with Scarlett. When she saw more of me than I wanted her to.

    I unlock my car door and pull it open as I unbutton my suit jacket. I get into the driver's seat—the cool leather welcomes me back. As I rev the engine and drive off, I see my family's estate in the rear-view mirror.

    You belong to it.

    I replay Father's words in my head. I can't escape him, even if I want to, and boy does he love to remind me of that.

    Rain calmly hits the windshield. Over the hood of my car, the city comes into view. I don't remember how I got here. I had to leave the house before I broke something, and my muscle memory must've brought me to the city that raised me.

    Tall buildings look down on me as I pull into the circular driveway of The Monte, a luxurious hotel in Boston. Valets rush over. I climb out of the car, adjusting my jacket, and I slide my bruised knuckles in my pant pockets. As I walk through the grand doors, I gaze at the familiar marble floors and bright chandeliers.

    Another night of secrets and silk. Time to play the part.

    I step up to the gold-plated elevator and take it to the penthouse. The doors open like a curtain revealing a scene in a play. A performance awaits.

    The polished floors shine beneath the soles of important people wearing Italian leather shoes. There are women in black gowns with red lipstick that stains the champagne glasses. Red pairs nicely with their fake smiles. Everything is beautiful, while everyone is rotten.

The room's full of people who hold authority in our small town. I see Roger Booth, who is the Sheriff of Millhaven and also Chase's dad. I continue to move through the room like a chess piece being shifted by someone else's hand. I nod to familiar faces, as I'm expected to, and avoid the gazes of the smart ones. They avoid me too. I don't smile and I definitely don't speak.

I make my way across the room to Harrison. He's near the bar. *Shocking.*

"Already counting down the minutes until you can leave?"

A thin smile crosses my face. He raises his finger, and a waiter comes over. He orders us drinks.

My phone buzzes in my pocket. I wonder if it's her, but I leave it for now—I have a part to play.

"Didn't know if you'd show." He sips the drink that was just given to him.

"You say that like I have a choice." I swirl the dark liquid in my glass.

"None of us have a choice." He stares across the room. My eyes follow his. A woman in a tailored red dress leans in too closely to an older man in a custom suit.

"She's new." He motions toward her. She moves around like she's someone who wants the attention, but I don't recognize her.

"Why should I care?" I ask flatly.

"Because that's Scarlett's mom."

My eyes snap back onto her, sharper this time. There's something in the way she carries her shoulders that reminds me of Scarlett. Her mouth is the same too—a similarity I don't want to see. Harrison takes another sip of his drink, his eyes on me. He knows I wouldn't do anything here, but he watches for my reaction.

My stomach twists when I look at her. With all the time we've spent together—mainly when I watch her—I haven't seen her spend any time with her mom.

"How long has she been involved?" I keep my voice low.

"At least eight years. Probably more." He shrugs like we're talking about the weather. "She keeps to herself. They like her, she's... compliant." He sips more of his drink.

"Does Scarlett know?" I sip mine, feeling like I know the answer but needing his confirmation.

"No. And she's not supposed to." He glances at me.

My shoulders tense and my jaw tightens. I can't help but look at her again. She clings to the man she's with, laughing at whatever he's saying. Her reactions look planned, and her smile looks fake. It's too late, the damage has already been done. The illusion that there's distance between Scarlett's world and mine is immediately cracked, and there's no fixing it now.

I can't be here, not around these men, knowing that she's in their circle.

"Thanks." I finish my drink and place the glass on the bar. Without another word, I walk toward a balcony with double doors and push them open. The chill of the evening ripples through my body as I walk outside. The city shines beneath me. I take a few deep breaths.

Scarlett's Mother.

Of all the twisted pieces in this game, I didn't expect her to be one of them. All I can think of is Scarlett's face if she finds out. My grip tightens against the balcony's ledge.

I need to get out of here, *now.*

I head to the elevator and press the button, waiting impatiently for it. Once I get down to the main floor, I grab my car from the valet and tightly grip the wheel. I need to see her. She needs to be okay and untouched by all of this. Trying to concentrate on driving, I drown out the thoughts of what could happen if she is impacted.

 I don't think before I get out of the car, and I walk over to the side of her house. Stepping over the green hedges, I grab the trellis. I don't struggle as I make my way up to her window that's cracked open. As I slip inside, she doesn't move.

Her limbs are wrapped under her bed sheets and the moonlight shines across her face. I stand over her and know that her world is closing in. I hate that I'm a part of it.

She looks so graceful when she sleeps, like the world has never touched her and no one has ever hurt her, but that's not the reality. I hold my hand just above her face, close enough to feel the warmth radiating from her skin, but not close enough to steal it. If I touch her, I don't think I'll stop. Even with her eyes closed, she makes me feel like I'm worth saving. She doesn't know it yet, but I'll ruin her. And the worst part? I'll do it gently.

I climb back down the trellis then light a cigarette. Cold hits my chest but the heat of her stays on my skin. She burns me without even knowing it.

Smoke isn't enough for me right now. I need something harder, something violent.

I try to leave quietly in my loud car— I don't want to wake her. The drive doesn't take me long, even though it's two towns over.

The alley behind the club, The Underground, smells like sweat and blood. It feels like the closest thing to a home right now. It used to be a night club, but now it's a place for people who need more, like me.

I hear loud, familiar voices as I get closer to the building. I push through the door, ducking past the bodyguard. No one asks questions here, that's why I like it. Through the lobby's low light, I can see the black paint flaking off the walls. I walk toward Johnny, the club organizer, and pay him my entry fee. I make my way through the crowd of people.

Standing on the sidelines, I watch the main fight until it's my turn.

The first hit lands sharp on my jaw and I smile—I've got this.

The crowd gets louder as the taste of metal fills my mouth, and just for a few seconds the world disappears. No warmth and no softness. No guilt, just pain. Just me.

Fire

Scarlett

Tonight, I need to relax. I've been so busy with exams and boxing that I haven't taken any time to unwind. I paint my toenails bright red, the lamp on my bedside table casting just enough light that I can see each coat I apply. *Cigarette's After Sex* plays in my headphones and almost instantly, everything else that's going on in my head tries to fade. Usually, I enjoy stillness and quiet, but tonight the lack of noise made me anxious. I needed something to distract me, hence the toenail painting.

I chew the inside of my cheek as the polish brush flattens against my pinky toenail. I twist the lid back onto the glass nail polish bottle and open my bedside table drawer, pulling out some Sour Patch Kids gummies. I pop them in my mouth, one at a time— yellow, red, orange, green, and blue. The order must stay the same. It's something I do when I'm anxious. Seven years ago, when I was sixteen, I read that eating something sour helps with feeling anxious, and it's always stuck.

My phone buzzes and the screen lights up on my desk. I carefully try to keep my toes separated and reach over to grab it.

Callum: You going?

No context. I know that he's talking about the party at the Bronsen brother's tonight. My thumb hovers over the screen and a hundred snarky remarks pop into my head.

Scarlett: Didn't think you cared.

Delete.

Scarlett: Why?

Delete.

I sigh and place the phone beside me, on the bed. I don't need to reply right away. My chest tightens in a familiar way. My phone buzzes again.

Sophia: I'm coming over.

I'm not going out tonight. I already said no to Sophia. She can come over and get ready for the party, but I plan to stay home and watch a movie.

Scarlett: Sure, but I'm not going with you.

Sophia: ;)

Ten minutes later, Sophia bursts open my bedroom door.

"Hey Scar. Where's Jake?"

It's not unusual for her to do this. We often show up at each other's houses on the weekends, but something about tonight feels different.

"My toenails are wet!" I yell as she jumps onto my bed.

"Oh, cute color. Are you doing your fingernails to match?" She grabs my hands and examines them.

"Nah, I've been boxing too much lately. They'll just come right off. Maybe you can do them next week?" Sophia is the best at painting nails.

My phone buzzes again.

Callum: It's rude to ignore people.

I snort. It's rude for him to assume I'm not busy. Sophia raises her eyebrows.

"Who is that?"

I try not to make eye contact with her.

"No one."

"Um, Scar! I can tell by your face it's not no one!" She moves closer.

"Fine, I'll tell you, but I don't want you to freak out."

She smiles and stares at me, waiting impatiently.

"It's Callum Mercer, but it isn't anything and I don't want you to get weird about it."

She lets out a small yelp.

"Tell me everything!"

"I don't know what it is yet, so please, let's drop it."

"Okay, but it's more of a reason to come with me tonight." She sighs.

"I don't want to deal with everyone tonight. Plus, those parties can be so annoying." I roll my eyes with my phone in hand, unsure if I'm going to reply yet.

"Well, I think you should. You can come with me and then we can say hi to your hot little problem." She smirks.

"Ew, do not call him that. He's not my problem." I nudge her side.

"Oh, so you think he's hot?" She won't let that one slide past her.

"Of course, I think he's hot. Have you seen him? He's not just hot, he's gorgeous." I look down at my phone.

"Oh honey, you're so done for." She rests her head on my shoulder.

"Stop it, I am not!" I yell.

She jumps off my bed and walks over to my closet.

"I'm not even going to force you to put something fancy on, just jeans and a shirt. Come on... please?" She pulls out a beige tank top and throws it onto my bed.

I grab the top, dig my favourite pair of jeans out from the hamper, and change. From my closet, I pull out a pair of black heel boots and show them to Sophia, asking for her approval.

"Yes!" She screams.

"Jeez, calm down." I laugh as I sit on the edge of my bed and slip them onto my feet. "I'm not staying for long."

"We'll see about that." Before we leave, she fixes her makeup in the mirror that sits on my dresser. I text Dad that I'm headed out and shove my phone into my clutch.

As we pull into the Bronsen brother's long driveway, my stomach tightens. I hear music before I even get out.

"Good God. I already have a headache." I look to Sophia and push the door open.

I get out of the passenger seat and glance at the house. Expensive looking lights line the walkway to the front door.

"You look hot. How long do you think before he comes over to you?" Sophia asks as we walk toward the back of the house.

"I'm not here for him." The denial seeps out of my mouth.

Sophia gives me a sassy side glare.

"Mhm. Sure."

As we enter, the back porch is overflowing with students. Sophia greets people she knows, and I trail behind her. My eyes scan the room as we step into the house. I don't mean to look for him, but I am.

And then I see him.

He leans against a taupe-coloured wall with a drink in his hand. His dark eyes land on mine, like he's been waiting to see me all night.

I look away.

Someone drags Sophia into the kitchen, and she disappears into the crowd of familiar faces. I stay behind and trace the edges of the room with my eyes—anything to keep me from looking back at him.

My skin feels warm, too warm. I need a drink that I won't sip, or a dark corner to disappear to. Instead, I slip between the crowd and down a hallway, toward the back of the house. The walls feel smaller, almost like they buffer some of the noise.

I feel his presence before I see him.

I turn around and Callum stands behind me, leaning against the wall, like he's been here the entire time.

"Were you going to say hi to me?" He asks with his low voice.

"Not everything is about you, Callum." I cross my arms.

He pushes off the wall, calmly but with tension at the same time.

"Could've fooled me."

I hate how he makes me feel so uneasy and safe all at once.

"Why are you always around?" Our eyes meet. "Why this... sudden pull to each other?"

"I got tired of fighting it." His answer is soft but raw. The silence that follows feels louder than the music that blares through the house.

I blink; my throat is heavy. I swallow and gaze at him like I'm going to say something, but I don't. Instead, my eyes focus on his lips.

His eyes pierce mine. He inches closer and grabs my neck, sliding his warm hands to the base of my skull, and cradles my head with enough force that allows me to stay locked on his eyes.

"I tried to stop wanting you." He steps even closer, our bodies barely touching. "I failed." Our eyes dance together in a familiar way. The tension builds.

His lips crash onto mine. The kiss is hard and uninviting, but not unwanted. My body tenses as he steals the breath from my lungs. He devours my mouth, forcing our tongues to meet. There's nothing fragile about it. His hands make their way into my hair and my chest heaves, in need of air while I give into him. My hands find his hair like they belong there. He pulls me closer, and my chest presses into him. His mouth is fire and control—too much and not enough.

The cold wall cools my back as he presses me against it. His warm hands move down to my hips, claiming them. I let him. His wet lips move toward my jaw, slow and deliberate, like he is mapping my skin with his mouth. My hands slide to the collar of his shirt. I tug on him, hard. He lets out a low, rough moan, as if his last shred of patience has snapped.

His mouth lands onto mine again, hungrier than before. I feel him in every inch of my body—the rush, the ache. I should pull away, but I press closer into him. Before I let myself become consumed by him, I stop.

I pull back and look at him, reminding myself of where we are and who we are— two people with opposite lives that aren't supposed to be together. I don't say anything. I don't have to.

I slip down the hall, back to the party. My lips still burn from him. Regret fills the pit of my stomach. I hate the way he kisses me like he already owns my body.

Lift. Your. Fucking. Hips

Scarlett

The outside lights are left on when I pull into the driveway. I expect the usual sense of relief when I walk into the house, but I feel nothing. As the door shuts behind me, I lean against it. I sigh and walk upstairs. My body stays tense, unable to relax.

Dad told me that he was going to a friend's house to watch the hockey game, so he'll be home late. I didn't expect to beat him home, but I also needed to escape. That kiss was a mistake.

What is Callum doing to me? I touch my lips where the heat from his mouth still rests.

There's something about Callum that makes me crave him. He's so mysterious and the more I talk to him, the more I want to peel back his layers and discover what's underneath.

I need to focus on school right now. As I get changed and tuck myself into bed, I lick my lips, removing any remnants of him that remain.

Minutes feel like hours. I roll over, trying to get in a comfortable position. There's no use.

Sigh.

I throw the covers off and sit up at the side of my bed.

12:40 a.m.

That stupid clock.

I stand and make my way downstairs, grabbing my gym bag from the front door. Since I'm already up, I might as well let out some steam.

I grab my gloves and step out to the punching bag in the corner of the garage.

The lights are off, but I know my way around.

I flick on a lamp on Dad's tool bench. The bright lights are too harsh, so instead, the gloomy low light welcomes me.

I pull my gloves on and hit the bag. With every punch, instead of feeling calm, my anger builds. I control my breath and continue to strike the still bag until my sports bra is covered in sweat.

I lift my glove and wipe the sweat that glistens on my forehead.

Suddenly, I sense that someone is watching me. The uneasy weight forces me to look over my shoulder. I don't expect to spot those dark sea eyes, creeping in the shadows. He leans against the inside of the door frame.

"What, are you following me now?" I try to catch my breath.

A calculated raspy chuckle escapes his mouth.

"No, Scarlett. You just seem to be noticing now."

I'm taken back by his statement, but I sense that he's telling the truth. I wonder if he's been watching and hiding in the shadows. I don't know if that should scare or comfort me.

"What do you want, Callum? You're at my house." I'm not a toy he can play with. He needs to understand that when he comes into my house uninvited.

"I know where I am, Scarlett." His arms remain folded across his chest.

"Then what do you want, Callum?" My temper is short. I'm already confused by the kiss from earlier.

He takes a step forward, but his body language doesn't change.

"Maybe I just wanted to see you again."

I know that feeling, but I can't show him.

"You've seen me, is that good enough now?" I throw my hands out to the side, fed up with his games.

His expression changes. There's a shift in his eyes as he takes another step toward me. I don't move back.

"No, Scarlett, it's not good enough."

I try to stay calm, but my chest rises and falls too quickly to control. *What does that mean?*

I silently stare at him.

"Why are you down here at one in the morning punching an old bag?" He breaks our eye contact and looks at the punching bag.

"I couldn't sleep." I don't mean to tell him, but it just comes out. "You either?" I picture Callum as someone who doesn't get lots of sleep.

"Something like that. I don't have people waiting for me at home like you do."

I know he isn't trying to make me feel guilty.

"What are your parents like?" For a moment, I doubt that he'll be honest with me.

He looks to the ground and leans against a car that sits in Dad's shop.

"My parents?"

He takes a few seconds before he looks back at me.

"My father only knows how to take. Respect, loyalty, love… he demands them like he's owed something from everyone. My mother… she gave up a long time ago. She sold herself to the highest bidder and called it survival. I was raised on duty and distance, not love."

I don't pity him. I *hurt* for him. He doesn't hold back. Silence fills the room. I want his parents to feel pain the way that he does every day.

"You deserved better, you still do." I shake my head with frustration, but I can't look at him yet. I step toward the bag.

Before he has a chance to respond, I throw a punch– quick and hard. I expect him to leave but he stays in place. *He shouldn't stay.*

The air thickens. I can feel him moving closer with his heavy and silent steps. His rough, steady hands stop the bag as he grabs it, mid swing.

My knuckles hit the leather, and I freeze. I can feel him against my back, and every inch of me burns like I'm on fire. I shouldn't turn around. I'm afraid if I do, I might forget all the reasons why I should stay away from him.

I feel his warm breath against my neck.

"Nobody has ever said that to me before."

My chest tightens.

"That I deserve better," he adds, his voice cracks like it costs him everything. Another beat passes. He lets out a controlled breath, almost like a laugh, but he remains serious.

"My whole life, I've known that better wasn't for people like me, Scarlett."

I can't hold back any longer. I turn and face him. My gaze is captivated by his parted lips. He moves his hand down the side of my arm and removes it quickly, like he'll ruin me if he touches me.

I grab his hand. I let my vulnerability match his. "You're wrong."

I stare into his eyes and really see him. The boy who no one fought for and the man who fights for everyone.

"You don't know that, Scarlett," he says, as if he holds so much darkness within him.

"Then show me," I respond, soft and daring. I'm no stranger to the darkness.

His hands trace my body up to my face.

"If I touch you, it won't be gentle." His lips hover above mine. "Say stop, lie to me, pretend you don't want this."

I don't respond. Instead, I bridge the gap. His lips come down on mine, hard and fast. I feel the pressure behind his hands as he parts my lips with his tongue.

His mouth is hot on mine, and his hands tighten at the base of my neck. He bites my bottom lip—not hard enough that I pull away, but with enough force for my mouth to taste the blood.

His hands work their way down my body and squeeze my ass. He picks me up and gently places me on the hood of the car that sits on the lift in the ground. Then sets me down, like I'm precious cargo.

I moan. His tongue licks the side of my neck.

"I tried to stay away from you Scarlett," he whispers into my neck.

I know exactly what he means—the tension, the pull.

"Stop trying." He pulls away and kisses the top of my head.

I need more.

"Please."

I wrap my legs around him. He comes back for more, devouring my mouth, while his hands trail down to my torso and land on my tits. He squeezes them.

"Fuck."

I moan and pull him back up to my face. This isn't a kiss, it's violent. It feels like I'm fighting for whatever lives deep inside him. I feel him smile against my mouth.

He trails his hot, wet tongue down my chest and pulls my sports bra down, exposing my nipple. He takes it in his mouth.

He grabs a fist full of my hair, forcing my head back.

"Now you're going to come for me, Scarlett." He lets go of my bra, leaving me raw and exposed.

"Lift your hips." He pulls at my shorts.

"Callum I was just boxing–"

"I'm a fucking man, Scarlett," his tone is stern. "I don't care what you've been doing– Lift. Your. Fucking. Hips."

I comply and place both hands on the hood of the car to lift my hips. He pulls my shorts down, slowly, like we've done it before.

My back slams on the hood of the car as he grabs my hips and thrusts me forward. He doesn't waste another minute. Callum's lips meet the wetness between my legs. He licks my swollen clit, sucking the life out of me. It's never felt like this before. I throw my head back.

"Callum, fuck." I moan.

He pulls away only for a moment.

"Eyes on me, Scarlett." I watch as he devours me, like I'm his reason for living.

Warmth builds behind my clit.

"Callum I'm so close." I wrap my legs behind his head. I want to hold back.

"Callum."

"Let go Scarlett." I pant, the pressure building, tighter and tighter, until I can't hold back any longer.

"Fuck." My hands pull his hair as I finish on his mouth.

He grabs my face and kisses me, making me taste my own come. I grip his face between my hands and his jaw shifts. I can feel his hard dick against my center.

I reach for his belt, but his hand stops me.

"Not yet Scarlett. When I take you, I want you to know who you belong to."

Burning

Callum

Silence startles me. I'm used to waking up in my bed alone, but today I wish I wasn't. My cock gets hard just thinking about the way she moaned my name. The taste of her sweet clit still lingers on my lips.

I throw off the covers and walk over to the large window beside my desk. I must distance Scarlett from my lifestyle. The Society knows all my worst parts—she should only see the good. I need to shield her from that side of me.

I look at the gloves that are on the floor underneath the punching bag. I don't use them. I never do. I deserve the pain.

My bare knuckles hit the bag, fast and hard. Again, harder. Again, faster. Each hit helps my thoughts escape a little more, but she keeps creeping back in. The bag jolts with every hit, her voice stuck in my chest. I can't get rid of her.

I hit with my left hand, then put all my force behind my right-handed blow. The bag swings back at me. I grab the cool leather and rest my head against it.

How could someone as pure as her want someone like me? I need to see her again—she has a class at 10 a.m. today.

I shove the bag out of my way, race to the bathroom, and start the shower. As hot steam fills the room, I grip the edge of the counter, staring at my reflection in the mirror. I look just like my father. Everyone tells me that and every time I hear it feels like a slap to the face. It isn't bad enough that I have his brutal expectations to live up to, I have to look like him too.

    I dry myself off and walk to my colour-coded closet to pick an outfit for the day—jeans and a black t-shirt. My worn leather jacket lies on the back of my desk chair. I grab it and head out.

    On campus, there's a shift in the air. My mood usually changes closer to winter, but this year is different. Maybe it's because this is my final year and I'm only just realizing it, but I feel more disconnected than I usually do.

    The Society hides within the bones of this place—in its traditions, books, and buildings named after old money. Most people are here because they have to be, not because they want to be. They were born into a system of entitlement, empty and rotten beneath a gold-plated surface—like me.

    I stay in my car and put the window down, watching as she pulls into her favourite parking spot—the same one she parks in almost every day. As she gets out of the driver's seat, she grabs her bag. I expect to see a change in her, maybe something in her step that's changed since last night. Instead, she looks untouched and pure, freely walking toward the campus buildings like she wasn't fucked by my tongue last night. It drives me *mad*.

    I've never cared enough to act territorial over a woman before. But I don't just want to claim Scarlett, I want everyone to know that she's mine—yet I don't at the same time.

As her perfectly outlined legs lead her toward the psych building, she pulls something out of her bag. *Gummy bears? No, sour gummies.* Scarlett, a sucker for something sour. I watch her examine the colour of each candy in her hand before she individually brings them to her mouth. She must eat them in a specific order. *Interesting.*

My mind shifts back to last night. *I'll have her on her knees for me soon enough.* I reach into my pocket for a cigarette without looking away from her. I bring it to my lips and light it, hoping to find clarity when I inhale, but the heaviness remains.

I watch her walk down the campus path. She turns back only for a moment and sees me. Her eyes meet mine, like they were looking for me. I feel a pounding in my chest, but neither of us react. She breaks our eye contact and turns to leave just as my phone rings. I hold my stare on her before I pick it up.

"Callum, we have a drop on Thursday." Harrison gets right to it.

"Just us?" I ask.

"Yeah, it's just a small one out of town but it shouldn't take too long." He's quick to respond.

I sigh.

"You good, Mercer?"

"Yeah, you at The Society tonight?" He usually spends most of his free time there.

"I'm just leaving. You want to meet up for a drink later?"

"Sure, text me." I'm about to hang up as he interrupts.

"Oh Callum, don't forget about the party at The Society next Friday."

"How could I forget?"

In the two times that I've seen Mother this week, she's mentioned it.

"I think I know the answer but... are you bringing anyone?" He doesn't miss a beat. I want to bring Scarlett, but she can't be placed in dangers way. Although, at this point, being with me is probably her safest option.

"I'm not sure."

Silence.

"Okay, I'll text you later." He hangs up.

I start the engine, ready to head home.

At the house, I can immediately tell that no one is here. I drop my keys on the marble table that sits just inside the door. It's quiet. The furnace lightly hums and the tick of the grandfather clock in the study feels empty and sterile.

I take my jacket off and throw it on a chair by the kitchen island. I pace into the study, straight for the decanter on the desk. I pour a glass of the amber whiskey, no ice. I don't want to dilute it. The first sip burns, but I don't wince. The pain is familiar.

I move down the hall and into my room— the only place where I can hide from the legacy that this house represents. I lean on the window frame with my shoulder against the wood, watching the sun set and trees sway in the wind. I think of her.

I don't know how to give love, but I'd burn for hers.

Forgotten Roses

Scarlett

It's just after dinner and it's already dark outside. My computer screen lights up the room. I need to finish this assignment. Although it's not due for another week, there's still more research to be done for my Early Developmental psychology paper.

I shift in my desk chair and hug a leg against my chest. I'm not sure why, but I find myself thinking about him, again. It feels out of character for me, but as soon as his mouth landed on mine, I wanted more. There's something about Callum Mercer that I'm drawn to, but there's a part of him that feels restricted and off limits.

My phone buzzes on the nightstand. I reach over and grab it.

Callum: Come outside.

I look out my window—I don't see his car. Within a few seconds, his Jaguar creeps down the street. *How did he know I was home?*

Scarlett: Why?

Callum: Don't make me ask twice.

I smirk as I read his text. *Who the hell does he think he is telling me what to do?* I should stay here just to show him he doesn't control me, but instead I shut my laptop and go downstairs.

As I put my sneakers on, Dad sits on a lounge chair in the living room and watches TV.

"I'm headed out for a bit, Dad, don't wait up for me."

"Okay, honey. I love you." He looks up from the TV. I walk over and give him a tight hug.

I grab my keys and purse—even though he'll notice that I don't take my car. The porch light is already on as I close the door behind me. I see him parked a few houses down and pray that he doesn't pull up in front of mine. The last thing I need is Dad finding out. Even though I'm an adult, he still worries about me.

I walk by the hood of his car and see him reach across, opening the passenger door from the inside.

Well, isn't that chivalrous of him. I fight a smile as I duck and slip into the seat.

"My dad would love your car." It's the first thing that comes out of my mouth. I feel like I owe him an explanation. "He loves fixing up older cars, but he has a sweet spot for a newer sports car."

He doesn't respond. Instead, he just looks at me, his eyes turning dark as the interior lights fade.

"Put your seat belt on."

"Why, are we going somewhere? I thought you were just stopping by to say hi," I say, with sarcasm. I reach and pull the belt across me.

He smirks and shifts the car into drive. My eyes scan the inside of his car. The leather of the seats feels stiff and new. I could taste smoke after we kissed, and I saw him smoking on the balcony at the party, so it doesn't shock me to see a pack of cigarettes and a lighter in the center console. Otherwise, there's nothing personal in here. It's like he walked into his garage and picked a car from the many his parents own and just hopped in it. Although, I know that's not true, I've only seen him drive this car to school.

The headlights pierce through fog as we head toward campus. I look over at him. He's got one hand on the wheel and the other on his gear shift. His car is automatic, but it's almost as if he had a manual before and the habit just stuck.

He doesn't look nervous. There's a calmness about him I wish I had.

"Where are we going?" I ask.

He doesn't take his eyes off the road. "There's a few different places on campus that not many people know about." I look out the window.

"But you do?" His head turns and peers at my reflection. I turn to him quickly, hoping our eyes meet. Instead, I'm met with his side profile.

Why won't he look at me?

"Something like that."

He has both hands on the steering wheel now. We don't say anything else. The silence is comforting. My hands are cold, so I put them under my thighs for warmth. He doesn't face me, but he reaches for the button to turn my heated seat on.

It's dark and I can't see much. His car slows as we pull into an area I've never been. It's still on campus, almost on the edge of town. As we get closer, I see a small, worn building with the vines crawling up its sides.

"What is this place?" I lean closer to the dashboard to try and get a better view.

He puts the car in park and turns it off.

"Do you trust me?"

This catches me off guard. I'm not sure. My gut tells me no but what comes out is, "Yes."

Finally, our eyes meet. He slowly moves closer to me, like friction is pulling him. Without breaking our eye contact, he places his hand on the door behind him and slides out. He walks in front of the car and opens my door, like he's done this a hundred times. I get out. He shuts it and heads toward the darkness. I follow him. Although the lights from his car remain on, I still can't make out what this place is.

When we reach the building, he rattles the knob and shoves the wooden door with his shoulder. *He's definitely been here before.* The smell of soil and moss overwhelm me. Callum reaches up and pulls on a string for a light to flick on.

A yellow bulb faintly shines, just enough that I can make out the room. It's a greenhouse.

"What is this place?" I walk over to a bench with a terracotta pot on it, running my finger over its broken edges. As I keep walking, the smell changes, now an elegant, honeyed spice. Its sweetness is familiar. Up ahead, I spot at least a dozen red and pink rose bushes.

"This place has been forgotten about, abandoned. No one tends to them anymore." His voice is low as he walks over to the other side of the table I stand in front of.

"But you do." I look at him. *He must.* He rubs a petal between his fingers.

"I wouldn't have picked you out as a flower guy."

His eyes meet mine, like they are trying to tell me something.

"I'm not, but these ones were left, forgotten. They shouldn't have made it. But with the right help they thrive. It's hard to explain, but they survived when they should've died."

I know he's referring to more than just the flowers. "Like you."

He looks at me for a beat and leans back against the table, his hands on either side of him.

"I could sit here and blame it all on shitty parents, Scarlett, but I'm the one who makes bad choices. I can't blame anyone else for what I've done."

"You don't have to blame anyone else Callum—you were raised in a house where you weren't shown how to be loved. It's your parent's job to show you, to teach you."

"It's not like that Scarlett, not for most people. You fight for your legacy, not what you believe in. You don't get a choice. Your only choice is to survive, and sometimes the price of that is yourself."

"I don't know what that's like, so I won't lie to you and tell you that I get it. My dad loves me unconditionally and supports everything I do. My mom is a different story, but—"

"Tell me about your mom." He interrupts.

"Um, she is," I sigh. "She's the opposite of my dad. She left us, for a life I'll never understand. It was before high school. I knew things were changing between my parents. I knew they were drifting apart... but she just became someone that I didn't recognize." I take a second to peek at the flowers, finding comfort in their smell. "I know she works at the steakhouse in town, but truthfully... I think she's an escort. I've heard things and people have told me that they've seen her out before. I don't know if Dad knows. I'm sorry, I didn't mean to overshare."

"You deserve better." His voice is low, almost angry. Our eyes lock. His jaw stiffens as he steps forward. I feel embarrassed.

I look down at the flowers, their sweetness draws me in. "It is what it is," I say. His footsteps get closer.

He stands in front of me and his hand grabs my jaw as his eyes meet my glossy sight.

"That doesn't make it right, Angel."

For a minute, my breath picks up. I can feel my heart in my stomach. His hand remains gripped around my jaw. "That doesn't make it right for you either, Callum."

His face tenses, like he's fighting something deep within. "Every time I feel nothing, I take something from someone else. Their breath. Their fear. Their control. I don't want to take anything from you." He slightly squeezes my jaw. My breath hitches. "I'll ruin you." He rests his forehead against mine, so delicately.

I shouldn't want him. There are so many versions of him that I don't know. But why does none of that matter?

"I'm already broken."

That does it for him. His hands rest on either side of my face and his mouth melts into mine. My hands find the front of his jacket, pulling him closer, but he's not close enough— I need all of him. My mouth opens for his tongue while his hands run through my hair. He grabs my head and pulls it back.

"Let me ruin you." He whispers.

His lips hover above mine.

"You already have." His lips land back on mine, more aggressive this time. For a second, he pulls away, brushing me off to the side while his arm pushes the broken pots off the table. They hit the floor; their crash startles me.

He lifts me by my ass and sets me back on the dirty table. His hands work their way up the outside of my shirt until he aggressively pulls it down, exposing my chest. His mouth salivates as he looks at me and flicks my hardened nipple, back and forth against his thumb. He places his warm lips on my neck and works their way down my breasts. With each kiss, he breaks me a little more. I can feel myself getting wet and shift my hips forward, trying to find some relief on his cock against the seam of my jeans. My head falls back. *It's ecstasy.*

"Fuck."

I reach for his mouth on mine. My tongue traces the outline of his lips. His Adam's apple bobbles as his lips graze my ear.

"Take these off."

I unbutton my jeans and pull the zipper down. He grabs them at the waistband and pulls them down my legs, peeling away the only dignity I have. He rubs his knuckle along the front of my thong before he pulls my underwear down and exposes me. He slides two fingers in, cradling my clit. His fingers swirl back and forth. I bring my lips to his, but he pulls back, not letting me kiss him. He moves faster against my clit, stops for a second, then positions his fingers down, plunging into me.

"See how wet you get for me?" He unleashes something feral in me. I move my hips against him, faster.

While his hand fucks me, I reach down and undo his belt. I unzip his jeans and pull them down, leaving him in his boxers. My hand trails down his stomach and slides into the top of his underwear. He sucks in a deep breath. I grab his hard cock and work my hand up and down his shaft, at times running my finger over his tip. His ass flexes. I quietly moan. He pulls his hand out. His thumb caresses my cheek before he shoves his fingers, with my wetness still on them, into my mouth. In a swift motion, he uses his other hand to pull his boxers down.

"I can't hold back anymore, Scarlett. Say you're mine." He looks down at me, his hard dick against my wet entrance. He removes his fingers from my mouth.

"I'm yours." He leans forward and slowly pushes his cock inside of me.

"Who do you belong to?"

He briefly pulls out. "Oh, fuck." I need all of him. His palms lie flat on the table as he braces himself around me.

"Scarlett, who do you belong to?" He asks again.

"You Callum, you. Just you." He shoves himself into me—it's better than anything I've felt before. As he leans forward, he rests his forehead against mine and plows into me, over and over. Strangely, there's something sweet about him being so vulnerable.

"Oh, God." I moan.

He slows down, running his nose runs over mine, and brings his hand up to my neck.

"I'm the only one you worship now." He pushes into me—faster, harder. My climax builds. Sweat runs down my back. I grab his ass, and he squeezes my neck harder.

"Callum, I'm going to–" He bites my lip, cutting me off. Blood enters my mouth as he slams into me one last time.

"Fuck, Scarlett." He lets out a deep moan. The pressure inside of me releases as I finish with him.

Our chests rise and fall in sync as we catch our breaths. His thumb brushes over my lip, where he bit me.

"You bleed so sweetly for me."

Clarity

Scarlett

I spray washer fluid onto my windshield, wiping away the frost. Long over are the days of t-shirts and jeans. It's the end of fall and I'm not looking forward to Millhaven's cold and dark winters. It's so hard to get out of bed most days when the sun sets early and rises later. But today, something is different.

Cool heat blasts inside my car on the way to campus. I keep thinking about how to explain last night to Sophia. She'll be able to tell that something's up, and I don't want to keep anything from her. Maybe I don't have to tell her *everything*.

What do I even say? I have no idea how to explain anything related to Callum. I try to make practical sense of what last night meant, but all I can think about is how bad I want it to happen again. He keeps opening up to me in ways I don't expect. *Does that make things okay?*

I pull into the campus parking lot, turn off the car, and give myself a pep talk. *Okay. You can do this, nothing has changed. Go to class, box, then go home. It's simple.*

Except it's so damn messy. Everything has changed. There's nothing simple about anything in my life right now. *Great pep talk.*

I grab my bag and walk toward the coffee bar. I pull a tube of lip gloss out of my bag and put on a thin coat.

Look good, feel good, right? I try to channel everything I've learned from the last four years to guide me. How am I supposed to help others if I can't stop spiraling about a guy. Or am I being too hard on myself?

I spot Sophia in the courtyard as I walk over to the coffee shop.

"Scar!" She holds two drinks.

"Thanks, Soph." I grab my drink from her and faintly smile.

"I was thinking, maybe next weekend we could go out together?" She always has a plan.

"Where?"

"There's this new club that opened. I figured a little post midterm fun wouldn't hurt?" I'm hesitant, but I do think I need a night out with Soph.

"Sure?" I respond, in more of a question than an answer.

"Sure?" She looks me up and down. "You aren't going to make me beg you or put up a fight?"

I shrug. "We both know that you'll convince me anyways, so I might as well just say yes now."

"Who are you and what have you done with Scarlett Voss?" She links her arm with mine. "Seriously. Should I be worried?"

I don't have it in me to hide the truth from my best friend. The momentary silence is enough to make her frown.

"I had sex with Callum," I blurt out.

Wow, smooth Scarlett.

Sophia gasps. "Tell me everything and don't leave out a single detail."

A small, awkward laugh escapes my mouth. "We just... had sex."

"Okay. You need to start at the beginning. Since when are you and Callum a *we*? I can't believe you didn't tell me things escalated." She looks slightly offended.

"It's not that I didn't want to tell you. And we aren't a *we*, Soph. He just..." I smile. "It's complicated. It might not work out. I'm just letting whatever happens, happen. Callum is complex. Dark. Messy."

"Do you want it to work out?" She asks me the question I've been too nervous to ask myself.

"I don't know what I want." I pause and stare at the people that pass us. "But the sex, I want that again." We laugh together.

"Callum Mercer looks like he knows how to fuck." She raises her eyebrows and squeezes my arm.

"Oh my god, Soph!" I screech.

"What, he does. And based on your reaction, I'm not wrong."

I fight a smile as I look down at my watch.

"Bye Soph, I'll see you later. Thanks for the chat."

"Anytime. Love you." We hug and walk our separate ways to class.

Professor Budgley calls on me for an answer. For the first time in a while, I wasn't paying attention.

"Oh um, sorry can you repeat the question please." She sighs with disappointment and moves on to a different student instead.

Professor Budgley's voice sounds muffled between my thoughts. All I can think of is getting to the gym—I need clarity today. When everyone stands to pack their things, I realize that class is finally over.

I throw on my jacket and walk to the car. I unlock it and throw my bag in, wishing I had heated seats.

The gym's fresh smell welcomes me as I open the door. It's only been three days since I was last here, but it feels like forever. I spot Ricco tidying around the cardio machines. As I walk toward my locker, it's not long before he sees me. I open its squeaky door as he comes over.

"Hey kid, it's been a while. You ready to get back in the ring or what?" I should have known he would've noticed my absence.

"Careful old man, it almost sounds like you missed me." I nudge him with my elbow.

"Oh yeah, I really missed your slacking off and smart mouth." He says sarcastically.

Deep down, I know he cares about me. He's put up with me for long enough that I've either grown on him or added more stress in his life. Likely both.

I crawl through the ring ropes. Something about placing my feet in the middle of the canvas calms my nerves. Ricco jumps into the ring, acting like he's still twenty years old.

"You remember how to do this?" He says as he puts his gloves on.

"You'll wish I didn't soon enough, old man." I bounce back and forth on the balls of my feet, prepared to unleash a fight. I never have to worry about going too hard on Ricco. I know he can take it. He understands that the further I go, the clearer my mind gets. He told me once he feels the same way.

I lift my hands to block my face. I throw the first punch, then move quickly on my feet, swaying to the dance we both know so well. We continue at it for about forty minutes. He blocks every shot I throw. Before I've even calculated my next move, he knows what to expect.

"You can do better Scar, come on." Although that may discourage others, it gets me going.

I put my full force into the next jab. I lick the side of my mouth, tasting the salty sweat that runs down my face. My legs burn.

I shouldn't have taken so many days off. I stop to catch my breath, take off my glove, and pull my mouth guard out.

Ricco removes his gloves and walks over to me. "You must've really needed that."

I chuckle. "Yeah, I did."

His face turns serious. "Does it have anything to do with the guy who followed you to the gym a while ago?"

I've never been good at hiding my facial expressions, so he must realize by my reaction that I have no idea what he's talking about.

"What, when?" *I never saw Callum here.*

"I didn't want to say anything at the time and make you worried. He left shortly after you came in. Are you in trouble Scarlett?" There's the overbearing man I know.

"No, I'm not in trouble Ricco, Jesus. It's just a guy with a crush. I'm fine, and for the record, we both know I can handle myself."

He laughs.

"Oh, I'd never want to cross you in a dark alley." He smiles, but his face remains concerned. "Just be careful, I know you're safe, and one of the smartest women I know... But there's bad people in this town. I'm always here if you need me."

I trust Ricco and know he would be there for me without hesitation. I step toward him and place my hand on his shoulder.

"You're the best Ricco, and you need new friends if I'm the smartest woman you know. I give myself credit where it's due, but come on dude."

We laugh together. "Okay, maybe smartest was a stretch." He adds.

I playfully hit his arm and smile. "Dick."

"I'll be back tomorrow. Save me a round." I climb out of the ring and make my way over toward my locker. I hesitate before I open it, my mind is stuck on the thought of Callum following me here.

I hate that I'm thinking about him, again.

Bliss

Callum

The roof's dark peaks come into view as I pull up the driveway. What used to be a beautiful place, is now so tainted. Dead leaves crunch under my car as I pull into my usual spot. I walk into The Society and up the stairs to the lounge. I have to find Harrison and finalize the details of the drug run. It's the middle of a weekday, so I don't expect to see many people here.

I spot the parlour door cracked open. Harrison sits on a chair in the corner with a drink in his hand.

"Callum," he says. It's not an unusual way for him to greet me.

"What's the plan?" I walk toward the bar and pour myself a drink.

"We just have to run a few bricks into the city. It shouldn't take too long." My back faces him as I move over and stand beside the bookshelf.

I hope this drink will calm my mind.

"Usual spot?" We drop drugs off to a house in Boston. The drive up is nice, and the drop has a low chance for anything going awry. We've dealt with the same guys there for almost six years, so they know the chain of command.

"You bringing someone next week?" I ask and sit down in the chair next to him.

"I don't know. You still not sure either?" I know that I can trust Harrison, I just don't want to bring him into my shit.

"Yeah, I'm not sure if Scarlett should come. I don't know if she's safer out there or here with me." I take a large sip of the dark liquid in my glass.

"I get that man. But I don't think anything will really happen that night. There will be lots of eyes on everyone."

He's right. A couple of the sororities will be here, and we can't risk anything. Plus, all the Highers and their flavors of the night will be present as well. That reminds me... Scarlett's Mom.

"Do you see Vanessa Voss often at the parties?" I look at him and hesitate. "Should I be worried?"

His subtle glance already reveals his answer. "I've seen her around more lately. I'm not sure who enjoys her company, but I can find out," he says.

"I need to know. If I bring Scarlett, Vanessa can't be at the party. It's important." My voice is hesitant.

"What is this with Scarlett, Callum? You know that once she gets closer, you'll need to tell her about your involvement with The Society." I take another sip from my glass, the burn in my throat makes his words sink in.

I know that I'll have to tell Scarlett about The Society eventually, I just don't know how much I want to tell her. I also don't trust all the pledges, and even though I can keep her safe, I don't want her exposed to any threats. She's already been a victim to the power and greed that controls most of us.

"I know, I will tell her. I just need more time. She can't see me differently yet." My words feel like poison, thick and crippling. I never want to be responsible for her pain, it's too heavy.

"You just about ready?" I ask, changing the subject. I finish my drink, walk over to the bar, and place the empty glass on the rail. "We're taking my car." Harrison doesn't say anything. It's very rare that I let anyone else drive, I need control in all aspects of my life.

The clouds darken as we pull out of the manor. It's almost like Mother Nature knew that the mood has shifted.

Rain droplets pound against my windshield as we pull up to the house in Boston. It's your average suburban red brick house, that looks like it belongs to a middle-aged couple, not a drug organization. I park the car and pop the trunk. Harrison gets out. I take a minute longer and flip down the visor to look at myself in the mirror, turning on the side of me that most of the world already knows. *No one will ever see the side that she does.*

I grab the product from the trunk and walk up to the side of the house. The old pledges that did this run used to say, "whatever you do, don't knock on the front door. Go around the side and to the sliding door at the back." We thought they were fucking with us. Turns out they have nosy neighbours who like to complain, well... they *had* nosy neighbours.

We reach the back door and knock on the glass. Our usual three suspects sit at a table visible from the back porch—they always wait for us there. I'm not sure if they live here or just use this as a drop house. The door opens.

"The cash is in the kitchen," says Tom, a balding man with a larger build, probably in his mid-twenties. He seems to run the show around here. Tom stands on the side of the sliding door and motions for us to come in. We step into a room with floral wallpaper and butter yellow curtains that look like they aren't from this century. Nate, an average thirty-year-old with dark hair and a crappy mustache, stands and reaches into a cupboard in the kitchen behind Tom. He grabs a stack of cash and puts it on the table. Harrison walks over and picks it up without counting it. We've done this enough to know that it's the right amount. Harrison faces me and nods. I put the tightly packaged drugs on the table.

"The next drop is already arranged. We'll see you in a few weeks." I say, then silence fills the room.

"See you shortly." Tom reaches his hand out. I don't shake it, and we leave the house—we're past formalities at this point.

The bright moon shines against the well-lit streets as we make our way back to the car. War time bungalows surround us, coming more into view as I drive down the road.

Millhaven's welcome sign greets us once we drive into town. Returning here never feels like home. Brick mansions come into view as we pull up to The Society. I park, Harrison gets out, and he walks over to his car.

"I'll find out if they plan on having Vanessa at the party. Don't say anything to anyone else or someone might get suspicious," he says, pulling his car door open. I don't answer. Harrison drives off.

I pull my phone out as I sit, parked in the driveway. It's only been a day, but I need to see her. I type a message.

Callum: Be ready in 10.

I can be at her house faster than that, but I want to give her a few minutes notice, which is unlike me. I stare at the screen, hoping for a response.

Scarlett: Yes, Sir.

That little brat. *Does she know what she does to me when she talks like that?*

Callum: Careful, Angel.

She must be glued to her phone, just as engaged as I am.

Scarlett: Or what...

I can't wait another minute. I pull away from The Society and merge onto Cambridge Street, heading into town. *She puts up a strong front, but how much will it take to break her?*

I plan on where I want to take her. Not my house—even though I know no one will be there, I don't want the toxicity of that place to impact her. I know the perfect spot.

Callum: Come outside and find out.

I idle a few houses down. The streetlights are different on this side of town—grey poles with dull yellow lights as opposed to the black cast iron lights I'm used to. Those would never be found on the East side of town, where homes look like they belong in a classic British novel, and the bright streetlights act as manipulative beacons of hope guiding the way.

Scarlett steps out of the house. My eyes gravitate to her legs, wrapped in tight jeans. I can see every curve. *Fuck.* I stretch my pants to adjust my growing length. She walks in front of the car. I reach across and open the passenger door, as she slides into the seat. Just seeing her does it for me. Without a word, I grab her face and plant my open lips onto hers. Her hot breath enters my mouth as she moans. I suck on her bottom lip then pull away.

"What's that for?" She looks slightly irritated and out of breath. Her plump lips and glossy eyes cry for more, but I don't give into her yet.

"Brats get punished." She has no idea of her punishment today. Slowly, I'll break down every wall she's ever built. I know she's not ready for it yet.

"Sure, Callum."

I hold back a response and accelerate, pulling away from the curb. The car engine roars as I drive to a familiar part of town. We usually don't talk much in the car, but today I don't want the silence, I crave her thoughts.

"I'm not close with my grandparents," I blurt out. She knows that I'm not done.

"My dad's parents are from the same world—wealth, power, greed. And my mom's parents are just like her—they can be paid to stay quiet." I have no respect for either of them. I don't tell her that, but I'm sure she can piece it together.

"Do you see them a lot?" I can tell that she cares by the genuine way that she asks.

"No, only on special occasions, at fundraisers and sometimes for family dinners." We're almost out of town when I turn down Fraser Street, a road we've never been on together.

The houses on this road scream a different kind of wealth—one that I'm sure Scarlett isn't familiar with. Sure, she's friends with Sophia, and her dad has some high-profile clients, but even I'm in awe of these lavish houses when I see them. We turn into the most extravagant driveway on the block—the home of my grandparents, my father's parents. The perfectly spaced oak trees precisely line the driveway.

I'm not sure if they were ever humble about their wealth. From a young age, I've known that they'd want nothing to do with me until I was ready to work with my grandfather's tech company. Luckily for me, that time is coming.

"This house is stunning, Callum. I've never seen anything like it." The moon's reflection glows in her eyes. I hate that I have to look away to park.

"Where are we?" She smiles and faces me.

"This is my grandparent's estate." Our eyes finally meet again as I shift the car into park. "I don't come here often, but I thought you'd like it." I don't bother telling her that they aren't home—she can clue in on that part.

I circle behind the car to open the door for her, but she's already opened it. *So damn stubborn.* I lead us along a path to the side of the house and enter a code to open the door, turning the alarm off as we enter. As we pass through the foyer, Scarlett looks around, in awe. Her boots sound heavy on the marble floors.

I lead us into the library. Books line the walls, and scents of lumber mixed with expensive wine fill the room. Scarlett approaches one of the shelves, her fingers trace the books. I lean against a shelf across the room and watch her take it all in. I break the silence.

"I grew up reading a lot, my parents weren't around, and I wanted to fill the void, so I lost myself in novels."

She looks up at me, her head falls to the side, like she didn't expect me to say that.

"Out of all the habits you could've picked up, I guess escaping reality in literature isn't so bad." She smiles. "Who knew Callum Mercer was a softy."

I smile back and lick my lip. *She's done it again.* The air gets thicker as I step toward her. Suddenly, I feel an urge to break her and protect her all at once. I take a few more steps until I stand directly in front of her. Her breath hitches, while her ocean blue eyes gaze up at me through her thick eyelashes.

"There's this event next week, would you come with me?" The part of me that wants to protect her comes out first.

I can't predict her response.

"Like a date?"

I fight with how I should tell her about The Society. I'm not sure how much she's heard on campus, and I don't want to get her involved.

"There's this group that I belong to. It's mainly made up of high-power men from town, and their sons." She looks confused but I can tell that she is trying to wrap her head around it.

"So, you're in it because of your dad?"

I mean, it's the truth. "Yes." I don't want to lie to her.

"What do you guys do?"

Does she really want to know?

I've thought about this scenario so many damn times. How do I tell her that I'm involved with the people that tried to hurt her? She can't know that yet.

"Not all of us are good, Scarlett. But we do different things for the town, a lot of the time we try to fly under the radar." I don't know where this is going.

"Like Scouts?" She covers her mouth as she laughs a little.

"No Scarlett, not like Scouts." A part of me wishes that we were.

I tuck a strand of hair behind her ear. The heat of her skin brushes against my finger.

"Are you scared to be like him?" The question comes out of nowhere, but I know immediately who she's talking about.

"No. I despise him. If I ever let myself turn out like him, I wouldn't want to live."

Her lip curls up at my response.

"That's a pretty firm statement, Callum." She frowns.

"If you knew what he stands for, what he does, you'd feel the same, Scarlett." I can't tell her everything today, but someday I will. I'll have to.

"So, will you come with me?" I ask, reluctantly.

"What should I wear?" She tilts her head to the side.

I slide my hand up her arm, trailing until it lands on the back of her neck. "I'd prefer if you wore nothing at all. But for the sake of dignity, any dress will be perfect."

Finally, her mouth meets mine. I can breathe.

Challenge Accepted

Scarlett

I close the front door behind me and rest my back against the wood. I tilt my head up and smile. Dad is asleep in his chair in the living room. I walk over, pick up a blanket from the couch, and lay it across him. I'm halfway up the stairs when his voice startles me.

"Who was that?"

I turn around. Dad stares back at me from his chair.

"No one." A blatant lie.

"So, you've been out with no one most nights? I'm not an idiot Scarlett. You're an adult, you can do whatever you want. Just be careful." There's sincerity in his voice.

"Thanks Dad, I just don't know what it is yet. And I know you catch feelings early, so I'm trying to spare you the heart ache." It's true, he does. But I'm also trying to brush off these feelings I'm having.

He chuckles. "Hey, that's not fair. I'm just a lover."

I roll my eyes. "Oh, I know."

He looks out the window then back at me. "You don't know something is worth it 'til you try, Scar."

I smile. "Thanks, Dad. I love you." I turn around and continue up the stairs.

"I love you too." He proudly shouts.

Before I reach the last step, I stop briefly, still facing forward. "His name's Callum, he's a good guy," I yell. I won't get into all the demons and trauma that make Callum who he is, but at least he'll know his name.

"Callum. Hmm... Interesting name," I hear him say.

"Night, Dad." I laugh.

"Night, honey. Thanks for telling me, I can't wait to meet Callum." He emphasizes his name.

He's being protective, not snarky.

I laugh to myself and head into my room. *In Dad's eyes, I don't think I'll ever find anyone good enough for me.*

I throw my purse on the floor, shut the door, pull my phone out, and roll over on the bed. I open my conversation with Callum. He's probably not home yet, but I contemplate sending him a text. I bite the inside of my cheek. I don't want to sound desperate...

Fuck it.

Scarlett: Thanks for a good night.

I don't hit send. Instead, I stare at the message, overthinking.

A bubble with three dots appears and then disappears.

Callum: Miss me already?

I smile. He must've had our conversation open and saw that I was typing. Two can play this game. I delete what I previously typed out.

Scarlett: You wish.

He must be home—that was quick. *I wonder where he lives?* I imagine he's in one of the nicer neighborhoods in town, with houses like his grandparent's place. I linger on the thought, wondering if he'll ever take me to his house.

Callum: No, I pray.

I fixate on his response before I pull up Sophia's number. The phone rings three times before she answers.
"Hey Sis. What are you up to?" We obviously aren't sisters, but she's been calling me that for years.
"Not much, just got home, was out with Callum for a bit."
"Oo-la-la. Go anywhere interesting?"
"Yeah, actually. It's kind of weird I guess, but we went to his grandparent's house. They were out of town."
"Oh shit, that's hot."
I laugh at her reaction. "You're ridiculous. Anyways, I wanted to see if you wanted to go dress shopping with me?" Sophia's got the best style.
"Oh, of course! I'd love to! What is it for?"
"Callum asked me to this party, or... event, I guess? I don't know which." I guess I should've clarified those details.

"Formal though?" She asks.

"Yeah, it's an event for this group. I'm not sure." I don't really know what to tell her since I'm also confused on what it is.

"Okay, no worries. I know the perfect spot. You have morning class tomorrow?"

"I only have a class in the afternoon, but I have my TA seminar after. Would the morning work?"

"Yep, I can pick you up. Will you be at home?"

"Can I call you when I'm done at the gym? Going to go scare a couple rounds out of Ricco first."

"Sure, just let me know."

"Perfect, thank you! Love you." It feels weird, but I'm excited.

"Bye, love you too." She hangs up.

I finish my bedtime routine, then look online for some dress ideas. I debate on sending one to Sophia to see if she approves of the style. Instead, I find myself in my conversation with Callum.

> **Scarlett:** How's this for the event. Is it an event or a party? I guess that matters for the type of dress I get.

I attach a picture of a black dress with an open back. It falls elegantly on the model and stops just above the ankles.

It's just tight enough to see every curve but loose enough to keep details hidden.

> **Callum:** Jesus, Scarlett.

Frig, is it too much? Before I type an explanation, he responds.

> **Callum:** I'm going to fuck you so hard in that dress. You're going to scream my name so fucking loud.

> **Scarlett:** Challenge accepted.

I smile bigger than I'd like to admit. Something about flirting with Callum fills me with warmth and jitters. I place my phone on the nightstand and turn off my light. I look up at the ceiling. *What is this man doing to me?*

~~~~~~~~

The next morning, I wake up to a loud bang.
"Dad?" No answer. I throw the covers off and run downstairs. He's not here. I rush out to the garage.
"God damn. Piece of shit." I spot Dad as he wipes his forehead off with an oily rag.
"Jesus Dad, what was that?"

"Sorry, did I wake you? The damn wheel well fell off." He has a car up on the lift, the same car that Callum exposed and explored my body on. I fight back a smirk.

"I was just worried that something happened to you, that's all." I reach over and pat his back. "Be careful, old man."

"I'm not that old Scarlett, I had you when I was twenty-one." I roll my eyes— if I had a dollar for every time he's used that excuse.

"I'm aware, Dad."

"You have class this morning?" He throws the rag on the bench and reaches up into the car.

"No, I'm going to have a few rounds with Ricco then Sophia and I are going shopping."

"Oh? What for? Do you have money?" He's always a caretaker at heart.

"I don't need money Dad, jeez. I'm an adult. And it's just some event, I think it's a party?" He looks over at me, his eyes squint. Like he's trying to figure out what I'm thinking.

"You *think* it's a party? You don't know what you're doing?"

"Well, I think it's a party. I don't fully know yet." I deflect. Callum didn't clarify on the nature of this party when I asked him last night.

"Okay, well, have fun shopping for the maybe party. Tell Ricco I said hi." He raises his eyebrows, shakes his head, and slightly laughs.

I run back inside and get ready for the gym. I throw my sports bra and shorts on, with sweatpants over top. Winter is almost here. While sunny days are still warm, the nights are brisk.

I snatch my school bag off my desk chair and take it with my gym bag downstairs. I pour some coffee and yell bye to Dad before leaving for the day.

Once I'm at the gym, I head over to my locker and follow my usual routine. Ricco waves at me from the ring— he's with another boxer. I wave back and gesture for him to stay. I can hit the bag today. A part of me feels slightly selfish for always taking up too much of his time.

I start toward a small area with different bags and find the one that I prefer. As I walk toward it, Ricco comes over.

"Hey Scar." He walks to the bag with me. "Up for some sparring today?"

"You're busy, and I don't have much time, so I was just going to hit the bag a bit and call it a day."

"Alright, let me know if you change your mind. He's just leaving." His head motions toward the guy in the ring.

He looks familiar, about six feet tall, and sandy hair. A chill runs down my back, making me shiver. I can't pinpoint where I've seen him before.

"Thanks Ricco, you're the best." I tap his shoulder. "But turn up the heat, it's freezing in here."

"No Scarlett, you're not working hard enough. Get moving." He walks away.

I laugh and look back at the ring. The guy is gone. At first, I find it strange that he left so quickly, but Ricco did say that he was done his lesson. *I'm overthinking this.*

I hit the bag, over and over. Today, I need to push—for something deeper, something within. I don't need an outlet—I need a spark.

After almost half an hour on the bag, I'm exhausted. My body aches but it doesn't stop me from thinking about our plans later. I call Sophia to let her know I'm ready for her to get me, then I quickly shower and get dressed.

I meet her outside, her red car pulls up, the country music is blaring.

I open the passenger door, and she moves her bag from the seat. I climb inside and put my seat belt on as she turns on to Main Street.

"Well, do you have any dresses in mind or are you going to see what you find?"

"I have something in mind." I grab my phone and pull up the picture of the dress I sent to Callum last night. I hold it out for her to see. She glances over for a second, paying attention to the road.

"Holy shit!" Her eyes pop and her brows lift.

"Is it too much?" I rummage through my bag on the ground and pull out my sour gummies. I eat them in my order of colours and offer a handful to Sophia.

"Honestly, it's perfect. If it's too much for the party, Callum can always just take you home." She smirks, with a mouth full of gummies.

"Oh, trust me, I think he will anyways. We've spent almost every night together. He'll come over at night or sometimes we meet on campus in this beautiful hidden spot. I forgot how nice it feels in the beginning when you like someone, and you just want to learn more about them." Sophia and I haven't talked about boys lately—I guess from the lack of action. That's changed for me.

"Are you talking to anyone? You haven't mentioned going on any dates recently." Sophia is usually the opposite of me. She goes on dates regularly and keeps her options open.

"I'm not. Well, it's complicated."

I gasp. "Sophia!"

"What? I didn't want to tell you... I'm still not telling you. It's complicated and embarrassing."

If she's not ready to share, she must be really confused. Sophia tells me everything.

"Oh, now you have to tell me." My eyes are glued on her. She doesn't say anything as we pull into a parking spot on Main Street. We get out and meet in front of the car, close to the dress shop.

"Are you really not going to tell me?" I open the shop's door for her.

"I don't know what it is yet, like you and Callum but a bit messier." She rolls her eyes.

"Oh God. I can't wait to find out. Take all the time you need." I pull her in for a side hug. She knows that I'm always here for her, just like I know she's there for me. Sometimes that includes figuring things out on our own, even in complicated situations. I know the feeling, so I let her be.

The store's dresses are colour coded. The walls are painted a soft yellow, and a bunch of frilly ball gowns hang near the front. As we walk over to the black dresses on the rack in the middle, a friendly, blonde middle-aged woman comes over to us.

"Can I help you ladies with anything?" The smile on her face tells me that she's likely getting paid commission.

"I'm actually looking for this dress, or something like it." I pull out my phone and show her the picture.

"What size?" She asks as she walks over to a different rack.

"Four?" I have no idea what size I am. I haven't bought a dress in years, and the sizing is always different from jeans or pants.

"Hmm. Maybe an eight or ten?" She says as she looks me up and down.

I'm not offended. I spend a lot of time in the gym. I try not to take her comment personally and remember that she does this job every day.

"I'll just try on both then." I wait for her to grab them off the rack, but she doesn't.

"We only carry one size of each, and I don't have any left in those sizes. I'm sorry. How about another style, one that suits you a little more?" She plasters on her fake smile and eyes me up and down, like I don't belong in this store.

"I'll look around a bit, thank you." *God, I hate confrontation, but she was being a bitch.* I'd rather raid Sophia's closet and get out of here.

I find Sophia. She holds two dresses in one hand while browsing through a rack with the other.

"Let's get out of here."

She looks to me, confused. "But you didn't even try anything on yet. Where's your dress?"

"The sales lady is being weird, and I would rather borrow something of yours."

She scans the store to find the sales lady. She rolls her eyes, places the two dresses in her hand back on the rack, and grabs my arm. We walk out.

Sophia looks to me as we head down Main Street.

"What did she say to you?"

"I'm probably just overreacting, but I didn't know what size I would be, and she said that they were sold out of the eight and ten in the dress that I wanted. It's not that I was offended about the size, I could care less what size I am, it's that she made it seem like I wasn't good enough for the dress or that damn store." I look down at the cement then back at Sophia.

She sighs. "Sometimes I hate this town. If you aren't filthy rich, people don't want anything to do with you."

Sophia smiles. Her parents always have brand new cars and lavish jewelry. She never had to worry about applying for scholarships or reheating dinners. Instead of trying to understand, she offers support in the best way possible.

"Want to get ice cream?"

I smile and squeeze her hand as we walk to the ice cream shop.

Later, she drops me off at the gym to pick up my car and gives me a hug before I leave.

As I approach my car, I notice something on my passenger seat. It's dusk and I can't see from across the street.

When I'm finally close enough, I see a long black bag lying across the passenger seat. I walk around to the opposite side and open the door. It's a clothing bag. As I unzip it, a note falls out.

You deserve everything.

It's the dress I wanted.

There's only one person who would've done this. I used to think I liked my world untouched, but that's before Callum Mercer got his hands on it and ruined anything else for me.

Watching From the Shadows

Callum

I arrive at her house five minutes early. I turn the car off and wait for her to come outside. While I should go in and say hi to her dad, she told me to wait out front. I'm tempted to remind her that I don't take orders well, but I'm not exactly the type of guy who dad's love. I pull my phone out of my pocket and text to let her know I'm here.

Her front door swings open and I can hear her laugh.
God Dammit, that laugh.

I smile every time I hear it. A tight black dress falls just above her ankles, with a slit that runs up, exposing her perfect legs. I couldn't imagine her in anything else. She wears cherry red heels with lips that match. I'll find it hard to keep my hands off of her with that colour.

I feel myself getting hard just looking at her. I adjust myself before she opens the door.

"Hey, I'm waiting for my girlfriend, so you better get away from my car or she'll kick your ass." I tease as she slides into the car.

"Shut up." She grabs my face, and her red lips meet mine. My hand finds her face. I slide my tongue between her parted lips, just licking the outline.

She pulls away. I'm met with her smile as I open my eyes. I smile back, naturally.

"Stunning doesn't even come close to how amazing you look, Angel."

"You clean up nice yourself, Mr. Mercer." She reaches over and rubs my neck.

My car lulls beneath us, steady and low. As we drive off, my hands sit on the steering wheel, even though they'd rather be touching her. I hate that I'm bringing her tonight. I wasn't going to let the Highers or my dad make me bring anyone else, like they usually suggest, but here we are. *Fuck.* I run my hands through my hair.

Scarlett quietly sits beside me in the passenger seat. She gazes out the front window, her eyes locked on the road, but every few seconds, her eyes flicker to me, like she is studying me out of the corner of her thoughts. We continue to sit in silence, comfortable in each other's presence.

"Are you excited to see some of your friends?" She breaks the stillness, her voice is soft and careful.

I shake my head. "No."

My suit is my armour—crisp and dark. It's too expensive for someone who claims that he doesn't care about appearances. Scarlett has already seen me at my worst, with bruised knuckles and blood on my shirt. I hate that she's seen that side of me, the side I wish I could control.

"You don't want to go to this thing." She states. It's not a question, but a truth.

"No," I admit. "But I have to."

"Because of the group?"

Silence.

I can't correct her. I can't lie.

Shadows paint Scarlett's face as she turns toward me.

"So, what am I tonight? Your date? Your distraction?" I glance at her—quick, sharp, pained.

"You're the only thing that makes this bearable." The words hang between us like smoke. Unfiltered. Unrehearsed. Her lips part as she swallows. I can sense her heart, hammering against her ribs like it wants to escape.

"Callum..." She starts. I gently place my hand on her thigh, moving my thumb in slow circles. It's gentle and grounding. I'm not sure if I'm trying to calm her or myself.

"You scare me," I say.

Scarlett blinks. "Why?"

"Because I don't know how to be what you need. But I won't stop trying."

I know she can feel it, *right there*, just under the surface. On the tip of my tongue lie the three words neither of us are damn brave enough to say. My feelings have grown into a need—the words are just an extension of that. But I can't say them. Not here. Not now. Not with the whole world watching from the shadows.

"I don't need you to be perfect," she whispers. "I just need you to be honest."

My jaw flexes. For a moment, I think about letting go and telling her everything. Instead, I slow the car down as its headlights catching the pillars of the estate ahead.

I don't want to be here. Not with her. *Maybe this wasn't a good idea?* I try to conceal the dread on my face. She doesn't know what these people are capable of, and I never want her to find out.

Although this may be our first official date, I've watched Scarlett for years, studying her from afar and we've been inseparable for a while now. Tonight, everything changes.

I stop the car and turn to lock eyes with her. One hand still rests on her thigh, the other brushes her cheek.

"I need you to stay close tonight," I quietly plead. "Promise me." I won't forgive myself if something happens to her.

Explosion

Scarlett

Callum shifts his car into park and the engine stops. He reaches over and unbuckles my seat belt. The silence between us is heavy, I can feel there is so much he isn't telling me. He steps out of the car and walks around to my door, holding his hand out as he opens it. He does this every time we're in the car together—such a small act of chivalry that makes me feel special.

My palm graces his as I get out of the car. I move closer to him. His fingers slowly caress the small of my back. The touch comforts me instantly.

The house looks like a Gothic manor, lit by the bright moon. Vines grow perfectly up each side of its dark stones. Flashing strobe lights peek through the tall windows and match the bass that vibrates under my feet as we inch closer to the red front door.

"Please," Callum says.

I grab his hand and kiss it. My 'Fire Engine' lipstick smears against the top of his knuckles.

"I'm not going anywhere."

He leans in, his hot breath hitting my pulsing neck. "You say that like you have a choice."

I don't expect him to introduce me to anyone. It's not the kind of party where you sip champagne and make small talk over caviar. We're here for one reason: he must make an appearance. I hope it's a short one—large crowds make me anxious. Although tonight, I know I'm safe beside him.

Callum takes my hand and pulls me through a sea of people. Inside, the manor is elegant and matches Callum's rich persona. Nothing looks out of place, even for a party. The glasses are perfectly stacked on one table with napkins neatly folded beside them. Everything has a purpose.

I don't see anyone I know, until Harrison comes into view. He saunters toward us, holding a girl on his arm like an accessory. She looks familiar. I've most likely seen her at school before, but I don't give it much more thought. A smile comes across my face but it's not genuine. I rub my fingers against my palms by my side.

Harrison lowers his head when he sees me.

"Scarlett," he says.

"You clean up nice Harr." Callum speaks up first. He scans the room, like he's searching for someone specific.

"Didn't have a choice on a night like tonight. Could say the same for you though. It's been a while since you've been to one of these." Harrison glances at me, as if he suggests that Callum is here for me and not himself.

"We need some drinks." The platinum blonde on Harrison's arm speaks up.

I contemplate it, but I'm not comfortable enough to get a drink yet. I smile, wondering if her and Harrison are a couple or if she's just here to support the group too. I have so many questions in this room of people I don't know. I feel alone.

Callum must be reading my mind. He pulls me close and kisses the top of my head. Crowds of people in gowns and tuxedos surround us. Callum runs his hand down my bare back. There's something about his touch that makes me crave his closeness.

"Dance with me." I pull him toward me.

I've never seen a party like this. I've been to many of them, but this experience is hazy, almost like a dream. His cool hands slowly trail down my burning skin. The heat of the room clings to my exposed chest.

I sway my hips under the weight of his hands. With every movement, my chest brushes against him. Our eyes lock. We share the same breath.

Lights pulse and the crowd grooves to the beat of the music. Tension builds between my legs. I don't look up at him, but his body moves closer to mine. Suddenly, it feels like there is no one else in the room, just him and I.

My cheek brushes against his. He opens his lips and moves his hands toward the slit of my dress. My nipples harden at his touch. He pushes the slit open, brushing his fingertips against the side of my thong. For once, I don't care that others might see. I trust that he would never push it too far.

And just when the tension is unbearable, when I think I might explode, something shimmery catches my eye.

On the stage in the corner of the room, I spot the back of her honey golden hair. I would recognize it anywhere. The hair that I've braided. The hair that smells like coconut and once comforted me like a warm embrace. She swirls her hands above her head, dancing naked with golden tassels covering her nipples.

I shouldn't stare, but I can't peel my eyes away.

I need to know.

My stomach drops.

Don't let it be her.

She turns around.

My heart pounds.

It's my mother.

Protection

Scarlett

My stomach churns as my hands drop by my sides. My gaze moves to the floor. He looks to the corner where my mom is. I can't look back at her.

"Get me out of here." My eyes search for the door while I run, faster than the pounding of the music.

"Scarlett." Callum runs after me, pushing through the swarm of people.

"Scarlett!"

I don't turn around.

A faint sliver of light guides my way as the heavy door opens and closes, letting more people pile in. I push the door open. I'm outside. Finally, I catch my breath. My head spins.

A sweaty hand grips my arm, forcing me to turn around.

"Scarlett, let me explain," Callum says.

My jaw drops as the blood drains from my face.

"I didn't know she would be here. I tried to make sure she wouldn't be. I wouldn't have brought you if I knew, Scarlett." His words spill out of his mouth like vomit. "I tried. Please—"

"You knew?!" I cut him off.

No. This can't be happening.

He reaches for me, and my hands shove him away.

"Do. Not. Touch. Me."

He steps back. The space between us grows larger than the knife in my heart.

"Scarlett, I'm not a good person. What I'm a part of—" Pain echoes in his voice. "I've hurt people. These hands, they have so much blood on them. But you—" His voice cracks. "I can't be responsible for your pain. That goes beyond my hands. It rips out my God damn heart."

"No. You don't get to guilt me." My eyes remain locked on his.

"Scarlett, don't you see? Everything I do. Every time I breathe, it's all for you. I would set the world on fire just to keep you warm."

The heaviness in my shoulders forces a sob out of my chest.

"Tell me how you found out. How do you know?"

He runs his hands through his perfectly parted hair, crouches, sighs, then stands abruptly.

"The Society. Your mom has done some parties for them. I thought it was just a casual thing, then Harrison told me he heard his dad talking about her. She's in deep with them Scar—" He looks over toward the mansion. "She's been working for them for at least eight years. I thought she was just dancing, but I don't know. I've been trying to find out so I could tell you everything. You have to understand—once you're in The Society, they make it impossible to get out. They will control you. Haunt you. Once they have their claws in, you can't leave."

He isn't just talking about Mom—this feels personal. Horror is written all over his face. Even when I hate him, I want to embrace him.

"How long have you known?" My tone is calm yet assertive.

He tries to speak. "Scar—"

"How fucking long, Callum!" Every ounce of control leaves my body.

"A few months." His words feel like a slap to the face. I step forward.

My ears ring as I tilt my head. "A few months?" I close my eyes for a moment. "You knew all this time, and you didn't tell me?"

I open my eyes. His sharp eyes impale me.

"Every insecurity I shared with you. All the times I told you how I felt about her. You just sat there and listened to me pour my fucking heart out. But you knew... you knew that she was what, selling her body? I've been with you almost every day. We spend so much time together and you couldn't tell me? You knew and you never told me. I can't Callum..." A drop of my saliva hits his perfectly ironed black dress shirt. "I can't trust you." I slowly back away.

He looks distraught, but I can't focus on that. I slowly feel him letting his guard down. I need to pull away before he sucks me back in. "Callum..."

He tightens his jaw. "Don't you fucking dare." His words are a threat, not a warning. "You want to hate me? Fine. Hate me." His voice is unsteady. "I hate me too, Scarlett. I have spent so long hating and hiding. I was trying to... I thought I was protecting you. The first real thing in my fucking life."

My heart betrays me as tears start to flow down my face.

"I'm sorry—for the secret, for not telling you. For thinking that silence was safer than the truth. For not being the kind of man who deserves to hold something as precious as you."

I can't listen to him anymore. I need to leave. We're surrounded by darkness, but I spot the many parked cars down the driveway. There's no one else out here, other than the valet driver. I rush over to him.

"Mercer." I stutter. "I need the keys for Callum Mercer."

The valet driver makes eye contact with Callum in the distance. He gives the valet one nod and then the man reaches behind the podium to grab the keys.

"I'll bring the car around Miss," he says and begins to walk off.

"No," I step in front, cutting him off. "Just give me the keys." I place my palm out.

He slowly places the keys in my hand and my fingers curl around them. I know that I must leave, but a part of me wants to stay. I shut my eyes—they feel so heavy.

I walk down the stone path to his car. The headlights flash as I unlock the door and slide into the driver's seat. I rest my head against the steering wheel. I turn the car on and drive off, leaving Callum there.

When I pull up to the house, the porch light is on. I park on the street and see my reflection in the rear-view mirror. I dry my wet eyes. *Dad will notice anyway.*

I push all the air out of my lungs to gain strength, then get out of the car and climb up the porch stairs. My fingertips brush the worn railing.

Dad sits in his lazy boy chair. "Hey honey, I wasn't expecting," his voice gets quiet as he spots my red face. "What's wrong, Scarlett?" He abruptly asks.

I can't tell him.

"Callum and I got into a fight. It's nothing"

"It doesn't look like nothing." Concern grows in his voice.

"Dad, please, not tonight. I'm just going to go to bed and sleep it off."

"Okay. Well, I'm here if you need anything. I love you, honey."

I know he'll be there, but it will break him when he finds out about Mom. Even though they aren't together, she'll always be the love of his life. He doesn't deserve this. We don't deserve this.

"I love you too, Dad. I'll see you in the morning."

Eventually I'll tell him, I just need to figure out how. And I need to figure out what the hell is going on. I make my way up the stairs, my legs carrying my tense body and broken heart. I reach my bedroom, push my shoes off, and flop onto the bed. The comforter swallows me whole and as I curl onto my side. I close my teary eyes and release a quiet sob.

For the first time in the last few months, I think about the possibility that Callum and I might not work out. Maybe we were never meant to survive each other.

Sympathy

Callum

The taillights of my car fade into the distance. I stand outside alone, watching her drive away. *I need to make this right.* I run my hand over my mouth and grab my jaw. I pull my phone out of my pocket and call Harrison, but there's no point. The music is too loud. I know he's inside, the last place I want to be, but I need to get to her.

I push the manor door open without resistance. Faded red strobe lights burn my squinting eyes. I search for Harrison and don't see him.

He's likely upstairs with the Highers.

I head toward the spiral staircase and run up, two stairs at a time. Once I get to the top, I stop, let out a deep breath, and straighten my jacket.

I can't let them see me like this.

The music is muted upstairs. These walls have heard too much, these floors have seen too much, and somehow, they always ask for more. I open the door to the lounge. The familiar scents of cigars and aged whiskey claw at my throat. I spot Harrison, drinking alongside half of the other pledges and a few Highers.

"Harrison." I make my way over to him.

"Callum." He grabs my arm and smiles. "Where's Scarlett?"

He can see the pain in my somber eyes. He doesn't let go of my arm. Instead, he guides me to the other side of the room. "What's wrong?"

I try to keep my composure while laughter fills the room—sharp and cruel. *I need to get the hell out of here.* I clear my throat.

"She left, can I uh—can I borrow your car?"

Harrison is my best friend. He's the only person who has seen me break down. He understands the pressure that we live with—from The Society, from our parents, and from ourselves. He pisses me off more than most people, but I'd still go to war for him. Blood or not, he's the only one who's ever come close. I trust him with my life.

"Vanessa is downstairs. Scarlett saw her." A small weight lifts off my chest before it comes crashing down twice as hard.

"Callum, shit. Man, how can I—"

"Did you know?" I cut him off. My fists build.

I'm distracted by one laugh that catches my ear, and the scent of cheap cologne becomes overpowering. I look over my shoulder and see Chase. My teeth grind beneath my clenched jaw. Harrison follows my eyes, then he brings the conversation back to Scarlett.

"Of course, I didn't know. You think I wouldn't have warned you?" We hold eye contact. I can tell that he's upset by my accusation—I'd be mad too.

"I know Harr, I just—fuck, I can't lose her." I look to the floor. I hate this feeling.

From his pant pocket, he pulls out a set keys and tosses them to me.

"You're lucky I don't like the valet driver tonight."

"I owe you man," I say, my voice is quiet.

He chuckles. "You don't owe me shit." His voice stiffens yet remains quiet. "Just don't make it worse with Scarlett. Listen to her. She probably has a million questions, and the answers will be hard, for both of you."

"I'll call you later," I say. He pats my back before I walk away and avoid everyone else in the room.

I hurry down the stairs, out of the house, and to Harrison's Land Rover. When I get in, I pull a cigarette out of my jacket pocket and search around his dash for a lighter. I find a Zippo. My hands shake as I light the cigarette that rests on my lips. I pull out my phone and check to see if Scarlett has called or texted me. Just like I suspected, she hasn't. I call her. No answer. I don't leave a message. She knows I'll come to her. She knows I'll fight for her—for *us*.

I pull up to her dad's house and cut the engine. The porch light is on. Once I'm out of the car, I flick my cigarette onto the pavement, and a long exhale escapes me. I reach the porch and knock on the door. No answer. I knock again, heavier this time.

"Scarlett." I'm about to turn the corner and head toward her window when the door opens.

"She doesn't want to talk to you." Her dad leans against the doorframe, his arms crossed.

"Jake, Mr. Voss, I just need to clarify a few things with Scarlett—"

"She doesn't want to talk, Callum. Go home." He stands up straight now. *He's taller than I expected.*

"I just need her to know that I was trying to protect her. I never would've put her in that situation if I knew she was going to be there." I try to keep my composure. Jake's face drops, his body stiffens, and his jaw locks in place. He takes a step toward me.

"What situation? If who wasn't there?"

Fuck. She didn't tell him. How the hell do I tell my girlfriend's dad that his ex-wife is a prostitute who is in deep with The Society? I bite the side of my cheek, but I remain in place. I know if I tell him, he will be there to comfort Scarlett.

"How much do you know about Vanessa's involvement with The Society?"

He cocks his head with confusion. "What did you just say to me?"

"Vanessa was at the party we were at tonight. She was... working." I don't know how much he knows. "She started a couple years back, stripping for some members of The Society. It has turned into more than that and now she's in deep." He squints his eyes, and I give him a few seconds to process what I just said. I don't know if he's aware of The Society or what we are in this town.

"And Scarlett saw her? What did she see?" He begins to pace along the front porch.

"She was dancing on a stage, naked." I pause. "And then she ran out and I told her I was sorry and that I tried to stop her from finding out this way."

He lunges at me, grabbing my jacket. "You knew?" He spits in my face.

"Yes, I knew. But I was trying to protect her. I didn't know everything yet. I've been trying to find out so I could give her the proper information. What would you do if you knew, tell her?"

He lets go of me. I know he's not a violent man—he's just breaking. I sympathize with him, a true father figure. I've never felt protection from a parent.

"I'm sorry. I didn't know what to do. I just wanted to keep her safe. From The Society, from the secrets, from it all. I don't know how to fix this. I want to give her space, but I want to tell her–" I swallow the lump in my throat, unprepared for what I'm about to say. "Tell her that I can't live without her." I look to the ground, unable to meet his eyes. "Is that love?" Slowly, I find the strength to lift my face and meet his. "Wanting to keep someone safe? Wanting to bleed for them when they are hurt? I don't know how to do this. I've never loved anyone."

He looks at me with pity and an unfamiliar weight builds in my chest. "Yeah kid, that's love." He pauses. "But she is also *my* daughter. And I've been loving her since the day she was born." His voice is steady yet firm.

He steps toward the door. "And she doesn't want to talk."

He reaches behind him. "So, it's time you leave. Goodnight Callum."

He shuts the door in my face.

Ricochet

Scarlett

The sun's morning rays poke through my curtain, warming my face. I've already hit the snooze button twice. I roll over and face the door. In my four years of studies, I have yet to miss a class. If I don't hurry, today I might.

My phone vibrates on the nightstand and thoughts of last night flood my mind. My cheeks burn—either from the sun, or the embarrassment of my finding my mom, naked at a party. I knew that she hasn't been honest about her lifestyle, but now I want to discover the true extent of what she does. I sit up, my head leaning against the headboard. My phone buzzes again. I don't want to look at it.

There's a faint knock on my door.

"Scarlett, are you awake?" Dad says from the hallway.

I don't want him to see me like this, but there's no point in hiding. He is my dad after all.

"Yeah, I'm up."

"I just wanted you to know that I'm here if you need to talk about last night." His voice is muffled through the door.

I don't want to push him away, but I can't help to think that if he knew the truth, he wouldn't be so calm about it. I don't answer him. Instead, I get up off the bed and open the door. He holds a coffee in his hand—a peace offering.

"I know about your mom, Scarlett." His words startle me. I try to read his face. His eyes have bags under them. I wonder if he knew or if Callum told him—I heard him here last night. He came to talk to me, and Dad wouldn't let him in.

"You know that she was at the party?" I take a sip of the hot coffee with a bit of cream and sugar, just the way I like it.

"I know everything, honey. Callum told me what happened at the party, and then I found out more from some people I know in town." His face looks older today, like stress has warn him down. The hair framing his face isn't pushed back with oil—I can tell he hasn't been into the shop yet.

"Who did you ask about mom after?"

He hesitates.

"Daryl from the Sheriff's office. You know that we've been friends for a long time. He's known for a while, but he didn't know how to tell me. I guess he's not sure of the full extent and didn't want to come to me with missing pieces. Can't blame the guy, I wouldn't want to tell someone that either."

I wonder how much he knows. "What did he tell you?"

He looks to the floor, then back at me. "How much do you know?"

"What does it matter what I know, Dad. I'm going to find out either way. Wouldn't you rather be the one to tell me the truth?" His eyebrows shift, each word firing directly into his soul. His frown tells me that this has broken him too.

"Your Mom works at the Steakhouse, that isn't a lie. But I guess that over the last few years, she has transitioned into, um, escorting men on dates."

"As a prostitute?" I ask. Nothing about this feels real.

"I think so. I'm not sure. I don't know Scarlett, this is just what I've been told." His words are scattered, like he isn't sure what to believe either.

"I just want to know why. I think it's more than that, Dad." My eyes focus on the mug in my hand.

"I don't think we'll get the answers we want, honey." He reaches for my hand and grabs it in his. We lock eyes.

"I know that you don't want to forgive her for leaving us Scar, but this didn't take her away from us. She couldn't be here. She wasn't with us for a while before all of this. It was time." The words hit me hard.

"I know you're just trying to help Dad, but I just need to sit with this for a while before we talk about it anymore." I face him with a broken smile.

He squeezes my hand, then let's go.

"I get that. Are you going to school soon?"

"I'm not sure what I'm doing today. I might just go to the gym and work on my paper after."

He nods and smiles. "Come say bye before you leave," he says and shuts the door. I hear him step down the stairs.

I place my mug on the nightstand beside me before I slide down, back underneath the covers. I don't want to face anyone today or show up at school, pretending like I'm okay.

When I can't hide behind fake smiles and boxing gloves, I need to embrace the darkness.

I throw the covers off and walk over to my closet. I stretch my arms above my head and examine the clothes hanging on the rack. *I'm definitely not going to school.*

I walk over to my dresser, pull on some sweatpants, pick out a sports bra, and throw an oversized hoodie overtop. In the bathroom, I brush my teeth. Before I turn the light off, I notice my reflection in the mirror. The person looking back at me isn't the girl I once was. My hair looks the same, but it feels heavier. My eyes are identical, but they feel tired. My body isn't different, but it feels beat down. I walk downstairs and grab my gym bag before heading out to my car. I don't see Dad in the house—he must've started working.

I open the garage door and poke my head in. "I'm headed to the gym. I'll be back in a bit."

He lifts his head out from the hood of a car and smiles.

"Okay honey. I was thinking takeout for dinner. Chinese?"

"Sure Dad, love you."

A thin layer of frost coats my windshield, slowly melting in the sun. I get in the car and wait for the window to defrost. I pull my phone out of my bag—I purposely haven't looked at it all morning. I open the screen to twelve missed calls and five texts. Two of the calls are from Sophia, she must've found out. It's likely that Callum told Harrison, and I'm sure he told Stirling, they are brothers. I click on the messages.

Three were from last night.

> **Callum:** Please, let me explain. I can fix this.
>
> **Callum:** Scarlett, please let me see you. I need to see you.
>
> **Callum:** You are everything good in my life.

Two are from this morning.

> **Callum:** You can ignore me Angel, but that won't stop me from trying.
>
> **Sophia:** I'm here when you're ready to talk. XO. I love you, Sis.

I throw my phone in the passenger seat and drive to the gym. I can't believe he thinks I'd want to talk to him. I shake my head and turn up the radio, trying to find an escape in the music. Radiohead pluses through the speakers but my mind drifts back to him. I need space to figure out what to make of all of this. I wonder if Callum is used to fights like this. *Surely, he's been in a relationship before. Hasn't he?* If he doesn't have a good demonstration of what healthy boundaries are, then this all makes a lot more sense. I linger on the thought—*will he ever understand the boundaries I'm putting in place?*

I pull into the gym parking lot, grab my bag, and walk in. I don't remember the drive. Today, the space doesn't greet me with the familiar smell that is usually comforting. Instead, it feels like a task I'm checking off a list, not something I love doing. I go over to my locker and shove my bag in the small space. I pull my gloves out.

"Hey Scar," a familiar voice startles me from behind. "I have thirty minutes until my next match. Hop up in the ring and we can have a quick round." Ricco doesn't move as I shut the locker and turn around to face him. Before I say anything, I know he can read my expression by the lack of enthusiasm on my face.

"I'm just going to hit the bags today, but thanks." I walk around him.

I don't hear him move.

"Scar, you okay?" He responds quickly. I don't want to tell him anything, but he knows me well enough by now.

"I'm just having a day, Ricco. Take the time to relax or clean the machines for the tenth time today while you wait." My jab hits him harder than my fists ever have.

"You're allowed to have bad days Scarlett, but don't take them out on me." He steps toward me. "Save it for the bags, give them one hell of a go." He looks me up and down. "Let it all out, kid." I break our eye contact as tears begin to pool. I smile at him, but he doesn't return it. He turns around and walks away.

I head over to my favourite bag, that's tucked away from everything else. I slide my gloves on, expecting to feel the rush take over my body, but it never comes.

I'm so furious— at Mom, at Callum, at this damn Society I know nothing about. I hate that I'm letting these issues consume me. I wouldn't be mad at Mom if she was just honest. Instead, everything stings that much more. I grab the bag, unable to swing at it, and gently push it away. I can't. Not today. I close my eyes and exhale.

When I open them, I take my gloves off and rush to my locker to grab my stuff. Before I can run into Ricco, I hurry out. I unlock the car door, throw my bag in, and grab my phone.

I go to my contacts and look for the only one I want to talk to.

Mom.

My finger hovers over the call button. Moisture gathers beneath my eyelids as regret washes in. I lock my phone and lean back against the head rest. I don't open my eyes as tears fall down my face. A lonely sob comforts me while a heaviness spreads across my chest. I'm welcomed back into the darkness that I've been fighting for too long.

Selling Your Soul

Callum

I lean against the wooden frame of the bar, holding a glass in my hand. Although it's empty, it's comforting. It has been almost a week since things went south at The Society with Scarlett. I haven't heard from her—I don't expect to. While I don't want to push, I need to see her. I pull my phone out from my pocket and open our conversation. *Dammit, doesn't she know what this is doing to me?*

I can't handle being ignored. All I've known is selfishness and I can't control it right now. I can't wait to teach her a fucking lesson.

Footsteps thud down the hall. I turn around and watch a tall figure walk through the door frame. By the way he carries himself, I can tell it's Harrison—with his shoulders held high and his pride beaming, confident with who he is. He shuffles beside me, reaches for a glass, and pours himself a drink.

"Still no word from Scarlett?" He lifts the glass to his lips and takes a sip.

"No." My tone is cold.

I push my glass away, sliding it across the counter. I hope it falls off and shatters. It doesn't.

"Is there anything I can do?" I know that if I ask him to hurt the people who've ruined Vanessa's life, he would, without question. But I can't ask that of him, not yet. "Do you know who it was?" He mentioned that he was looking into it, but I haven't got an update and it's driving me crazy.

"I don't know who it was, but she's been spending time with one particular member lately." He looks down.

"Who?" My eyes stay fixed on him. *I'm going to fucking kill them.*

"My dad." He looks up at me, the pain in his eyes goes beyond what we're taught to conceal.

Unlike my father, who's always had other women that he spends time with, Harrison's dad is a family man. I've never seen him with another woman other than Amelia, Harrison's mom. In the public eye, he can't be seen with anyone else. He wouldn't just ruin his reputation—he would destroy his family.

"I'm sorry," is all I can offer.

"I guess it was always bound to happen." His Adam's apple bobs as he takes another sip. "In our world, men like us don't belong to anyone."

I used to believe that. Now, I don't just belong to one woman, I'm controlled by her. And I'm determined for her to respond to me.

I push off the bar and grab Harrison by the shoulder.

"I'm sorry... about all of this." We share a deep-rooted look, one that goes far beyond the surface. We both know that things can't change.

As I prepare to leave, voices echo into the parlour from the lobby downstairs. Mumbles fill the room. I look to

Harrison. He seems calm, like he knew other pledges were coming.

"Expecting anyone?" I ask. My back faces Harrison as I keep a look out for who's coming.

"Some of the pledges are coming by to discuss a new run in the city."

A few pledges from different initiation years step into the room. Their attire ranges from khakis and a golf shirt to tailored suits that scream wealth.

Leo Belmont, a Higher with The Society, walks in behind everyone. Born into this life much like me, Leo is loved by no one and hated by many. He's someone who understands that power comes first. As he walks in the room, his chest rises naturally. He makes his way to the corner chair—a spot that the Highers take to assert their dominance. A spot that soon, I'll be asked to fill. He unbuttons his Louis Vuitton jacket and sits down.

"There's some tension lately. With final initiations coming up, everyone must be committed. Anyone in question will be eliminated." The room grows quiet— everyone knows that you don't make it out of initiation alive. You either sell your soul to The Society, or you die. Those are the only options.

"Which brings me to the next issue." His voice grows louder. "A few of you have been sloppy lately. You have come too close to exposure and for that, second chances are not given. When you were chosen, you knew the rules. You don't tell anyone what we discuss, and you don't ride the line of getting caught."

My eyes scan the room to find Jasper. I know that he is on their hit list after everything that happened with Emily at the beginning of the year.

"I need all of you to be on your A-Game for this run. It could be the beginning of a great relationship with a few dealers in town. That means, I'll need my best men on it." He turns to me and Harrison.

Harrison looks up at me, knowing this comes at the worst time.

The silence in the room is broken by a scoff. All eyes fly to Jasper as rage boils over within me. He's *done*.

Leo's eyes shift onto Jasper, then back at me. He nods his head once, enough to summon me. That's all it takes to be reminded of my role here. I walk toward Jasper, my fists balled at my sides.

"We all know that your head hasn't been in it lately, Mercer." Jasper throws at me. That's all I let him get out before I make contact. Without hesitation, my fist lands on Jasper's face. Blood pours down his nose. I grab his shirt with my other hand, steadying him. My knuckles hit him, repeatedly, his blood splattering all over my white Tom Ford button up shirt. I can't stop. The sound of his face caving in doesn't slow me down, it pushes me further. He had his chance, and he blew it when he killed Emily. Everyone knows that you don't get two chances, not with The Society.

Jasper loses his balance as I slowly lower him to the ground and hover over top of him, on my knees. Blood and spit fly from his mouth.

"Please…" He faintly pleads.

My swollen fist meets his face one more time. I pick up his head and smash it into the ground. I stare into his lifeless eyes. This is my job—defending The Society. And I don't have it in me to stop.

My mind goes to her and all the ways that I've let her down. *This is why she shouldn't want me.* The pain compels me. I grunt loudly and grab his head in my hands.

Just then, I feel a warm touch on my shoulder, and I look to Harrison. He doesn't have to tell me, I know what I've done.

I let go of Jasper and roll off of him, landing on my back. I look up at the crown molding that lines the room— a display of elegance and class in a place full of darkness and horror.

"Thank you, Callum. You never fail to show The Society your loyalty." I remain on the ground, unable to look his way. "Everyone, clear the room." Leo stands and does up the button on his jacket. He leans into Harrison as he passes us. "Make sure this gets cleaned up. I'll deal with the others."

He stands over me and nods. Everyone leaves the room after Leo—a sign of respect mixed with fear. Fear of what they just saw, and fear of their future.

"She shouldn't have done this. Doesn't she know what I am?" Harrison doesn't answer, he just listens. "Doesn't she know what I do? That I hurt people? That's what we always fucking do... for them. For all of them." My voice turns hoarse. I sit up and cradle my hands between bent knees. I feel Harrison's eyes on me, watching me combust.

"She doesn't know because you won't show her." His voice breaks the silence. "Do you want her to know this side of you? The one that kills? The one that craves darkness?"

"I don't want her to see it, but I know if I don't show her, it will ruin us." The truth that I've been concealing from myself finally slips out.

"If she doesn't see all the different sides of you, how are you going to let her in?"

She's already in. She's crawled her way inside of me, unable to escape even if I try to force her out.

I don't tell Harrison that. I stand up, fix my shirt, and look at the mess I've made— the life I've taken. The fact that I've "shown my loyalty" makes it worse. I did it for them. They know that as long as I have nothing to lose, they can keep using me as their weapon. And they've already hurt the one thing that I want. The one thing that I need. *Her*. I see red.

I pick Jasper up by his arm and his leg and throw him over my shoulder. I don't care about the mess that follows.

"I can help you." Harrison pleas as he follows, downstairs to the crematory. I don't answer.

I place Jasper on the big metal table, flick the machine on, and watch it warm up.

Flames scorch my eyes as I watch heat fill the small space inside. The Society won't take this pleasure from me. I don't hear Harrison, but I know that he's sitting at the bottom of the stairs, quietly waiting and plotting. I say the only thing that I know.

"I can fix this."

"What do you need me to do?" Harrison asks. I need to handle this myself. If something goes wrong, I can't bring him down with me.

"Clean this up." I walk past and squeeze his shoulder.

I get to the top of the stairs and find Leo waiting for me.

"What are you going to tell his parents?" I ask.

"His dad knows what's at risk." His eyes are as cold as his tone. He glances at the blood on my shirt. "Your dad will be happy with this. I think he's been worried about your loyalty after you left the party." *Why is he telling me this?* We aren't close, and it's disobedient to give away another Higher—especially my father, their silent leader.

"He should question my morale more than my loyalty."

Leo smirks. "Comments like that will get you into trouble, Callum. What you do for The Society should never question morale, only strengthen it."

I stare at him with a flat face. They have created a monster who is afraid of no one, even them.

"I've been in trouble my entire life." The words spit from between my teeth. I know he's not threatening me, but it doesn't help that I'm already on edge. If Father has noticed, it means that they are paying attention to me. Suddenly, I feel an urge to protect Scarlett, something that I haven't felt so strongly since that night four years ago.

"I never question The Society, Sir." The lie seeps from my mouth like poison, but I'll do anything to protect her.

"Good man." He reaches for my shoulder and grips it. It takes everything in me to stay in place. When he finally breaks the contact, I dig my fingers into the palms of my hands, almost cutting my skin.

I walk outside and get into my car. I need to see her. My engine rumbles as I back out of the driveway. From the centre console, I grab my sunglasses and look into the rear-view mirror.

The place that made me who I am and ruined all that I have stares back at me.

This fucking place.

Silent Gestures

Scarlett

Rain is back in the forecast for the next week. It's not unusual for November, but I'm not ready for the nice weather to leave. Wind hits the back of my neck. My wet hair is contained in a clip. I walk across campus to the lecture hall, constantly looking over my shoulder. I feel uneasy, almost like I'm being watched.

There is no one behind me, but the whole situation with my mother has shot my nerves completely. I'm surrounded by so many people in the halls, but I still feel so alone. I open the lecture hall door and take a seat in my usual spot. The room quickly fills as everyone takes their seats and pulls out their notebooks.

As I place my bag on the ground, my phone vibrates. I pick it up, turn my notifications off, and check my messages—two from Callum and one from Sophia.

I should answer Sophia, she hasn't done anything wrong. I pull up our conversation.

Sophia: Miss you. Can I bring you coffee later?

I know that even if I say no, she'll likely show up. Deciding to text Sophia is the first step to get past this.

Scarlett: I'd love a coffee. After class?

I hit send before I can change my mind. Lately, I feel like I'm making decisions without even thinking about them. Even my usual anxiety never hinders me this much. Her response comes through fast.

Sophia: Can't wait! XO See you soon.

I put my phone away. Professor Elliot lifts his briefcase onto the podium, before he pulls out his textbook and laptop. He scans the class, landing directly in my eye line. Our eyes meet. If I was into the whole 'hot for teacher' thing, I'd think he's cute, but it's never been my niche.

I react with a small, partly forced smile. He returns it, like it's a habit.

"Good morning, everyone. I hope that you all did your readings." He picks up the textbook.

"Today, we're going back to different brain imaging techniques. Does anyone remember the different techniques that are used?"

Well, is he talking about in each State or in general? I raise my hand, along with a few others.

"Scarlett." He looks at me.

"Well, Sir, here in the States our first options would be an MRI or CT scan. But in Europe, they tend to do an EEG with an MRI instead of the CT scan sometimes." I didn't have to read this week's syllabus to know the answer to that—we've discussed this topic many times in various classes.

"Why do you think that is?" He leans against the podium, his hand brushing the stubble on his face.

"Well, we still do EEG's here, but they are mainly used to test brain activity in real time. Meanwhile, the CT scan is used more for diagnostics. But with the EEG, the test can be impacted by exterior factors, like no sleep and various medications. A CT scan focuses more on the anatomy of the brain instead of what's going on inside of it. I think that both have a purpose and are useful for different things. Overall, an MRI is the standard practice." The words come out so easily, like they're second nature to me at this point. As someone who hated speaking up in the beginning of my program, finding my voice has boosted my confidence.

Today, I needed that.

"Exactly. Let's dive into EEG's first." He sets his textbook down and opens his laptop.

The rest of class flies by. A few other students participate at times, but Professor Elliot looks to me for most answers. I don't always want to speak, and sometimes I wish other people would step out of their comfort zones and engage more.

As class comes to an end, I gather my papers and laptop off the small desk attached to my chair. I throw my bag over my shoulder, my palms are sweaty. A hand reaches over me and holds the door open on my way out of class. I turn to see Professor Elliot.

"Oh, thank you," I say with a smile.

"Thanks for the participation today, Scarlett. Good to have you back." He looks over my shoulder, then disappears past me through the crowd of students. I look up and don't see anyone directly in front of us, but I notice a tall figure with sandy hair, almost like Chase's, briskly walking past.

I make my way across the courtyard to the coffee shop. Sophia sits at a table with both of our drinks. She frantically waves, then stands and embraces me with a tight hug. "Hi," she says into my hair. Our hug is longer than usual.

"Hi," I say back. She doesn't know how much I needed this. Until now, I didn't either.

I place my bag down on one of the seats and sit across from her, taking a sip of my coffee.

"Thanks for this. I needed it." I take another sip.

"Anytime. How was class?" She picks up her iced concoction and stirs it with the straw.

"It was good actually."

"Okay, we don't do small talk. How are you? I wanted to give you space, but I'm worried Scar." I know that it's probably been hard for her to see me so closed off.

"I'm okay. I'm just going to class, going to the gym, and trying to focus on the good." That's a lie, I haven't been able to box. I've walked into the gym a couple of times, but I keep giving up once I'm there. Maybe I'll try again tomorrow. I know she isn't buying it.

"Are you okay?" I want to say no but instead I nod. I don't know how much she's been told.

"I thought you would've heard all about it by now."

"I begged for Harrison to tell me, but he wouldn't budge. And Stirling said he didn't know all the details. All he told me was that Vanessa was at the party... I'm sorry."

"Ha!" I let out a sarcastic cackle. "At the party? No, she was working it, Soph."

Sophia's eyebrows dip as her face contorts.

"She's a hooker or something I guess, Soph. My mother left us to be free and fuck men for money."

"Jesus, are you sure?" She stutters.

"Well, unless you can think of another reason why she would be dancing naked at the party with men all around her and tassels on her nipples. It didn't look like just stripping to me. She didn't look like someone there to dance, she looked like someone there to sell herself... and it seemed like the men there already knew her and what to expect. It's not the job, I respect anyone who can do it. It's that she left us, Soph. And he didn't even fucking tell me, yet he knew. *He. Knew.* He fucking knew Soph. I opened up to him about my feelings and he kept that from me." Tears fill my eyes, but I don't let them fall. Not today.

I don't need to tell her who, she knows.

"Scar, I'm sorry. That's really awful." She grabs my hand.

"And the worst part is how much I miss Callum. This is why I didn't want to start anything. I should focus on what the hell I want to do after I graduate and the last thing I need to worry about is guy drama. But I want to continue this, I just don't know how." I pause for a minute, thinking about what I really want to say. "I just feel like maybe I'm more into this than he is."

Sophia squeezes my hand. "I'm not taking his side, and you know that you're my ride or die. But do you think, maybe there's a reason he didn't tell you? Guys like Callum don't date, and they sure as hell don't open themselves up, Scar. It sounds like it wasn't nothing to him. I'm sure it will all come to the surface soon."

I have thought about that, but it still doesn't excuse the lie.

"Yeah, I know. But it doesn't mean that it's okay. Where do we go from here? We aren't even together, are we?" I look to her, hoping she can provide the answers but knowing that she can't.

"Well, I think the first thing you need to do is talk to him. And I dare you to tell him that you aren't together and see how he reacts to it—might get kind of steamy."

I snort, she's probably right.

"Thanks, Soph."

"I'm here for you, *always*. We're best friends, we don't shut each other out." She's right.

"I know, I just needed some time to breathe."

"I understand that. I'm sorry about Vanessa. I swear, when I see her again, I'm going to punch her for hiding all of this from you and Jake. What do you think is going on?"

"I have no clue, but I think Callum knows more. I guess I should talk to him sooner than later."

"Yeah, I think so." She takes a sip from her plastic straw.

I decide that I'm going to hit the gym tonight and ask Ricco for a round before I work on my paper. I walk out to my car, faster than normal. The wind feels stronger than this morning. My hair that has fallen from my clip swirls in the breeze as dead leaves dance to their own tune around me.

I can barely see my car in the distance, parked beside a streetlamp yet consumed by the evening's shadows.

As I get closer, the street light flickers. Although this aged campus is beautiful, it creeps me out sometimes. There have been stories that different buildings on campus are haunted. I usually don't buy into them, but it's evenings like this that make me question my beliefs. There are other cars parked, but I don't see anyone else in the lot.

I unlock the driver's door and glance into the window. A single red rose lies on my seat.

Callum.

I pick up the rose, it's free of thorns.

He's taken them all off. I look around, expecting to see him. I don't. While it doesn't make everything okay, it's a beautiful gesture.

I get in my car and can't help but smile. The gym can wait, I know where to find him.

Protection

Callum

The air is thick. I'm used to it by now, but every time I open the door it hits me, like it's my first time here all over again. As I walk further into the greenhouse, each rose comes into view under the ceiling lights. It's just past six in the evening, but it's that time of the winter where depression is deepened and the moon shines longer than the sun. I'm better acquainted with the moon anyway.

I know Scarlett doesn't want to see me yet, but that doesn't stop me from watching her. I always will. I inhale the sweet rose scent and walk over to the bushes that haven't bloomed yet, their beauty still hidden. The soil under all the rose beds is dry.

I remember when I found this place, after a drop in my first year. I needed somewhere to clear my head. I was driving from campus to The Society and pulled off the road to notice a small path. I followed it and saw this old building—surprised I'd never heard of it, but glad it was unknown by many. The moss growing on the roof intrigued me. I didn't know what this building was until I walked in. The smell of the half dead roses drew me in before I saw them—much like today.

She creeps back into my thoughts. I'm struggling to accept that she doesn't want to talk to me. She doesn't know how crazy it's driving me to watch her from afar. *How did I do it for so long before?* We've spent almost every day together, and being away from her this long just feels wrong.

Lately, everything at The Society has been setting me off—from the pledges and my father to school stuff. I'm stuck in the vicious cycle of blaming everyone but myself.

I think about the night where I saw her at that party, four years ago. She still doesn't know what happened, and if I tell her, I worry it will break her even more. I can't see her go through this agony again, but the risk of not telling her is greater than saying something.

I walk over to the hose on the other side of the greenhouse and glance at the bench where she moaned my name not long ago. I fill a bucket with water and evenly spray the flowerbeds.

Just then, I spot headlights as a car approaches the path. I recognize them immediately—it's Scarlett. She gets out of the car and slowly walks up to the worn door, opening it with caution. As soon as she steps in, her cheeks turn a bright red. I place the bucket down and lean against the bench, keeping my distance. My arms fold over my chest. I don't approach her, it takes everything in me, but she's finally here and I don't want to push her away.

"Hi," she says and looks toward the ground.

"Hi, Angel." My tone is low.

A moment passes before she speaks again. The whole time I stare at her. She's so beautiful with fury in her eyes—it's her best look yet.

"I'm mad that you didn't tell me about my mom. You knew and you didn't tell me, Callum." Our eyes lock. Sadness sweeps across her face—she's not masking it at all.

"I didn't want to keep it from you, I just didn't know how to tell you without hurting you. I didn't want to see you the way you are now. I'm the only one that should bring you pain, Scarlett—pain that you'll enjoy." It's true, I will break her, and she will bask in it.

"The fact that you didn't tell me hurts even more, Callum. I opened up to you about what she's done that has hurt me, and instead of sharing this, you held it from me. If I knew something about your family, I would tell you. Because I care about you." She looks to the roses, like she can't trust me. *I need to make this right.*

"I'm sorry, I should've told you." I take a step toward her. "But Scarlett, you have to understand...I've never done this. I don't know how to do this right. I know that what I did was shitty, and it doesn't justify my actions." I take another step closer to her. "I'm sorry. You must know that I'm sorry, and that the last thing I want is to hurt you like this. The only way I'll hurt you is so fucking sweetly. I'll bring you pleasure you've never felt before."

I stroke the side of her arm.

"You think you hate me now, wait until you see what I become for you."

Her breath hitches. I don't lean in and neither does she. Instead, she pulls back. I can tell it's because she's trying to stay strong. So, I let her.

"I know why you did it, Callum. I know that it was your way of protecting me." Her saying it makes it real.

"Is that why you think I did it?" She still doesn't understand.

"Well, why did you do it then?"

"You still don't get it. I don't just want to protect you, I want to break you. I want to hurt you so badly that you scream for me to stop. I'll never be done with you, Scarlett. You've dug under my skin into whatever is left of me, and I'm not letting you go, not now." I expect her to fear the beast that's been tamed within me. Instead, her eyes meet mine and she licks her plump lips. The intensity between us shifts.

"I want to trust you. Can I ask you a few things?" I'm not afraid of much, but her quiet tone worries me. I don't want to lie to her anymore.

"Anything."

"What is The Society really about? I know by what I saw and the way that you talk about it that it's more than what you've made it out to be."

I pause to process my thoughts before I say anything.

She can't know too much.

"It's tied to the university," I finally say. "The group is made up of a lot of powerful men in the community who dictate what some of us do and how we control things."

She takes in what I'm saying, but I know that the answer will lead to more questions.

"Are the things that you guys do legal? What kind of things are we talking about?"

It's a loaded question.

"I can't tell you too much because then you'll be at risk, Scarlett."

"You can trust me—I won't tell anyone."

"I know that you wouldn't but it's more than that. It's the fact that you could get hurt if they know that I've told you. I've done too much, Scarlett. Once you know, things won't be the same."

"So, try to help me understand. I want to know all of it. The good. The bad. I want to know what I'm getting myself into and what my mom has gotten herself into."

She's worried about her mom's involvement.

"She isn't just a stripper, is she?" She quietly adds.

"No."

"What does she do then? What's her part in all of this?"

"I don't know the full extent of her role yet, but I'm trying to figure it out. These men don't tell anyone anything unless they need someone to know. I have some sources with the Highers—that's what we call some of the guys that lead us. What I do know, is that she spends a lot of her time with one particular Higher."

She frowns. "Who is it?"

Shit.

"Scarlett, he's a really powerful man. I don't want to-"

"To what Callum? The worst has already happened. I already found out about her double life and all this bullshit that comes with it. Her safety is at risk. What could be worse?"

"It's Archer Alden."

"Harrison and Stirling's dad?" Her forehead scrunches up.

"Yes." Her eyebrows come together and form lines above her nose. Doubt fills her face. "I know they look like the picture-perfect family from the outside, fuck, we all do. But he isn't a good man, Scarlett."

Her eyes drop with worry.

"Is she safe?"

"I don't know." My honesty punctures her like a bullet to the chest. She might not be close with her mom, but she still loves her.

"I'm sorry, Scarlett. I'm trying to get as much information as I can."

"What if something happens to her?" Tears fill her eyes, but they don't fall.

Honesty is the best thing I can offer her.

"I've seen it all, Angel. It's hard to make it out of this life any other way."

My words aren't comforting, not when I know that she wants honesty. I grab her hand. The heat between our fingers pulls us closer. She takes a step and wraps her arms around me, melting into my chest. The smell of her sweet hair under my jaw overpowers the scent of roses. I rest my chin on her head.

I must tell her about that night four years ago. If she knew the things I've done, she wouldn't be clinging to me.

Emotional Confessions

Scarlett

We stand in this still embrace for a few minutes before I back away and leave him just as I found him, alone in the greenhouse. I need to think about what he just said to me, and I know that if I stay any longer, I'll likely give into his lust.

My headlights shed a bright light on our dark house as I pull into the driveway. Dad didn't leave the porch light on—he must be out. I get out of the car, go in through the side door, and enter the kitchen. I lock the door behind me and turn the porch light on. Chinese takeout is my only option as I glance into the fridge. I open the paper box, grab a fork, and inhale the noodles. I haven't had much of an appetite over the last week, but now that I've vented to Sophia and had the dreaded conversation with Callum, I feel like a weight has lifted off my chest.

Worrying about Mom isn't new for me. Growing up, there were many times where she didn't come home. I should've known then. I think of myself as a young teenager, finding out that my mom is a prostitute for some of Millhaven's finest—my full body shivers. I wouldn't have been able to process that then—I barely can now.

I finish my leftovers and leave the box on the counter. I head upstairs and open the bathroom door. I'm too tired to jump in the shower, so instead I wash my face and make my way over to my room. I change into fresh sweatpants and a baggy t-shirt, climb into bed, and pull the covers over my head as I lie on my side. It's been a long day. I need sleep, but my mind won't let me rest. I roll over and look up at the ceiling.

I can't help but think about Callum and The Society.

What kind of things have they made him do? I wonder if he'll ever open up to me about any of it. I can tell by the way he speaks about them that he harbours a lot of resentment toward these Society men. His father must be involved. Callum said they're made up of the upper echelon of our town and his dad is within that circle. His father also went to Langford—there's a hall named after the Mercer family. All the Mercers went to Langford. Their legacy must be the reason why Callum can't get out.

I think about Harrison and Stirling, and wonder if they know what's going on behind closed doors. I know what it's like to have everyone critique what you're doing, but the events taking place in their lives are on another level. I can't imagine how they feel versus what they must conceal.

Silence.

I hear the furnace kick on, followed by a scratching noise that I'm unfamiliar with. I look to my closed bedroom door and hear faint footsteps.

"Dad?" I call out. Usually, he wouldn't be this quiet coming in. He doesn't answer.

"Dad!" I call out again, my pulse picks up.

There's no response. I sit up and push myself back, against the headboard. I look around the dark room, wondering what I can use to defend myself against an intruder.

Before I can reach for anything on my nightstand, my door slowly opens. A tall frame appears in the shadows. He lifts his hand and runs it through his hair. His familiar broad figure steps toward me.

"Jesus, Callum, you scared the shit out of me. You couldn't knock or call me?" I catch my breath as he approaches the edge of my bed.

"If I asked, I knew you might say no. I couldn't take the chance."

"So instead, you show up in my room?"

"Yes, Scarlett."

I glance at the clock—it's been about an hour since I left him in the greenhouse. He has a different shirt on and wears black leather gloves on his hands.

"Why do you look like a serial killer?" I study him. The room is dark, but I don't miss his stark reaction.

His laugh surrounds me, pulling me in. I drown in it and close my eyes. His leather covered hands run up my body as his warm breath hits my lips. He doesn't kiss me. Instead, he hovers there for a moment, our lips an inch apart.

"You're the only person I've ever bled for," he whispers. My neck pulses in his grip.

I can't take it anymore. His hand grounds me, weaving through my hair. I press my lips against his and find his jacket with my hands. I rush to take it off.

"You said that you want to break me." The words come out as I pull my lips away from his.

He doesn't say anything, but I feel the corners of his mouth lift against mine in a smile.

"Show me," I whisper.

He stands, breaking our connection, and takes off his jacket, then pulls his sweater over his head. He leaves his hands covered.

"Callum, I don't know if I like gloves." Something about them makes me feel on edge, but I don't tell him that.

"You don't get a choice, Angel."

Cold leather trails down my body, covering me in goosebumps. At first, I don't know how to feel. But as he traces the outline of my skin, each leather covered finger grazing me, my physical reaction grows into a wetness I can't control.

I lean back on my bed and take my shirt off. He stays bent over top of me as I lift my hips and slide my pants down. He watches carefully as they fall to the floor.

Callum presses against my body, pushing me into the bed. He drags his cool fingers up my stomach, all the way to the tip of my chin. I forget how to breath.

"You know why I call you angel?" He says and licks the bottom of my neck.

I shake my head, unable to answer.

"Because even in my world of hell, you still make me believe in something more." His tongue lands on my bottom lip, sucking it. I reach down and slide my hand into his jeans without undoing them.

He pushes his pants down, exposing his hard length. As I wrap my hand around his cock, pumping it up and down, his body quivers.

He rests his forehead on mine. "Fuck, Scarlett."

I grab his hip with my other hand, pulling him in. He reaches his lined, thick middle finger down, circling my wetness. A moan escapes me. He pulls his belt out from his pants. I try to look at him, but he blocks me with a kiss. I can't see what he's doing.

I feel leather slap against my wrists as he loops his belt around them, pulling tight. I squirm beneath his hold, but our bodies move in sync. My wetness coats his tip. He shoves into me, slowly pulling out before he slams himself back in. My hands remain bound above my head. He sucks my neck, bringing me closer to ecstasy. I feel my inner walls tightening as the pressure builds. I'm so close, he must feel it.

"You don't finish until I say so." He pulls out and flips me over. My ass sticks up while my hands stay in the same position. His hands interlock with my hair as he pushes my head into the bed and plunges into me.

"Callum!" I yell, muffled by the bed. His firm grip pulls my body up by my hair. My arched back leans against his chest.

The belt loosens around my hands. He brings it to my breast, slapping the firm edge of the belt against my hardened nipple. A shock runs through my body, electrifying every inch of me in the best way. His hips press into my ass as he pushes deep inside me. He moves my head to the side with his.

"Do you trust me?" He whispers into my ear.

"Yes, Callum, please, I'm almost there."

"I know, Angel." His free hand reaches for my clit, rubbing the aching sensation away. I squirm. He moves in and out of me faster, the pace of his hand mirrors the speed.

He brings the belt to my neck and wraps it around. He pulls it tight. My throat feels like it's closing in as my body fights for air.

"Let go, Angel." I try to fight it. The moment I stop, my head falls back, and my hair mixes with his sweat. I feel myself on the edge.

He thrusts into me hard, hitting every nerve as he breathes heavily.

"You." Thrust.

"Belong." Thrust.

"To." Thrust.

"Me."

One final thrust finishes us both. My vision clouds as he lets go of the belt. His warm liquid slowly runs down my leg.

I'm so weak, I can barely hold myself up. Just before I fall onto the bed, he wraps his arms around my hips and holds me up. There's something delicate about it.

"I may be a monster, but you tame the beast inside of me." He kisses the top of my head and pulls us toward the headboard. I wonder if this is the closest thing he's ever felt to love.

I roll over and rest my hand on his chest, catching my breath as I drape my legs over his.

His face looks like he's somewhere else in his head and not here, beside me.

"Are you okay?" I ask. He looks down at me and strokes the hair out of my face.

He stares at the ceiling and sighs, like he's about to tell me something he's been fighting with.

"I overheard some of the pledges talking about wanting to take advantage of you. I didn't know you at the time, and it was well calculated, it always is. But then I saw you, and I knew I had to do something."

What's he talking about?

"I was by the pool. You were wearing a black bikini top with shorts. Your hair was a bit longer, almost all the way down your back. But it wasn't your beauty that I was drawn to, it was how you studied everyone around you. I knew that you were better than us, better than this."

He knows?

Blood drains from my face as I recall that part of the night, four years ago.

"Do you remember any of it?" He asks.

The pain in his eyes matches mine.

"I swear Scarlett, if I knew, I would've done more to try and stop it. I should've done more."

"You know?" I've tried to block that night out so many times. Nothing about this feels right. I push off him.

"I tried—fuck." He sits up and runs his hands through his hair, like he does when he's worried.

His eyes turn a dark shade that I'm not familiar with.

"They were all dealt with. I took my time and made them pay a debt they'll never be able to fully get rid of."

"Was this the first time something like this happened? Why did they do it?"

"You need to understand, The Society won't stop. It's a business, everything is a transaction. They will do anything that they want without much justification."

A transaction. His words strike me—they don't feel soft.

"Do I know them?"

His shoulders tighten. I must.

"You know of them, but you never have to worry about the one mother fucker who chose you."

I close my eyes and transport to that night once again. The smell of sweat and alcohol floods in. I'm not sure that I want to know more.

"He's still around, but he doesn't have his eye on you anymore. He was power hungry and shouldn't have been there." Callum's eyes tell me so much that he can't.

"I'm sorry," he says. It's raw and deep.

Now is not the time to find out more about The Society, even though I need to know. I can tell that this has been eating him alive and I don't blame him. He's helped me in more ways than he knows.

"I wish I could take your pain away, but, instead, I'll bleed for you." It's subtle but intense.

"Thank you for telling me." I graze his arm.

"I wish there was so much more I could've done Scar. I've replayed what they said so many times." Although I want to ask him of these words that replay in his mind, I want to remember them on my own.

"I think this helped a bit." I give him a faint smile.

He grabs my face and kisses me, apologizing with his lips as our emotions feed into each other.

"I didn't want you to carry it, so I've tried to carry it for you." His thumb brushes my cheek.

"Thank you for not letting me become forgotten." I whisper quietly.

A stampede of different emotions race through me—anger, and even a bit of relief. After all the pain and grief that I'm left with, maybe a tiny piece of me has mended its way back together.

Times are Changing

Callum

I leave her house knowing that things will never be the same. I have so much to fight for now. While she may think that I'm holding back, I just can't watch her break anymore. With time, everything will unravel, and she'll see all sides of me.

I get into the car that was gifted to me—it's so fucking tainted. *How many people did I have to kill to get this recognition?* My phone rings, and Deluca's name appears across the dashboard.

"Callum," he says. It sounds like he's taking a sip of something, like I'm interrupting him.

What a prick.

"Deluca," I say and accelerate the car.

"We need you here, we're calling a meeting." His voice is calm.

"I'll be there in ten." He hangs up before I say anything else.

I call Harrison.

No answer.

Something is off. It's unlike Deluca to call a meeting and ask me to attend. Usually, I'm aware of a meeting or if my presence is requested far in advance.

I call Harrison again.

No answer.

What the hell is going on.

I exhale and my grip on the steering wheel whitens. Before I know it, I'm at the mansion.

Dust rises from the gravel as I rush down the lane way. Grey clouds fill the sky. When I pull up to the building, I don't see Harrison's car. I park in my usual spot and pull out my phone.

Where is he?

I scroll through my messages with Scarlett. Sometimes just looking at them when I'm away from her brings me clarity—I need that right now.

The clouds rumble as I open my door and make my way toward the side entrance. I walk up the stairs and into the lounge where I expect to see all the pledges. Instead, only the ruthless ones are seated, alongside a few of the Highers. Deluca and Leo are there, but so are others that I haven't seen in a long time.

Leo leans against the bar addressing everyone, as Deluca sits on his throne.

"There's been another incident," Leo says. "We need to proceed with caution in our final initiations, there are lots of eyes on us right now."

"Legacy won't protect them anymore. Tradition is not enough. With the public eye on this case, we need to be more—" Deluca hesitates. "More selective in the future." Deluca's response is well versed.

He's referring to Emily. Her parents went to the press about her death and are demanding answers—ones they'll never receive.

Deluca looks at me. "And most of all, we need to be careful with who we trust," he threatens.

I twist my neck to one side as I adjust my shirt.

"Respectfully, as the one who cleans up everyone else's fucking messes, you don't need to worry about me." My sharp eyes lands on him.

"You need to be careful, Callum. Protection is earned, not given."

"Glass houses." A voice I often avoid speaks up from the bar. Holding a drink in his hand, unbothered, he raises his glass at me.

What the hell is he doing here?

Although I try to avoid him, it's hard when we share the same spaces. I almost ended him four years ago, but money can buy you anything, including protection, in this vile world. I've struggled to watch him talk to Scarlett. My teeth clench as I try not to give him the reaction that he wants, but it's too late, I'm unraveling.

"What the hell are you doing here?"

"Just came to show my support to The Society, since I'm also a member." He reminds me.

Leo looks at me and then back at him.

"Gentlemen." It's a warning.

He leans against the wood, his shirt freshly pressed, all to maintain his polished image. He proceeds with caution. Everyone's eyes are on him.

"We need to remember that our loyalty to The Society comes first. There's always a bad apple in the basket, sometimes you just need to eliminate it before it rots the entire bunch."

"And you've already been eliminated from her life, I still don't know what you're doing here." My response is quick.

"I told you, I'm here to support The Society, that includes you, Callum."

"I don't want anything from you. The only thing I want, is for you to stay away from me and stay away from her." He knows exactly what I mean. I close my eyes and picture her, lying on the bed, trapped underneath him. I'll never be free of the memory, just like she'll never be free of the trauma. She *trusted* him.

"Are we done here?" I need to get away from him, from all of them.

Leo nods toward the door, motioning for me to follow him. "Yes."

As we make our way down the hall, he turns to me.

"You need to distance yourself from her, Callum. You need to remember what's important right now." Leo's always been one of the only Highers that I've seen eye to eye with— even though he's sharp and closed off. I can sense that he comes from a place of worry.

"I can't do that Leo." It's the truth, I don't trust anyone else to protect her the way that I can. Even though she might be better off without me, I'm too fucking selfish to let her go.

His softening gaze holds mine.

"While I will always put The Society first, you do what you need to do. Just don't trust anyone. Clean up your own messes, Callum."

He grabs my shoulder and walks back into the parlour. His words stay with me.

Maybe I can let Leo in, just a little.

I can't help but fixate on why they let *him* come to the meeting. I should've asked Leo, but there's no point—especially with the recent events. Deluca must have brought him as a warning. Leo wouldn't have had much say in it.

My phone vibrates and I pull it out of my pocket.

Harrison.

"Where the hell are you? I've been trying to get a hold of you for the last hour."

"I've been tied up with a Society matter. What's going on?" I start to wonder if they didn't want Harrison here because they didn't want anyone to defend me.

"I'm here. Deluca called a meeting."

"Yeah, they wanted me to clean this mess up before I came." *Clean-up crew member number two.*

"What mess?"

"I'm just trying to tie up some loose ends." I know what that's code for—he's not alone.

"Who is it?"

"Nathan, Emily's brother. He heard something and was on his way to the press again."

I sigh. *That goddamn family needs a break.* I don't say that out loud—Harrison knows. He was friends with Nathan in elementary school.

"What happened at the meeting?" He asks as I walk outside to my car.

"They want everyone to proceed with caution as we come to the final initiations. Can't decide if it was a warning or a threat. And they fucking invited that slime ball in for the meeting." He knows who I mean. I hear him let out a sigh.

"Why was he there?"

"Apparently to support The Society. He reminded everyone on the importance of loyalty."

"Loyalty." The word rings loudly. I lean against the driver's door.

Harrison knows our history. Hell, he witnessed it.

I close my eyes and the flashback returns. I'm on top of him, my fists flying into his face. It wasn't just Scarlett that I protected that night, it was all the other women that he's laid his nasty hands on. If only she knew who was really in her life. My eyes slowly open to the dim moon in the sky—it reminds me of what I'm fighting for, who I'm fighting for. Although I'm still pissed with Deluca and Leo, there's more to worry about right now.

I open the car door, get in, pull out a cigarette, and light it. I need to see her, even if it's just from a distance.

I check the time on the dash—she's either at the gym or at home. I'll go to the gym first. As I drive across town, I think about how I can add a GPS to her car. I could do it easily. Maybe I should track her phone as well. With everything that is happening at The Society right now, I need to be able to find her.

I pull up to the gym's aged red brick exterior and scan the parking lot for her car. I don't see it. She must be at home. I look at my phone, click on her contact, and call her.

"Hey, Callum," she answers. I hear laughing in the background.

"Angel."

"What are you up to?" I guess we're doing the small talk thing before I skip to territorial boyfriend. *Boyfriend.* I'm stunned by my own thoughts.

"Just wondering where you are?"

"I'm just out with Soph. Did you want to do something later?"

I laugh.

"What's so funny?" She asks. I can hear her smiling.

"You think you have a choice. Text me when you're home."

"Actually, my dad is home. I was hoping that we could go to your place?"

My place. My parents house. The place I dread the most. She will never understand what it's like to exist in a place that's supposed to provide comfort but feels like it's ripping you a part.

"Scarlett, I'm not afraid of your dad."

"No, but you should respect him, Callum. It's important to me." She's silent for a minute.

Her relationship with Jake is something I must tread against lightly. While I don't have many boundaries, I'd do anything to have a father like him in my life. I won't ruin that for her.

"I'll be over later."

"Callum—" She starts.

"I'll be quiet, don't worry. He's hasn't heard all the other times I've sneaked in."

And all the times that she doesn't know about. She doesn't respond.

"I'll see you later, Angel."

"Bye, Callum." The softness of her voice stabilizes my mood.

I drive to my house to have a shower and change before I see her. As the night passes in my rear-view mirror, I can't shake the thought of how much power she holds over me.

Things Left Unsaid

Scarlett

I come home after a much-needed night with Sophia. Laughter, ice cream, and her company cured some of my broken pieces. I haven't been able to slow down and enjoy life with everything going on lately, and although I want to tell her about it all, I can't, not yet. Still, I would be lost without her support.

I open the car door and quietly shut it. While it's not too late, Dad is likely in bed. I slide my key into the lock and push the door open. Dad's not sitting in his recliner, but the kitchen light is on. I throw my stuff on the table and walk upstairs.

The bed meets me as I enter my room. Heat washes over my face and my vision blurs. Suddenly, it's not my own bed that I'm looking at. The walls become red, instead of the white that coats my room. I begin to relive that nightmare of a night all at once.

I'm lying on that bed; my limbs are flaccid. My hand reaches for the wall as I steady myself.

I moan, but I can't make out what I'm trying to say. I seem intoxicated, even though I didn't drink much. Three men surround me.

The air feels heavy as I try to take a deep breath. I close my eyes and push it out. *A distinct smell fills my nose, a common cologne, one that I've smelled since that night. Its citrus pulls me in—a scent that isn't as sophisticated as the typical Langford man. I can't shake it. Its woody undertones wash over me, and notes of cinnamon pull me in further.*

I can't stop the memories from flooding in. *Suddenly, I'm no longer looking at what happened to me. I feel his hot breath on my neck. He tries to pull my shorts down. I want to use my hands to stop him, but I'm unable to move them. I try regardless.*

I open my eyes to a warm hand, gripping my hip. I yell. The hand quickly covers my mouth. I turn to see Callum's eyes and my breath steadies.

His hand wraps around my head as he pulls me into his chest.

"Shh, I'm here now."

Relief washes over me—I feel safe in his arms. His smoky leather scent grounds me as I bury my face in his shirt. I want to tell him what just happened, but a part of me is scared.

"Callum, I ..." I struggle to get the words out.

He pulls back and looks at me, his hand gripping my face.

"Don't hide from me, Angel." His thumb traces my jaw, and his eyes meet mine—so dark and mysterious, yet so beautiful and soft. They stand for everything he is.

"I saw something. Well, I guess I felt it." I don't know how to tell him. "I remembered some of what happened at um... the party."

"What do you mean you remember? What did you see?" His brows meet as he looks toward the ground, concerned.

"I remember being in the room. I remember I was so hot, and I felt like I couldn't breathe." My throat tightens. I don't know how to tell him about how vulnerable I still feel and that I can't remember everything. "There was someone on top of me, he was trying to pull down my shorts." My cheeks burn. I want to crawl inside a hole and never come out. Suddenly, I feel ashamed. "I don't know what happened after that."

His face drops and he takes a step across the room. His hands ball into fists at his sides and his shoulders tense.

"Callum, I was drinking. I should've been paying attention. I'm—"

"Don't you fucking dare say sorry. Don't you ever say that, Scarlett." He stops pacing and looks at me. "I don't care what you think you did, no one deserves what you've been through." Pain ripples in his voice.

I didn't know how badly I needed to hear those words—they mean so much more coming from him. A sob escapes me. I close my eyes and fall to my knees. I don't talk about what happened to me for a reason, I've never wanted to become a victim.

Callum wraps his arms around me—a safe haven.

"I know Angel, you're safe now. I'll never let anything happen to you." His hand glides through my hair, comforting me. "I'll never let anything happen to you," he repeats.

It's a promise he shouldn't make, but I believe him.

He doesn't say much else—he doesn't need too. He just holds me, as years of tension leave my body. I begin to relax and lift my head to look up at him. His lips draw me in, and I lean forward, unable to deny his magnetic pull.

My lips land on his. I grab his face between my hands, and the kiss intensifies. His arms slowly lower us to the floor, and I straddle him. He doesn't try to take control. Instead, he gives me the power I crave.

Our lips meet again. I grind my hips against him and feel his length grow. I pull my shirt over my head and reach for the door to lock it. For a moment, I forget that Dad is two rooms over.

Callum's hands surround my hips.

"Scarlett, I can't... not like this."

His hands trail up my side. For a moment, I feel defeated, and I drop my hands to my sides, but I can't ignore the spark that lives deep inside.

"No, Callum, I need this."

I grab his hands and pull them above his head, trapping them there. We both know that if he wanted to escape, he has the strength to.

"Scarlett—" He brings my hands down to his chest.

"No, Callum. I need this. Please. I need the control. I need you. I need to feel like I'm more than what happened to me."

He brings his hands back above his head—mine follow.

"I'm yours." He sees me as I truly am. He wants my control. My hands hold his in place. I lean in and trace my tongue along his lips, then down his chin. I kiss his neck—it tastes smoky. There's a lust in my body that I can't fight. My lips land back on his and I move my hips, riding him. I pick up speed. Even with our clothes still on, I feel like I might finish if I don't slow down.

"Use me, Angel." I close my eyes and tears fall down my face. "That's it," he adds. His hips move with mine.

I pull my jeans off and move my thong to the side. I unbutton his slacks and pull them down with his boxers. Our eyes remain locked as I lower myself on to him. My hips move down then slowly back up, working his cock inside of me.

"Take it, Scarlett. Take it all." I move faster and moan. My head falls back as my eyes close. Tears leave my eyes—not out of sadness, but from relief. His hands grip my ass, and he holds me up, allowing me to gain full control.

I lean forward, my hands on his chest as my ass moves faster. I need this. *Fuck.* I need him. But this isn't about him or his needs—this is about me.

"Callum, I'm almost there." My mouth inches toward his but our lips don't meet. I hover just close enough to feel his warm breath on my mouth. I move my hips even faster, bringing us both to the edge, until my pelvis shifts forward and all tension releases. I lie my forehead on his chest. Our heavy breaths sync.

"Thank you." I say quietly.

In a brisk motion he flips me over, onto my knees, and roughly pushes inside me.

"You're not done yet," he whispers in my ear and covers my mouth from behind.

My moans are muffled under the palm of his hand as he drives into me, again and again. His hands move down to my hips, keeping me still. I reach back to touch him. He pushes my hand away.

"This is for you." The wooden floor is cool against my face as he places my head down. He knows I can take it, he knows I *need* it.

I push my ass out further and feel the tension building again. His cock hits me deep, over and over. I squirm as he holds my head against the floor. I'm almost there. Just when I think I can't take it anymore, another orgasm escapes me. He pulls my hair further, bringing my head back as far as it will go. He shifts his body, and I feel his warm come land on my face as he shoves his cock in my mouth. He degrades me in the best way possible. To remind him that I'm still in control, I lick the length of his shaft and look up at him.

"Open your mouth." His firm grip remains in my hair. "Show me you're mine, Angel."

I open my mouth as the liquid runs down my chin. He uses his other hand to caress my cheek. "Now swallow." He closes my mouth with his thumb.

I swallow all that remains of him as I sit back up.

"Good girl." He pulls me on top of him as we lie on the floor. I look up at the ceiling while his fingers trail up my neck.

"I hate that they took so much from you, Scarlett. I can't give it back, but I'll do everything I fucking can to make sure you never feel like that again." There's a pain in his voice I've never heard before.

"Do you know them?" I don't know why I ask, he's made it clear I'll never know.

He looks to me, his eyes saying everything he can't. He sighs and pulls his pants up. He can't give me the answers I want.

"I don't blame you, Callum. You didn't know. I just want—"

"I blame myself!" His loud tone startles me. "I blame my fucking self!"

I stand and grab my shirt. I can't look at him. I don't know what to say. I pull it over my head as I hear his belt fasten.

"What are you not telling me?" His footsteps come closer, then I feel his lips on top of my head. He lingers for a moment.

"Callum—" I turn around, "fucking look at me!"

His eyes fill with unfamiliar tears as he squints.

"That's all I can give you, Scarlett." He doesn't break eye contact and runs his hand through his dark hair. "Please. I can't." He's not asking, he's begging.

I don't move to watch him leave. Instead, I stare at the empty place where he stood. The door shuts and anxiety floods back in.

I'm so fucking mad at him. He doesn't understand—nothing he can say is worse than not remembering. I walk over to my bed and flop on it. I turn off my bedside lamp and get under the covers.

I want to call him, but I can't. I need space. I pick up my phone and call Sophia. She answers on the second ring.

"Hey Scar. Whatcha up to?"

"Not much. You?"

"Oh, just trying to finish this damn assignment."

"Sorry for bugging—"

"You could never bug me, you're my best friend."

"Want to go for a drive tomorrow?"

"Uh, yeah sure." The suggestion of a drive means I have something to talk about. "Is everything okay, I can come over now?" Her tone changes.

"Oh no, everything is good. I just wanted to chat."

"Okay, yeah. I'm free after my first class. I'll grab us coffee and meet you at the parking lot?"

"Sounds like a date."

"Can't wait. Love you, Scar."

"Love you too, Soph."

I hang up. I don't know if I feel better or worse. There's so much I haven't told Sophia about, and I can't really explain without telling her everything.

I place my phone on the table and try to turn my mind off.

~~~~~~

I wake up before the sun, grab my housecoat, and head downstairs. Dad sits at the table reading his newspaper. The smell of coffee helps me wake up.

"Morning, kiddo." His eyes lift from the paper and up at me.

"Morning, Dad." I walk over, grab a mug, and fill it with coffee, hoping it will bring me back to life after tossing and turning for most of the night.

"Did you know this kid?" He opens the paper so I can see.

A picture of Jasper Fontaine is placed in the top corner of the obituaries page. I went to middle school with Jasper—he was a couple of years younger than me, but I know his family.

"Yeah, what happened?" I just saw him at Langford a couple of weeks ago.

"He died. No details. His parents are having a celebration of life next week. You didn't hear anything on campus?"

"No, I'm surprised that I didn't."

"Two young town members dead in a couple months—things like that don't happen here in Millhaven." He sips his coffee and goes back to reading the paper. I don't know how to answer.

"I'm headed to the gym soon. Busy day?" I take a sip, unable to shake the flutter that creeps into my chest.

"Yeah, not too bad. Want to have dinner together later?"

"Sure. Let me know if you want me to pick something up on my way home."

"Okay honey. Be safe, text me when you get to school." He puts the paper down and stands, facing the shop.

I laugh. "Dad, nothing is going to happen to me."

"Well, I'm sure their parents didn't think so either."

"Okay, you're overreacting. I'm going to shower then head out. Love you." I put my hand on his shoulder before I make my way up to the bathroom.

I think about what Dad said. "Things like this don't happen in Millhaven."

I try to brush my uneasy feelings away and get in the shower, but thoughts of Jasper and Emily fill my mind. *What happened to them? And why do I have the urge to ask Callum about it?*

Signed, Sealed, Delivered

Callum

I needed to get out of there. I couldn't bare it. *Will she ever be able to forgive me when she finds out that I'm not who she thinks I am?*

The yellow light from the old lamppost leads me to my car, even though I don't really need the help. I've walked this path a thousand times before.

I sit in the driver's seat and grip the steering wheel. *I need to feel something, I need to stay grounded.* She's the only thing I want to protect, and instead it feels like I'm shattering her. I can't look back at her house.

I hit the wheel with the palm of my hand, repeatedly. I can't be what she wants me to be, but she's already everything. My hands shake as I grab the cigarette pack on my dash. The violent urge to hurt someone overpowers me.

I pull a cigarette out of the pack and light it with the Zippo. *Finally.* The sweet inhale doesn't feel like it's usual release. There's so much I want to tell her, so much she needs to know. My head falls back against the headrest—her world is currently crumbling. I need answers, and there's only one place I'm going to get them.

I shift my car into drive. The engine roars as the pedal meets the ground. For a split second, I forget about protecting myself. I pause and look up at her window. The curtain moves.

She's watching me leave.

I can't care about protecting myself anymore, it's all about her now— it has been for a while.

Ashes fall from the cigarette and onto my pants. I don't understand why everyone around me cares so much about fashion. Of course, it's a reflection of who we are, but what is it for those that try to hide parts of themselves? Mother does it so well. She pretends that she's royalty, even though she was raised to obey someone else. She was taught at a young age that even a hair slightly out of place could cost you your future husband, and I was taught to recognize that perfection.

Amid the dark sky, the moon lights the path to a place I've grown to hate. It has never felt welcoming to pull into The Society. I have no doubt that once I'm no longer useful, they will dispose of me.

There aren't many cars in the lot. I scan the area for Deluca's Lincoln. I don't see it. He usually parks near the entrance or in the garage—of course being a Higher comes with its perks. Next to getting away with murder, you get the best parking spots. *These men and their control.* I shake my head. I can't stop thinking about her as I make my way inside. She's in everything I do.

I try not to draw attention to myself as I enter the house. There's a security room on the main floor, near the back exit. Only Highers are allowed in.

I need to get there.

I already know that the cameras are following me, but I pull a knife out of my pocket and pick the lock anyway. I shake my head at how easy it is—you'd think some of the most powerful men in the town would protect their surveillance a little better.

Inside the dark room, I'm met with the shine of computer screens. Filing cabinets line each wall. I pull my leather gloves out from my jacket pocket and slide them onto my hands.

I'll do anything to watch this place fucking crumble.

I stare at the wall of screens. *I don't have much time.* I open the drawer closest to me and examine its filing, trying to pinpoint what I'm looking for. Files are organized by alphabetical order, each with a pledges' last name listed. I search for 'M.'

I think about how a Higher's mind would work. *Would they put her in my file since I'm the one who interrupted the initiation?* No. I should look for his name instead. I flip back through the files, closer to the beginning rows, and pull out the manila folder with his name on it. His stupid fucking picture looks back at me as I open it—I can't stand it. I sift through the pages, looking for something, anything—I don't find it.

There must be more. I know there's record of it. They are proud of these kinds of things—they fucking gloat about them. *I know it's in here.* I look toward the other clusters of cabinets and open the first drawer on the left. Instead, I find her: "BLACK, E."

Emily.

I open the file. There are no pictures, but Jasper's name appears on a page with the date of the party when she died. The file also holds all the newspaper clippings about her death, the receipts from her funeral, her dad's car payment... wait. I flip back. *The Society pays for her dad's car?* My eyes fall to the date at the top of the reciept—it's from six months ago, after Emily was killed. There must be more to this.

But this isn't what I came for. I can't do anything about Emily. I'm here for *her.*

I move to the last row of cabinets and open it quickly.

VOSS, S.

There was a brief moment where I thought I'd never find this, but now that I have, it changes everything. The leather of my glove carefully opens the folder. It has the same layout as Emily's. There's no picture of Scarlett, but there is one of her mom. I flip through her rent receipts, car payment loans, and cell phone bills. *Fuck, Vanessa.* She's in so deep.

A small yellow sticky note falls out onto the floor. I spot what I've been dreading to find.

His name is on it, next to the written words, *Initiation disrupted by pledge—Callum Mercer.*

233

My name is next to his. There's a specific curve to the M in my last name. *No.*

Bile builds in my stomach and rage erupts in my veins. *He won't get away with this.*

I take the entire file and stuff it under my vintage Valentino coat—one that has been passed down for generations. My grandfather saw it as a symbol for our family's determination and will. Right now, it conceals a monster.

I look around and make sure that nothing is out of place. On the computer, I delete all video evidence of my entering. I also set a timer on the cameras, so they won't turn back on until I'm out of here discreetly.

I hear a voice coming down the hall as I pull the door shut. *Leo.*

I scurry toward the basement stairs—my personal haven, but everyone's hell. It's not out of character for me to be there. Especially with everything happening, Leo knows I try to spend as little time as possible around the other pledges.

"Callum."

I roll my neck to the side and attempt to mask my rage. *Get it together.*

I turn to face Leo with the second years beside him. He tilts his head at me.

"Just tidying up some loose ends," I say. He stops before heading up the stairs and looks suspiciously at me. I feel the tension in the air.

"That's what you do best." His face doesn't change as he proceeds upstairs.

There's no camera's downstairs, there can't be. It's the one place in here that isn't monitored.

I pull out my phone and pull up his number, one I usually avoid. He picks up on the first ring.

"Well, Callum." He pauses.

I can't let him know.

"I swear if you go near her again, I'll end your life. You think that you're protected by The Society, but I clean up all the messes. And right now, you're looking like a big fucking mess."

His low laugh taunts me.

"You think I'm scared, Callum? If I was a threat to The Society, I would already be gone, but I'm still here."

"You're only here because I let you. Test me and find out."

Losing my patience, I pull at the collar of my shirt.

"I watch her, but one day... I'll get close enough to feel her warmth against me again, and there's nothing you can do about it."

I grip the phone tight, wishing it was his neck.

"You're dead." I hang up and stomp back upstairs. I take the back exit to avoid everyone.

I get to my car, take the file out from my coat, and shove it in the glove box. I pull out my phone, but I can't call her. Not like this.

I need a release—I need to make my pain someone else's. I do the only thing I know and go to the place where titles don't matter. A place where no one knows who I am, and they don't make eye contact when I walk in. Not because of my legacy, but because I'm nobody to them. A place where my fists are all I have, and where money and status won't buy your way. A place where I become who I truly am, and the monster in me is free.

Secrets

Scarlett

I wake up feeling anxious about the way that Callum left. I can't help but to focus on his silence throughout the day. I'm not one to be clingy, but he hasn't texted or called me since he left. Talking to Sophia after class today will help with all of this. And it felt good to be back in the ring this morning with Ricco. I haven't been avoiding him—I've been avoiding myself.

My stress is harder to turn off lately. In and out of the ring, I become my own worst enemy, but Ricco helps motivate me. He can always tell when I'm overwhelmed. He says it shows in my form. I don't get sloppy with my blows, but my arms drop, and I let more swings get past. With Ricco's guidance, I'm brought back to reality.

The library is the last place I want to be, but I figured it's best to finish some work while Sophia is still in class. I've withheld so much from her that I don't know where to start when she gets here. She knows that Callum and I are together, but she doesn't know how serious it is. She doesn't know that he's the last person I think about before I fall asleep and the first person I think about when I wake up and that he drives me crazy. The old me would've hated who I've become—relying on someone else for my own happiness. But I'm not sure if that's how I would describe him. Callum just gets me. When I'm around him, I don't have to hide all that I am. He sees the darkest parts of me and helps mend the broken ones that I'm not willing to face.

Shit. It's 2:40 p.m. I am going to be late meeting Sophia for 2:45 p.m.

I collect my books and shove them in my bag. I grab my coat from the back of the tall oak chair and walk by a study group from my physiology class. I smile at them, but they don't notice me. It used to bother me that people didn't often invite me to their library groups or study sessions held at their fancy houses. Unless I provide notes or essay tips, the invitation isn't there.

I rush through campus to the parking lot where Sophia and I usually meet. I scan the area for Callum. Sometimes he's out here. Although now that I think about it, I've seen him less around campus lately.

I spot Sophia's light wavy hair in front of me.

"Soph!" I yell.

She turns around. "Hey! I was just going to call you. Jump in my car?"

Her car comes into view as I catch up. Just then, we're cut off by a silver Mercedes, its front windows are down while G-Easy blasts. From the driver's seat, Chase makes eye contact with me as he slows the car.

"Hey, ladies." He waves.

"Ew," Sophia whispers.

I don't answer him. I can't. A familiar citrus smell escapes from his car as he laughs and peels away. A smell that recently sent me into a spiral.

I clutch the strap of my bag— anything to try and ground myself.

"*Stay still, sweetheart.*"

The quiet voice flashes in my head, each word making my stomach curl. I know this feeling.

I frantically search my bag for sour gummies. *I always have some in here.*

"Scar?" Sophia looks back at me. She was talking to me, and I wasn't even paying attention.

"Sorry, I, uh, I just need a minute."

"Are you okay?" I avoid her gaze as I riffle through my bag. Tucked under my books, I spot the bright coloured candy wrapper. *Thank God.*

In the middle of the cross walk, I stop to pull out a handful and put a yellow gummy in my mouth. I catch up to Sophia and we walk to her car in silence.

I get in the passenger side and reach around to throw my bag in the back.

"What just happened?" She asks.

"I, uh. I guess I've been seeing things. Flash backs really. To... that night." I struggle to get the words out.

She reaches across the gear shifter and grabs my arm.

"Scar, why didn't you tell me?" She pauses for a minute. "What have you been seeing?"

"It started the other night. I don't really know what triggered these memories. I just walked into my room, and the first one came. It was a lot, Soph." I look out the front window. "I wasn't just seeing that night, it felt like I was reliving it. Like I was paralyzed and couldn't move."

I glance at Sophia. Tears fill her eyes and match my own.

"You know you can always call me. I'm always here for you. Day or night, we've always said that."

"I know." I sigh. "It's not that I didn't want to call you, it's just that Callum came... kind of when it was happening, and I didn't really want to talk about it again after that."

Her faint smile is encouraging.

"You know that we don't have to talk about stuff if you don't want to. You can just call me and say that you need me, and I'll come over and sit with you. I just want to be there for you. You're my best friend and I feel like I don't really know what's going on in your life lately."

I nod. "Yeah. I feel the same. I'm sorry that I haven't been around much since things have gotten more serious with Callum." I feel like a shitty friend.

"How are things with him?"

"Good. He's kind of amazing in a dark and mysterious way. I don't know how to fully describe him. He's such an intellect—like he doesn't try to figure out what foods I like or what my favorite movies are, he just knows... although I'm pretty sure he's hacked my Netflix account just to see what I watch."

Sophia snorts. "Jesus, he sounds intense."

"Yeah, he is. But it's a connection I've never had before. With Chase…" I don't have to say that it didn't feel right.

"Yeah, I know. You were a fucking mess after Chase but it's because he tried to change so many amazing parts of you. Parts that make you, you."

Her reassurance comforts me. It's nice to hear that I wasn't just making those parts up in my head.

"How's the sex?" She wiggles her eyebrows and smirks.

I laugh before releasing a huge sigh.

"Holy shit, I always knew Mercer was packing."

"Sophia!" I slap her arm.

"What? I'm proud of you!"

Oh, God. She knows I hate this kind of confrontation. "It's unlike anything I've had before. It's more than just physical, and the way he…" I don't want Sophia to think I'm a freak. Although, I know that she's into a few weird things herself.

"What?!"

"Dominates me." I look to her and she gasps.

"Scarlett!" She slaps her hand over her mouth, and we giggle like schoolgirls. "I always knew you were into kinky shit… welcome to the club." She smirks.

Sophia has always been into different things, based on the sexcapades she's told me.

"So, it's good then?" She adds.

"Oh God Soph, it's so good. I never knew it could be this good." I can feel my cheeks flush a little bit. "I don't know what to do, Soph. I like him a lot, but it's so complicated. I can't help but wonder if this will all blow up in my face."

"You won't know until you try, Scar." Her faint smile brings me the warmth I was looking for.

There's so much she doesn't know. And I have a hard time believing that someone like her father, the District Attorney Victor Roberts, wouldn't know what was going on with the people that Callum spends his time with.

"Have you heard of an underground elitist group that supports Langford?"

"What kind of group?"

"The one that Callum's dad, Stirling, Harrison's dad, and many others in your social circle belong to?" I try to gauge her reaction.

"Look, I don't know what you think you know Scar, or what you've heard—"

"I haven't heard anything! No one will tell me anything." I don't mean to lose my temper, but I'm sick of everyone hiding this from me.

"No one will tell you because they are trying to keep you safe, Scarlett. Once you know…you'll wish you didn't."

I bring my hands together and begin picking my nails on my lap. There's no easy way to ask this.

"Does it have anything to do with the two students that have died recently?"

"No, Scar. Please. You don't want to push this. I'm not sure about the deaths, I don't know anything about that, but please, don't push any further."

I don't. I'll just have to figure things out on my own.

"Okay, it's okay Soph. I'm sorry. I shouldn't have brought it up."

"It's okay. Just listen, don't ask around about this. Please." The plea in her voice makes me worried.

"Okay. I love you, Soph." I reach out and wrap my arms around her. We've been there for each other through so much, but I need to find out what's going on—before any other tragedies happen in this town.

"You know I love you too." She pauses. "Well, I guess we don't need to go for a drive anymore. Unless you still want to?"

"No, I should get home. It was really nice just to talk about things with you. Let's not go that long with spilling our guts out again, please?"

"Agreed." She sighs.

"Anything new with you? I feel like we're always talking about my shitty life."

"Oh, you know. Just the usual—Stirling won't let anyone else near me, but he won't fucking admit anything."

"Seriously, that man needs to grow some balls."

"Yeah. That or let me go." Her voice goes quiet.

"You don't mean that."

"I don't know anymore, Scar. I'm so sick of this back and forth between us. It's been years."

Stirling's been in love with Sophia since we were fifteen, but he won't admit it—he's too proud. Yet, he threatens any man who tries to date her. When he found out that Sophia was hooking up with some guys from the hockey team last year, he just about committed murder. Sophia pretends to hate it, but I know she's secretly in love with him too—it's the only reason she puts up with his nonsense.

"I get that." I can tell she doesn't want to talk about him anymore. "Anyways, I'll call you later? Maybe we can get coffee tomorrow before your seminar?"

"Sure. Love you." I get out of her car and walk toward mine. Sophia rolls down the window.

"Love you!" She yells back.

I wave. As I turn toward my car, I notice something sticking up on the windshield. I get closer—it's a piece of paper. I pick it up and I look around. There's no one in the lot. Perfect penmanship stands out against the stark white paper, each detailed letter connecting to the next.

Stop searching for answers you don't want to know.

Beneath the Surface

Callum

Walking through The Society's door brings no comfort or sighs of relief. If anything, my blood pressure spikes a bit. The physical reaction starts to set in as my back tenses. It's hard to imagine anyone feeling happy in a place like this. When you have money and everything you want in life, you're constantly chasing a happiness you can't find. My Father has been searching since he was a teenager. I wonder if Mom ever thought that she was his happiness.

My mind wanders to Scarlett. She fills me with a joy that I didn't know existed. Bliss that I never want to let go of.

Vines cover the home's dark stone build, matching the personalities that live within it. *He better be in here.* I reach into the glove box for Scarlett's file, before entering through the side door.

The silence of the empty, lavish marble hallway greets me as I enter. It's dark in the sitting room, but I spot a small light on in the study. I tuck the folder under my jacket as I walk toward it.

He sits in a leather armchair, his back facing a wall of books. He has the newspaper in his hands. On the side table, his heavily poured drink accompanies him.

"You knew."

He doesn't look up.

"I know a lot, Callum." His tone is sharp like his physique.

Benedict Mercer's personality wasn't shaped by privilege. He worked for his position within my grandfather's company. It almost makes me hate him that much more. He was brought up by nannies and boarding schools and did everything he could to make sure that I would turn out successful. Instead of trying to break the mold and become involved in my upbringing, he chose to do the same thing that was done to him, but worse. He saw what he could've changed and let the things that he resented define me too. Amid it all, he built a fortune five hundred company and claimed his role as a Higher within The Society. Now he's the silent leader that many follow.

"Do you know about what happened to Scarlett?" I ask.

"Who's that?"

Liar.

"Scarlett Voss. She was almost raped four years ago. Her dad is Jake Voss, and her mom is Vanessa, the one who's bills you've been paying. Don't pretend like you don't know what I'm talking about."

His right eye twitches and he doesn't answer. I can't take my eyes off him. I look for a sign, anything that might give him away. His silence is powerful. I pull the folder out from beneath my jacket and slam it onto the table next to him.

His dark eyes rise to meet mine. Finally, I have his attention.

"It's below you to steal, Callum."

"Oh, but it's not below me to kill, as long as it's for The Society, right?"

I recall all the times he's used me through The Society to clean up his messes. Something he could never do—he doesn't have the strength.

"You're willing to give up on your brothers for this?"

Brothers. Family. They try to instill these values in us early on, that way you're less likely to betray them. They provide a sense of belonging just to take advantage of your name or your skill. My downfall is both.

"I don't have brothers. You were too busy fucking around to produce another heir."

"Watch it, Callum."

"Watch what? The lies? Watch you drag this family through hell with you instead of protecting us, like a real man? Watch you turn into everything you always hated." His face turns cold. I can't stop. "And yes, I know. About how you were raised, about how you resent it. Yet, you've become just like him."

He slams his glass down on the table and stands. His height matches mine and our noses barely touch as he grabs the collar of my shirt.

"You think you know? You have everything! I gave you everything!" He spits through his teeth. "And in return, all you have to do is what you're fucking told."

I push my chest up against his, unafraid. He's created this beast within me.

"I'm so close to having it all. So fucking close. And I never will. You did that. *You* did that!"

He lets go of my shirt but doesn't back away.

"You aren't protecting her, Callum. You're putting a target on her back. *You* did this."

A part of me shatters because I know he's right. I step back, my teeth firmly pressed against each other. *Have I made things worse by trying to help her? Would The Society have left her alone after that night? No.* This is what he wants.

"No one touches her. You make that known. Because I can protect her. I *will* protect her. From them—from *you*."

My breath picks up as my nostrils flare.

"Keep down this path and see where that gets you. See where that gets *her*, Callum. There was a Society before you, and there will be one after you. Just know that the future you've worked toward will be gone. What will you have to show for all of this?"

He isn't just referring to my career, he means her. Fists form at my sides.

"Don't mistake your obsession for love." He smiles.

I picture wrapping my hands around his neck and squeezing the life out of his body. *I need to get out of here before I kill him.* I grab the file and leave.

As I walk away, I shake the manila envelope toward him. "Next time, at least get someone else to do your paperwork. Your calligraphy is too obvious."

I shove the door open and rush to my room. I don't bother turning the light on as I enter. I'm glad I didn't pass my mother on the way. She's probably already drunk in bed or at another event for one of her charities.

The room's darkness feels like home. I throw the file in the top drawer of my desk, then walk over to the punching bag in the corner of the room and shove it away from me.

"Fuck!"

I need to be sure that she's safe, but that means I can lose everything. All of my work for The Society will become nothing. It's eating me alive. I hit the bag to stop my skin from crawling.

I should stay away from her. And if she stays away from me, they'll leave her alone. *Lies.* They'll never leave her alone. Not after this, not after *me*.

I hit the bag until my knuckles bleed. For the first time in a long time, I'm severely torn. I can't keep her safe if she's not with me, but I can't protect her if she is. I've done this—I sealed her fate, and I need to make it right.

I pull my phone out of my pocket. The tracker I put on her car tells me she's at home.

I lock the top drawer to my desk, change my shirt, and head out toward my Jag.

As I pull onto her street, the sky rumbles and fills with lightning, almost cinematic. I spot her car in the driveway, and the lights are on in the kitchen. Heavy rain hits my windows—I can't tell if her dad is in there.

I sit in stillness. My breathing syncs with the droplets of rain against the hood. She didn't ask for this. She wanted me to leave her alone, but my obsession couldn't keep me away. I smirk at the irony.

Is that what this is, obsession. I can't let him be right—

The passenger door opens.

Scarlett pulls her hood down, revealing her wet hair and faint smile. She slides into the seat.

"Hey." She says, shyly.

Scarlett's never shy, especially around me.

"What's the matter, Angel?" I grab her chin.

Her skin between my fingers feels like heaven might exist.

"Nothing." She looks out the front of the window.

"I'm not going to ask again." I squeeze her face enough to force her eyes on me.

"You left. You practically witnessed me having a meltdown and then you left me…"

"Scarlett—"

She pushes my hand away from her face. "No, you don't get to do that. You don't get to come and go whenever it's convenient for you, Callum. Am I not worth more than that?"

She's worth everything.

"I get it your scared, but I'm scared too Callum," she adds.

"Scared?! You think I'm scared? No, Scarlett. I'm fucking *terrified.*"

Her face drops, telling me she didn't expect it.

"You are the *one* good thing in my fucking life. The reason I do as I'm told. The reason I go to class and try so hard. The reason I do things you'll *never* understand. I don't care about this." I grab my shirt and point at the interior of my car. "I care about you. I've cared about you for four years, and now... now I'm realizing I can't fucking live without you."

It kills me that she thinks of herself as an issue, when she's the solution. My heart pumps faster and I force the air out of my chest. I stroke her face with my thumb. Her wet eyes lock with mine.

"I can't say those words, Angel." I don't tell her, but the moment I say them is the moment I'll die for her. Instead, I take her hand and place it on my chest.

"But this— this beats for you. I'm yours. Until my last fucking breath."

She quietly sobs. There's so much I can't tell her, so much I'm protecting her from. But the one thing she should fear the most is what I can't protect her from—me.

Familiar Fries

Scarlett

I can't stop the tears from falling down my face. Even if he can't say it, I know that Callum loves me. I want to protect him, like he protects me. And that starts with not mentioning the note.

Before I came outside, I already knew he was parked out front. Something just feels different when he's nearby— like a magnetic pull I can't escape. So, it wasn't a surprise when I spotted his car from my bedroom window. As I approached, I saw him sitting there. He was probably debating whether to come inside. I know him too well at this point—or at least it feels like I do. I'm not naive to the parts of him that I'm not familiar with. I know I must accept them all regardless.

Sitting here with him feels heavy. There's tension in the air. I know he feels it too. We both need a distraction, so I let him kiss me.

A fire is ignited between my legs when our lips meet. His tongue pushes into my mouth, the pressure building on my clit. Wetness builds as he gently grabs a handful of my hair and pulls my head back. *I need this, I need him.* His arms are the only place I seek refuge lately.

My hand finds the back of his neck as he pulls every bit of sanity from me. I don't want to do this here, but I can't tell him to stop.

His hand snakes its way through my jacket and up my shirt—the sensation causes my skin to feel alive again. He caresses my nipple between his fingers. My hips rock to relieve the burn, before he pulls me back to reality.

"Not here, Angel."

"So, you'll fuck me while my dad is in the next room but in your car is where you draw the line?"

"No, Scarlett. We're in the open, anyone can watch us. And if anyone sees you like this, I'll have a body to clean up." By his tone, he doesn't sound like he's bluffing. *He'd kill for me.*

"That's not funny, Callum."

"Oh, it's not a joke, Angel." Disgust washes over me but quickly turns to a yearning between my legs. My breath picks up.

"Does that turn you on, Scarlett?" His hand trails over my other nipple. "Thinking about me ending someone's life for you?"

It's so wrong. I shouldn't be turned on by that thought.

"Answer me, Angel."

Without hesitation, I nod my head yes. I couldn't possibly admit it out loud, and that's all I'm willing to give him.

He removes his hand from my chest and returns it to the steering wheel.

"Callum—" I whine.

"I said not here." His voice is assertive.

"Where do you want to go then?" I try not to pout, but he's never denied me before.

"I have a meeting I can't be late to. I'll be over after."

"Okay." I hide the disappointment in my voice.

He glances at me for a minute, like he's trying to read me. I remember all the times I've seen him vulnerable—like when he opened up to me about his family and his father. All he needs is to be loved. I stroke his face, and he flinches.

"I'll see you later." His eyes turn into slits as he watches me get out of the car.

I walk up the driveway, more confused than before. I know that there's more to this secret society that he's mentioned.

"Dad!" I yell as I open the door to his shop.

"Back here!" I see him over by the tool bench. A flashback of Callum and I in the garage sets in.

"Scarlett?"

I didn't realize that Dad was talking to me.

"Oh, sorry."

"You okay?" He wears a concerned look.

"Yeah, just came to ask what you want to do for dinner?" I scan the shop—he's worked so hard for all of this, for me. Anger washes over me. *How could my mom leave him?* He did everything for her, for us. He hasn't dated since, and I don't know if he ever will.

"I was thinking of ordering something? What do you feel like?"

"Um…I think I'm feeling Thai?" I think about it for a minute. "Or we could go grab some burgers," I add.

The Burger Bar in town has the best fries—crispy with seasoning. They've been in Millhaven since the town was formed and it's stayed in the Morrow family since. The interior has classic red and white checkered floors with matching red booths. Julia, the daughter of the current owner, went to middle school with me. I feel like if I wasn't so close with Sophia, we could've been friends, but I'm the type that doesn't need many close friends—I like to have one good one. She was always kind to me, and I see her behind the counter or serving tables when we go in. I always make friendly conversation.

"Now you're speaking my language." He responds with a smile. "I'll just need a bit more time in here. There's a fresh loaf of banana bread on the counter from Gerry's wife."

"Okay, I'll be inside if you need me. Come get me when you're ready."

The kitchen greets me with the warm smell of baking. I walk over and cut myself a slice of the warm loaf. It's completely dark outside now.

Just then, I spot headlights coming down the street.

I squint, trying to see if it's Callum's car, but the glare against the window stops me from confirming it. I sigh and walk around to the living room window to see if it's him.

"Scarlett, I'm going to call it a night, want to head out now and save the loaf for dessert?" Dad yells into the kitchen.

I jump as he walks around and into the living room.

"What are you looking at?" His grey eyebrows meet.

"Oh, I um, thought I saw something."

He moves to the kitchen sink and washes his hands, just like he does every day after working in the shop.

"Ready when you are." I grab my purse and rain jacket off the kitchen chair and head toward the side door. We always take Dad's truck when we go anywhere together. The pride in him won't let me drive. I don't even remember Mom being allowed to drive when she was around.

I open the passenger door and step up. As soon as I'm in the cab, the smell of leather and grease welcome me. It's Dad's distinct smell—I love it.

He backs out of the driveway, and we make our way to the other side of town, by the riverbank.

The red neon *Milkshakes* sign flashes beside the Burger Bar entrance. Dad locks the truck's doors before he shuts it. There's no remote locks or power windows. He's restored it multiple times. Always working on a different part of it and refuses to buy anything new. "Why would I do that when I can fix this one," he'd say.

The door dings as we walk in—matching the rings that escape from the kitchen. Julia rushes over to grab the ready plates.

"Sit anywhere!" She yells from the kitchen.

Dad motions for me to go first. I pick a booth near the back. It's a typical steady evening. Even on slow days, most tables are full. They are easily the busiest spot in town.

Julia brings menus and water to our table. "What can I get you guys?" She asks, hiding gum in the back of her mouth.

"Oh, I think we know what we want without needing these." Dad chuckles. "Right Scar?"

He asks me like I'm thirteen again. She smiles at him—it's genuine, everything about her always is.

"Yeah, I'll have the Country Burger, no mushrooms, with fries and a Diet Coke please."

"Of course, and for you?" She looks at Dad.

"The Big Country with mushrooms, fries and a Diet Coke too, please." He grabs our menus and hands them back to her.

"So, have you made any decisions about next year?" I know he's not trying to pry. He just wants what's best for me, but I don't have the answers.

"Not really, to be honest, I'm just trying to get through this semester."

He looks down at his water then back up at me. "It's taken a lot out of you. I can tell. Is there anything I can do to help?"

I smile up at him. "Thanks Dad. Nothing you can do. How are things with you. How's the shop?"

"Well, it's the same that it's been the last twenty-six years that I've owned it. It has its slow times, but customers always come back for good work. Especially with these damn new cars, I swear I fix them more than I fix the old ones."

There's a sense of pride in his tone. He's the hardest worker I know. He takes everything on himself and has never wanted to employ anyone else in the shop. This one time, I remember he was working late on a client's car, and she had to pick up her daughter from dance. So, his client and I got in his truck with him and picked her daughter up from her dance lessons. That's just the kind of guy he is.

It's not long before Julia returns with our drinks.

"How's Sophia?" He asks as he takes a sip of his Diet Coke.

"She's doing okay. You know her, always has something on the go."

"Yeah, she always takes on too much. She tries to impress her damn parents." He sighs.

"She misses you. She said she's going to come over for dinner soon. Maybe we can convince her to stay and watch a movie, like old times?"

"I'm sure it wouldn't take much convincing. She's always welcome. I worry about you girls. You both have a lot of big decisions you have to make over the next year. Is she going to continue in law school?"

"That's the million-dollar question. I'm not sure. I think she will end up sticking with it. I know she started down that path to impress her dad, but I think she is enjoying it now."

He smiles at me, content with my answer.

Sophia has spent countless hours seeking refuge in our house. Her parents live a different lifestyle—one I'll never understand. It often involved her being alone. So, she'd come over, whether it was for dinner or a weekend stay, she was always welcome. My Dad never makes her feel like a friend whose time at our house is limited. If she ever asked, I know he'd take her in.

"I have to ask, how are things with Callum?" His voice changes. I know that he doesn't love the idea of us together.

"Things are," I sigh, "complicated." I don't have to look up at him to feel the disappointment in his eyes.

"I just want you to know that I'm always here to talk or listen." He reaches for my arm. "You're the most important thing in my life, and I'm always going to be here for you—even if we don't see eye to eye on certain things."

"Thanks Dad. I really appreciate that." Hearing that gives me just enough courage to open up a little. "I just feel like, Callum has a part of him that no one else sees, because he doesn't let them. He's been so beaten down his whole life, and I sometimes don't know how to properly support him."

"That's fair, and brave to admit, Scar. Just listen. It sounds like support is what he needs. And you're great at that."

"Ha, thanks."

Julia appears with two overflowing plates. "No mushrooms for you, Scarlett." She rests my plate down in front of me. "And mushrooms for you, Mr. Voss."

"Thank you." I smile and grab a fry. *Yep, just as good as I remember.*

"You guys need anything else?" She asks and clasps her hands together.

"I think we're all good. Thanks," Dad says as he reaches over for the ketchup.

It's these little moments that I could live in forever. I eat my food and try not to think about all that's crumbling around me.

Glove Boxes

Callum

The cool air mixed with the lingering snow creates a layer of fog on the ground. I sit outside the gym, waiting for Scarlett to finish her early morning session. I haven't slept in over seventy-two hours, but for her, it's worth it. Watching her keeps me awake. I don't need any stimulants when I have her. She went in about forty-five minutes ago. *I have some time to kill.* I reach into the glove box and pull out her file.

I open the manila folder and read it again. They describe everything about that night on paper—from what she was wearing to who slipped the drugs in her drink. *Why was she chosen? Why did she stand out to them? Maybe they ran out of girls who aren't from here to take prey on.* There's always an increased population in Millhaven with the University.

I keep my eyes on the gym door, waiting for her to come out. It took me a while to understand why she boxes. I know that it's an outlet for her that I used to consider cute—now I find it fucking brave. *What pushed her into it?* Boxing isn't something that you just fall into—you have to claw your way in. And considering Scarlett's soft appearance, I wouldn't have guessed that it would be her thing. She's the countries average height, five six, with skin that should be kissed and not punched.

Being pushed to the edge too many times shoved me into boxing. I didn't adapt easily. I fought my way up to the top in different underground leagues. At first, boxing was a form of release. I'll never forget the way I felt after I killed someone for the first time. I needed to turn all my emotions off. I didn't want to feel the pain or guilt, just like I didn't want to feel warm blood all over my hands. I knew that The Society had pledges fight underground sometimes, I asked a couple of second years about it before I was even done my first week. They didn't know where the league was, or when it was held. They were being used for their money or power, not their ability to take lives.

I quickly learned that it was every Tuesday and Thursday, behind one of the local downtown buildings. You wouldn't know by walking past it. The men who run it don't care about your social status—just that you'll keep your mouth shut.

I've never kept track of how many people I've killed. That would makes each death too real. It makes them worth something, and they can't be, not to me. Living in a small town forced me to attend most of the funerals of the people whose lives I've ended. I shook the hands of their loved ones and told them that I was sorry for their loss. But really, the only thing I'm sorry for is letting The Society control who I kill. If it were up to me, there would be a hell of a lot more.

Now, boxing isn't a coping mechanism, it's a need. A craving for more blood on my hands.

The gym door opens. A well-groomed man comes out. Immediately, I know who it is—the owner, Ricco. I've seen him train with Scarlett before. He's a middle-aged Puerto Rican man with his hair parted and pushed off to one side. You can tell that he takes care of himself in an athletic way. He doesn't seem very tall from where I'm sitting. My eyes follow him to watch what car he goes toward. He turns to mine.

He approaches my window, and I roll it down.

"Can I help you?"

I look behind him and notice the gym's outdoor cameras. He's probably been watching me sit here since Scarlett went in.

"Just waiting for someone," I say.

"Oh, who are you waiting for?" The curiosity in his tone doesn't fool me. *He already knows the answer.*

"Just a friend." He leans against my car. One of the most insulting things you can do to a man is touch his car, especially when it's as nice as mine.

"I know everyone inside, and I know who you're waiting for." He's not playing nice anymore. *He thinks he can intimidate me—cute.* "Don't show up here looking for her. I know who you are, I know what you do. She—" he hesitates. "She is good. She doesn't deserve all the bad that you'll bring into her life. The danger, the lies. I know she's an adult and she can do what she pleases, but this will *always* be her safe place. And you aren't welcome here."

I'm not offended. Most people know who I am. He's looking out for Scarlett and that means something to me. The fact that he knows who I am and still came out here to threaten me shows me that he's willing to protect her, and that's all I need to know.

"You protect her in there, I've got her out here." I say, just loud enough for him to hear me.

He stares at me long and hard, like he doesn't know whether he should trust me. He doesn't say anything else. Instead, he looks around the lot and walks back inside. We aren't enemies—we're playing the same game, for the same person.

I know that Ricco and Scarlett have a good bond. He's been there for her through some of the darkest times in her life. I respect him for that. He's lucky that conversation went the way it did, it was off to a rocky start when he leaned against my car. I guess I can forgive him for it.

Not long after Ricco goes inside, Scarlett pushes the exit door open. She has her gym bag in one hand, and her car keys in the other.

Her rosy cheeks are flushed, and her hair is pulled back out of her face. She has no idea how beautiful she is.

It's just about winter and there's no snow on the ground yet, but she only has a sweater on. *She's going to catch a damn cold.* She scans the parking lot, like she's looking for someone. When she crosses the lot toward her car, her head moves from side to side, and it looks like she's biting the inside of her cheek. At this rate, I don't know how she hasn't noticed me. *What is she looking for? Or worse, who is she looking for? I must know.*

I slowly get out of the car and quietly shut the door. She unlocks her door as I come up behind her.

"Who are you looking for, Angel?" I whisper in her ear.

She jumps and turns around. Once she realizes it's me, she hits me with the bag in her hand.

"You idiot!" She yells in a high pitch tone.

"What? You were looking for someone, I figured it was me." *It wasn't, but I'm not going to be the jealous boyfriend.*

"I wasn't... I was just making sure no one was coming." She looks to the side. *Doesn't she know anything about lying.* Trust is shown by keeping eye contact, but not too harsh, or else it looks like you're trying too hard. Just enough and with a smile. That usually shows that someone is trustworthy. I add teaching her this to the long list of things I have to show her.

I don't say anything, I just raise my eyebrow. By now, she must know that I know she's lying. Her face turns my new favourite colour. *Scarlett red.*

"You were looking for someone, who was it." Just about all the patience I have has gone out the window. *I'm going to go from nonchalant to serial killer boyfriend in about two seconds.* "Scarlett." I warn.

"I didn't want to worry you." She looks to the ground.

"Worry me with what? What happened?" My heart beats faster. A million different scenarios run through my head before she tells me what happened.

"I got a note on my windshield. The other day, Sophia and I were talking in the parking lot on campus, and when I walked back to my car there was a note. I'm sure it's nothing."

"Where is it?" It comes out a bit abrasive, but I need to see it.

"It's in my glove box, just let me get it." She reaches in across the driver's seat, opens the compartment, and pulls out the note.

I look at it, trying to decipher the handwriting. At first, I wonder if it's Dad's writing. Luckily for him, it's not.

"Was there anyone around when you saw it?"

"No, I looked through the lot and didn't see anyone."

"When was this?" My tone is short.

"A couple days ago."

"When, exactly, Scarlett?"

"I don't know Callum, um, two days ago?" She expects comfort that I can't give her right now.

"And you didn't tell me?" I look away. *I can't give in, not when her safety is at risk.*

"No Callum, I didn't want to tell you because I didn't want this reaction. I didn't want you to get upset. I know that we both have a lot going on and I didn't want to add to it."

"What do we both have going on?" I know what she's been up to, but she can't know about all that I've done.

The only person I can be mad at is myself. She somehow received a written threat, and I didn't know. It slipped through the cracks on one of the only days I didn't wait for her when she was done class.

"From now on, you don't go anywhere alone."

"Pft, yeah right. That isn't happening, I—" Her face scrunches as she tries to finish her sentence.

"You don't have an option anymore, Angel. I won't follow you to classes, but if you're at school, I'll be on campus. If you're at the gym, I will be waiting outside. And if you're at your house, I'll be staying the night. And when I can't, someone I trust will sit outside your house down the street. Do you understand?" She needs to understand the severity.

She gulps and nods, sensing that none of this is a joke.

I rub her face with my thumb, finally giving her the comfort she wants.

"Your safety is my main priority."

She closes her eyes and moves her cheek against my palm.

For a moment, we stay there. The softness of her skin against my tainted flesh reminds me of what I have, and that I'll do everything in my power not to lose it.

Trauma

Scarlett

I was fourteen when I feel in love with psychology. It started with abandonment and progressed into more. It's fascinating to learn about how the brain responds to the different decisions we make. I sit in my favourite class, 'The Psychology of Trauma,' and remind myself of the memories and flashbacks that have been speaking to me lately.

I'm torn on how to feel about them. Part of me feels like a weight is slowly being lifted from my chest, while the other part feels anxious to learn the truth. I've been trying to relate to our lectures and case studies. Basically, the brain becomes overwhelmed when it experiences something traumatic, and our emotional part takes over. When this happens, if we block out or forget about trauma, we often lose those memories completely or struggle to put them back together. Sometimes, specific sights, scents, or textures trigger certain memories. *Great.* More things that *could* bring the feelings back.

I've been searching for a logical explanation of what could be triggering my memories. So far, I know that when I walked into my room, something about the lighting and the way I looked at my bed triggered the flashbacks from the party. Although I've encountered the sight of my bed a million times, that one time, it got me. It's all circumstantial.

Another trigger was that damn citrus and cinnamon smell in the parking lot. I've smelt that so many times that it doesn't make sense. *Why is it reoccurring things that are triggering me.*

 I focus back on the screen in front of me. Professor Elliot speaks about trauma responses and attachment. I think about mom. She hasn't texted me much lately, and when she has, I've ignored it. I pack away the feelings and save them for another day. *Look at the screen. Focus.*

 Professor Elliot feels like a broken record today. I've already finished this week's readings and know about everything he talks about. I try to avoid his eye contact, so he doesn't call on me. But no matter how hard I try, I can never avert his gaze. I always look like a teacher's pet whenever he calls on me. Which is at least once per class. I hate it.

 Once the lecture is over, I gather my laptop and place it in my bag. I throw the strap over my shoulder and head up the stairs, toward the door.

 "Scarlett, can I see you a minute?" I turn around to notice Professor Elliot.

 I hesitate before I walk down the stairs, toward him.

 "Yeah?" I try not to seem uneasy and look around at my peers who leave the lecture hall. Usually, I wouldn't care about being left alone with him, but today has been unsettling.

 "I noticed that you were a little off today in class. Is everything okay?" He studies me.

"Oh, yeah. Sorry about that. I'm just tired today."

"Troubles at home?" His head tilts to one side and his lips slightly purse.

"No, not really. Just didn't get a good sleep."

In second year, I thought Professor Elliot was cute—everyone did. But I've never had a crush on him like some other girls in his classes. He loves the attention and carries himself differently when he knows that someone notices him. Since we're only eight years apart, if I wasn't his student, we'd probably be friends. We share a lot of the same interests.

"Okay, I just wanted to check in."

"Thanks, I appreciate it."

A strong hand pulls on the back of my arm as I turn to leave.

"You could tell me, you know. If things weren't okay at home." I look down at his cold hand then back up at him.

Even under my long-sleeved shirt, the chill of his fingers washes over me. He doesn't let go. I take a step back and try to pull away. With a subtle jolt, he lets go.

"Things are fine. Goodbye, Professor." I look back at him as I walk up the stairs. The same nauseous feeling that I had during my first flashback fills my stomach. I shove the door open and scurry across campus. I need to get home.

I head straight to my car, open the door, throw my bag across to the back seat, and press the lock button. I tightly grip the steering wheel and try to control my breathing.

Blow out the candles, smell the roses.

I repeat it.

Blow out the candles, smell the roses.

I open the center console in search of my emergency sour gummies stash. It's empty. *Shit.*

I reach into the back for my bag and pull out my other rescue pack. I tear into the wrapper and dump some gummies into my hand. I find a yellow one, pop it into my mouth, and close my eyes.

Just when I think the agony is over, I'm taken back to that night.

The room is dark. I feel so drunk that I'm starting to fade. My legs feel heavy as I crawl across the bed.

As my head lands on the pillow, the door opens. It's too dark to see who's coming in. "Soph?" I moan.

She doesn't respond. Two more figures pile into the room. I want to tell them that I'll be here for just a few minutes, but I can't get the words out. Three of them surround the bed—one at each side. The tallest figure stands at the bottom of the bed.

They say something quietly to each other. I can't see their faces, but the tall one's body looks familiar. He doesn't have a bad posture of a hand in his pocket like the others. The way that he carries himself is different.

The tall one stands up straight. Clearly, he's the leader of the pack. He places his hands on the bed but doesn't come toward me. He just leans there.

I open my eyes. *Another flashback.* It was different this time. I focus on my breathing and close my eyes to try and make out their faces, but I can't. I just want to know who they are.

I reach for the next gummy in my hand and my phone dings in my pocket. I pull it out.

Callum: Where are you?

I left so fast, I forget to call him. The only way I'm off the hook from him escorting me is if I call him after the lecture, preferably before I walk out to the car. He knows that my class got out twenty-five minutes ago.

Scarlett: Just on my way home. See you soon?

I place my phone down in the cup holder, put the car in reverse, and back out of the lot.

What Money Can't Buy

Callum

I watch her from across the parking lot, yet she doesn't see me. *Did she really think I'd leave her alone after the note?* She stares at her phone. Her cheeks are flushed, like she's been bothered or out running.

I swear if she's hiding something else from me, I will have to fuck it out of her. It isn't safe for me to have this kind of aggression, not toward her. My grip tightens around the wheel.

She pulls her mirror down and looks at herself. But she isn't trying to fix her makeup. It seems like she's supressing a cry. Her ocean blue eyes turn icy. I can't handle it. My teeth press together, and my chest rises and falls at a noticeable speed.

Scarlett is tough, there's not much that she can't handle. But when I see her upset, I turn into a predator. I feel the urge to hurt anyone who even looks at her the wrong way. I want to feel their bones break in my hands and watch as they squirm under my shoes, their glare meeting mine as they suck in their last breath. I want to take everything from them, because even though I don't want to admit it, a piece of me disappears every time anything happens to her. I'd give her all of me just to keep her safe.

She pushes the mirror back up and pulls out of the parking lot. I start the engine and keep a far enough distance, so she doesn't see my car. She's been high alert lately and pays attention to everything, but I'm always two steps ahead of her.

Her last class was Elliot's. As much as I hate that slime ball, I don't think he'd try anything in class, but maybe I'm giving him too much credit. I need to figure out why The Society trusts him. *Should I ask Harrison for another favor?* I can't. He's too tied up in overseeing a few of the bigger drops right now.

I pull up the contacts list on my phone and click on Leo.

"Callum." His voice echoes as if he's also in a car.

"Do you have a minute?"

"Depends on what for." A chuckle follows his stern tone. He pauses, waiting for me to go on.

"It's about Elliot."

He's quiet for longer than I'd like. "What do you want to know?"

"Everything. Has he been given responsibilities? I thought he wasn't allowed too."

"He has. He said that he wanted back in. Daddy has the rest of the Highers in his pocket, it was only a matter of time before he was fully back, Callum."

"He's scum, Leo. After what he did… I thought interfering with an initiation was an immediate removal?"

We've been over this before. I've heard the answer. I just want to hear it again.

"He's a Professor at Langford, Callum. He doesn't need a reason. His parents throw money at everything he ruins. It doesn't faze him. He'll never learn."

I wonder how much money his parents have wasted to clean up his messes.

"Callum, I know why you're asking." He pauses. "You need to ask yourself if it's worth it, if *she's* worth it."

"She's worth everything." I don't hesitate.

"How do you need me to help?" I think about what I'm willing to ask. Once I say it, I can't go back.

"I need his file."

"I can't give you that, but I can tell you what you're looking for." I'm locked in as I continue to follow Scarlett back to her house.

"The summer before Elliot went into teaching, there were a couple of girls that went missing. They weren't local, but it happened just outside of Millhaven. He was the last person who was with them, but you'll never find that information on the police file."

Nothing is ever on the police file in a town where the highest members of society hold the sheriff's department by a choke hold. The Society basically funds it, so of course they can get away with anything. I remember hearing about those women. They were twenty—one of them had just transferred to Langford, and the other was helping her friend settle in. I wasn't a part of The Society at that time, but I remember overhearing a conversation that Dad had with Archer, Harrison's dad. Their disappearances were chalked up as a boating accident.

"That isn't it, Callum. I need you to give me your word that you won't do anything irrational." I can't do that. He knows I can't control what happens when I find things out. I don't answer him. Words echo through the speakers of my car as my ears ring. I focus on Scarlett, a few cars ahead of me.

"Callum?" His words hum in my ears. It takes me a minute snap back to reality.

"Why are you telling me this?" Leo doesn't owe me anything. While he's my friend, his loyalty isn't mine. It belongs to The Society.

"I had a Scarlett once, but I lost her. Don't let them take that from you. I can't change anything, but you can stop it from happening."

Leo was engaged but never married. It was forbidden to talk about, but that didn't stop rumours from spreading. Some say that she took off with another man, others say she died. Only the people who were involved know the truth. I can't imagine losing Scarlett. It would kill me, I'm not sure how Leo is still alive.

I don't want to say that I'm sorry, it would insult him. We were raised the same, and I know that he doesn't want my sympathy. He wasn't telling me this to get a reaction—he was using it as a warning. I know what I must do.

"I'll be in later today," I say and hang up.

Scarlett pulls into her driveway. I stay down the road, not letting myself get to close.

She gets out of the car and walks toward her dad's garage, then up to her room. She stays in there for a while. Her dad is probably working late. She checks her computer. I know that grades and school matter to her.

I don't go in yet. I can't. I sit and watch her for an hour before I pull away and drive toward The Society.

Just as I'm driving away, her name flashes on my dash. I pick up her phone call.

"Hey, are you coming soon?"

She has no idea how badly I needed to hear her voice.

"I can."

"Oh, I forgot something at school, so I was going to head over to campus. I'll call you when I'm back?"

What is she up to.

"What did you forget? I'm in that area, I can grab it for you?"

"Oh thanks, but I actually need to grab a paper that I handed in to Elliot. I must've submitted my rough draft, and I just want to explain myself and resubmit." She would never submit something that wasn't perfectly polished. *Another fucking lie.*

"You shouldn't go alone."

"He's a Professor Callum."

"Don't trust him." My foot pushes heavily on the gas as my hands turn the wheel in the opposite direction. I drive to campus.

"Callum, you need to trust me."

It's hard when you're lying, Angel. I'm such a fucking hypocrite.

"Call me when you're back then. Don't be long." I hang up.

She's up to something. I should find her on campus and call her out, but instead I do what I've been doing for the last four years, I try to protect her.

Even if she's unaware or resistant, I'll always keep her safe. I smile, thinking about when she does resist, making this all much more worth it.

I pull into the campus parking lot and pick a spot near her usual space. I fight the urge to go in and confront Elliot. I watch her car pull up. We're back to where we were not long ago. Again, I watch her from afar while she sits upset in her car.

She holds her bag of sour candy and pops a few in her mouth. I know her well enough by now to know that this can't be good.

What the fuck is she doing? She lets out a big exhale and steps out of her car. She walks through the parking lot, toward the main building. By the way she carries herself, I can tell that she is hesitant to do what she's on her way for.

She has three minutes before I'm coming in. She's lucky I'm giving her that when she's this anxious. Especially when I can tell something is bothering her this much.

No one messes with what's mine and gets away with it. *Especially not him.*

That Night

Scarlett

I've grown up surrounded by people who love me. It's the kind of love that conquers all and gets you through the hardest of days. I've always had the most support from Dad and Sophia. They'd do anything for me, and they know I'd do anything for them. Today, I need to do this for all the good times that were robbed from us. But more importantly, I need to do this for myself. I need to face my monster.

I finally remember that night.

I'm halfway through my drink when something feels off. I've always been a lightweight, but this is different. I need to lie down for a while before I can get back to the party. I stumble into a room upstairs.

The room is dark. I feel so drunk, fading in and out. My legs are heavy as I crawl across the bed. I just need to rest for a few minutes.

As my head lands on the pillow, the door opens. It's too dark to identify who's coming in. "Soph?" I moan.

She doesn't respond. Two more figures pile into the room. I want to tell them that I'll be here for a few minutes, but I can't get the words out. Three of them surround the bed. There's one at each side with the tallest figure standing at the bottom of the bed. I recognize him. It's my psych professor.

They speak quietly to each other. I can't see their faces, but the tall one's body looks familiar. Unlike the others, his figure doesn't have bad posture or his hands in his pockets. He carries himself differently.

Professor Elliot stands straight. He's clearly the leader of the pack. He leans over and puts his hands on the bed. He doesn't come toward me, he just stays there for a minute and looks at me.

I close my eyes, unable to prepare for what comes next.

His hot breath hits my neck, and he tries to pull my shorts down. I try to move my hands to stop him, but I can't.

"Stay still, sweetheart," he whispers in my ear.

The pillow under me gets wet from my tears as he pulls himself out of his shorts.

Someone barges into the room. It's too dark to see him. Professor Elliot is pulled off from on top of me and a fight breaks out between the two of them. Once the perpetrator is taken away with the other two that were with him, the fourth man comes over to me. His hood is up as he stands over me. Something cool runs across my face and I drift to sleep.

I wake up and my head is pounding. My hair sticks to my face in the hot air. I can't spot anything that I recognize. The walls are a deep red, and I'm on an unfamiliar bed. I pat my clothed body down. My ears ring as I sit up. A small light shines in the corner of the room and I spot a closed door. I look around for my phone and find it on the floor.

Tears run down my face. I bend over, grab my phone, then lunge for the door. Something doesn't feel right. My legs ache. I don't remember coming here.

I open the door and hear the loud music. I'm still at the party.

I stand outside of Professor Elliot's office. My hands shake as I open the door.

"It was you."

He's slow to lift his head from the paper he's grading.

"What was me?" He doesn't look phased. While I'm spiraling on the inside, he sits there in his perfectly paired shirt and styled hair, like he has it all together.

"That night, I remember. It was you."

"What night, Scarlett? You're going to have to be specific."

"Don't act stupid!" His silence lights a fire deep within me. "The night you tried to rape me!"

He adjusts his glasses. "Scarlett, I must say, I'm really disappointed. I would never expect this from you of all people."

"How did you do it?" I won't let him make me think that I'm crazy.

"I expect this from a couple of women in the class who can't keep up, but blackmail? Scarlett...really?" He sounds annoyed.

"How did you fucking DO IT!" I yell.

He gets up from his desk, slowly circles around, then leans against it. Leaving only a few feet between him and me. Scents of citrus and cinnamon fill the air.

"What do you think you remember?" He slowly looks me up and down with his arms crossed, waiting for an answer.

"You on top of me. Then someone coming in before you were able to do anything." My voice doesn't shake but it stings to get the words out—it's the first time I've said them out loud.

"Are you sure that wasn't just a dream? Hmm? Are you sure it's not just something you want to happen, so you made it up?"

"No, I remember. There were other people there."

"Oh, let's go ask them then."

I scan the office, embarrassed. I really shouldn't have come here alone. I feel like an idiot.

"I don't remember them. I didn't see their faces."

"Oh, isn't that a coincidence that you saw my face but not theirs? It almost sounds like maybe you aren't telling the truth. Or maybe, your trauma has recreated this in your head." He takes a beat. "Trauma can do that, Scarlett. It can recreate memories in your head to fit what you want to see. It's okay, I won't hold it against you."

I fight back the tears in my eyes.

"No, I know. I remember. It was you, and everyone is going to know." I feel defeated. *He can't be right, can he?*

"No one will know, because you can't go around spreading rumours that aren't true. It would be unbecoming of you when you're about to graduate and get into a master's program. No one would want to work with someone who lies about their colleagues."

"But it's not a fucking lie!"

He takes a step toward me.

"Do you know why I wear this cologne, Scarlett?" The scent causes memories to flood in. "All you tacky fucking women love it. There's something about this mediocre scent that makes you pathetic women drawn to me. It was the first thing you noticed in my class. I could tell by the way you looked up at me on your first day in my lecture, like something caught your attention."

I look to the door, just realizing that I shut it on my way in. He steps in closer. My heart beats faster.

"It makes you think that I'm relatable and not too expensive—or else I would've been out of reach."

"I never wanted you."

"Oh, but you did. You showed me without ever needing to tell me." The confused look on my face pushes him to go on. "Your curious face always told me you wanted more."

"I wanted to *learn*." I spit from between my teeth. He's created this illusion in his head.

"You wanted more than that. No one is that interested in psychology, Scarlett. You don't need to lie."

"You must be an idiot to believe that considering *you* specialized in psychology."

"You believe whatever you need to tell yourself, to play the victim." He takes another step. "It's too bad that you didn't finish that drink. I think we could've had a lot of fun." His lips come close to mine.

My body tries pulls away and my right jab lands on his cheek. He's not going down without a fight, not this time. He touches his face as I step further back.

"Jesus, Scarlett, you don't need to hurt me."

"Isn't that what you're trying to do to me?" He lunges for me and grabs my hair, pulling me back. My fists try and connect with his head, but he holds me too far away.

"It didn't have to be this way, Scarlett." He says, trying to dodge my next punch that connects with his shoulder. He grips my hair harder and drags me toward the back of his desk.

He slams my body against the ground and crawls on top of me.

I claw at his skin, trying anything to distract him. Nothing seems to slow him down.

"I'm going to enjoy this. You have no idea how many times I've thought about—"

Just then, he's pulled off from me. Callum holds him by his hair on his knees. He wears a leather glove on the hand that squeezes Elliot's face. He stares deeply into his dark eyes.

"Finish that fucking sentence, I dare you."

Garbage Day

Callum

When I spot her underneath him, everything comes flooding back in. Although she still doesn't know that I intervened that night, I'm ready for her to find out. About that night and everything since then.

We were in high school together briefly—she was in grade nine while I was in grade eleven. Most would call the colour of her hair light brown, but I've always thought of it as a mixture of darkened autumn leaves, faded from their bright fall colours but not crisp yet.

From the first time I noticed her, I became utterly obsessed. I was at the Burger Bar with a couple of my friends. When she walked in, time stood still. I'd seen her before, at school and around town, but I never recognized her beauty until that day. I was instantly curious about her. She sat at a booth by herself and read a book about the brain's functionality. She seemed so consumed by it. After that day, I began to gather little bits of information about her. I watched her from time to time, but not too intensely. I convinced my grandfather to donate a bunch of money to the university that went toward scholarships for psychology majors. I may have tweaked her application. If I didn't, she probably wouldn't have been able to go to Langford.

My obsession didn't escalate until her name came up during initiations. She didn't deserve what was going to happen to her. Braden, a third-year pledge, wanted to drug and rape her. She caught his eye at the gym. Usually, townies are off limits, but she didn't have anyone to protect her. Until she had me.

I tried to convince Braden to pick someone else, but he wouldn't listen. I couldn't tell him why it couldn't be her, but then I saw him slip the roofie in her drink, after I warned him. I sat by the pool and watched her. She briefly caught me looking at her. How I wish she could've seen the warning in my eyes.

At The Society, initiations are conducted to pledge one's allegiance. What they don't tell you is that they're also used as something to hold against any guy that wants to leave. The Society holds people captive against their will—that's why once you're in, you're in for life. Unless you kill someone and try to frame someone else in The Society, like Elliot. That's how you get kicked out, and what he did was a strict violation of club policy. Elliot was asked to step back, so he involved Braden in his initiation task. And when the time was right, he decided to commit the crime.

I watched her walk upstairs, staggering all over the place. Shortly after, Braden, Mack, and Elliot went up as well. I stood by the pool, knowing that something wasn't right.

I slipped my gloves on and made my way up the stairs, unsure of what I was about to see. All I knew was that I couldn't let her become a victim. I've seen how pain ruins people, how it rips them apart, and I didn't want that to happen—especially not to her.

I opened the door and saw him on top of her. I could hear her whimper before I saw her face. Lava flowed through my veins. I grabbed him from behind and pulled him off of her. Before I knew it, I was on top of him, my fists smashing into his face in swift motions. Braden called my name, begging me to stop. He didn't want the blood on his hands. Elliot should've never fucking been there.

I stood and threw Elliot toward Braden. "Take him. Far away from here," I said. Elliot reached for help as he tried to stand. Mack helped him up and they left the room. As the door opened, the light from the hallway reflected against Scarlett's face. A beacon of light, shining on someone so innocent, someone who needed my protection—an angel.

I walked over to her with caution. I didn't want to scare her. For the first time, I felt the need to comfort someone. I saw the pain through her closed eyes and stroked my cool gloved hand over her porcelain skin.

"Never again," I promised. She didn't hear me.

I pulled her shorts back up and looked around for a blanket. I didn't see one.

I walked out of the room. My hand lingered on the handle before I closed the door. I never wanted to leave her, *but she didn't know me like I knew her. I didn't want to scare her. So instead, I waited for her.*

I pull Elliot up by his hair and bring his face close to mine, so he can feel my spit on his face.

"Finish that fucking sentence, I dare you," I repeat.

He smirks. A small laugh escapes his mouth, and in that moment, I decide it will be the last sound he'll ever make.

I grab a larger fist full of his hair and bash his head off the ground. I don't stop—I can't.

Blood pours from the back of his skull as I repeatedly hit it off the ground.

Then, I see her. Standing over in the corner, watching me. She doesn't look away. Now, she sees all that I am and all that I've become. The pain in her eyes brings me back to that night—the pain I swore she'd never feel again.

I let go of him and my hands fall at my sides. Blood pools underneath my feet. I slowly walk over to her.

She stands motionless as I approach her with my bloody hands. Her face is frozen in a permanent state of shock.

"He's dead." Her eyes trail upon Elliot's lifeless body.

"I had to," is all that I say.

She doesn't say anything, she doesn't have to. Instead, she reaches up and strokes the side of my face. Even after I showed her the worst parts of me, she still treats me with such kindness and love.

"I couldn't hide it forever, now you've seen all of me. You have me, forever." My blood covered hand reaches for hers.

I pull her in close.

There's a passion between us that I've never felt before, and my heart picks up as she steps closer. Love and lust combine as I place my lips on hers. The fire that lives in me ripples through our mouths, creating harmony.

Just as I begin to get lost in her taste, she pulls back.

"Callum, what are we going to do about..." She nods toward Elliot's body.

"I'll take care of it."

"I can help, I just—"

"No, I don't want you involved. You've already seen too much. I didn't mean for you to see all of that, but when I heard him laugh, a rage built inside of me that I couldn't hide. After all he's done to you, he needed to pay."

I touch the back of my hand to her cheek, calming her.

Her eyes grow as she meets my gaze.

"Callum—" She covers her mouth. "It was you." Her words rock me to my core.

"It was you that night that stopped Elliot. You dragged him off of me, and then you brushed the back of your hands on my face, but they were cool?"

"I had my gloves on." She remembers. I don't react.

I search my pocket for the small pack of sour gummies I placed inside.

I pull out a yellow one and hold it up to her mouth. She looks at me as she opens it—there's something sexual about it.

I break our eye contact and walk over to Elliot. He's stopped bleeding.

I sigh. "Good riddance," I mumble.

I scan the room for cameras and find none. I pull out my phone and call Harrison.

"Hello." He answers on the second ring.

"There's been a situation."

"What do you need?"

"A large bag, some tape, and some bleach." He knows what that means.

"Who did you kill?"

"Shane Elliot."

"Jesus Christ, Callum."

"Where are you?" He adds.

"In his office at Langford."

"I'll bring supplies. Think of a way to get him out of there before I get to you."

He hangs up.

I wish I could say that I'm not happy with myself, but the truth is, I'm so fucking proud. Excitement seeps out of my pores. This man was the definition of trash. He killed people, he lied, he violated women, he stole, he cheated. He was everything that everyone hated.

I know there will be consequences, and I've already accepted them. I'm willing to pay whatever price to help Scarlett fight her own demons.

Strength in Tears

Scarlett

As I drive home, the shock wears off and dread settles in. *I just watched Callum kill Shane Elliot.*

I don't know what's worse—the fact that I'm okay with it, or that I feel so numb. All the hate and anger I've felt toward Elliot feels different. Within hours, I went from finding out that it was my professor all this time, to watching him die.

I know that Callum has his secrets, I'm not naive to that. But there was something about the way that he flipped so quickly into someone else. Someone I don't know.

I stare at the stop light in front of me, unable to look away. There's blood on my shirt, Elliot's blood. It must've transferred from Callum. *I'm wearing Professor Elliot's blood.* The shed of Elliot's blood isn't just on Callum. I also did this.

I try to rationalize this. I remind myself of what he's done. *Even though he harmed so many women. It's awful that he's dead, right?* I can't convince myself. I don't know if I can live in a society where we accept rapists and murderers. *Wait—The Society.*

I assume that Elliot must have been a part of The Society—his dad is one of the most influential investors in town. There's no way someone that superior isn't in an elitist society that is only for the wealthy and powerful. Callum has always hated Elliot. *I bet he knows more.*

I pull out my phone before the light changes and call Callum.

Even though I know that he's cleaning up Elliot's office with Harrison, I need answers. He picks up one the first ring. I hear his breathing before he says anything.

"Elliot, I need to know, is he a member?"

There's a brief pause.

"Yes."

I knew it.

"Was he still a member?"

"No."

"Dammit Callum, I need more. I need—" *don't cry for him,* "I need to know it wasn't a mistake."

"It wasn't a mistake. You didn't do anything, Scarlett. It was my decision, I did this. But if you need to hear that Elliot was a selfish bastard who raped many and likely killed two or more women, then yes... he deserved it."

The tears that fall don't represent my weakness, they represent my strength.

I don't say anything. I keep driving home as we sit together in a comforting silence.

I pull into the driveway and put the car in park.

"Thank you." I say softly.

"I'll be by later," is all he says before he hangs up.

I step out of the car and walk up to the front door. I stop before I open it to collect myself. I don't want Dad to see me, not like this.

It's still early in the evening. When I enter, I hear him working in the shop. It's the only time in my life I've been thankful for him working late. I throw my keys on the table and go upstairs.

The shower always takes a minute to warm up, so I turn it on before I get undressed. I peel off my jacket, smeared with his blood. I look in the mirror at the person I've become, knowing now that my life will never be the same.

I step into the hot water and close my eyes as it splashes against me. Visions from earlier flash in my head. If Callum didn't come, Elliot would've succeeded this time. That thought feels like a knife in my chest, causing pain I won't let consume me. Everything I've been working so hard for and everything I've fought for, it all feels wasted. My light feels dim.

I walk across the hall to my bedroom. I send Dad a text saying that I'm not feeling well and will be in bed. Sadness starts to settle in as I crawl into bed in my fresh pajamas. *The pajamas that I washed, because my mom isn't around, and she hasn't been for so long.*

There are certain times where a girl just wants her mom. Tonight, I long for her—just like I did four years ago. The sting of her absence sinks in.

I pull the covers over me and cling to the duvet, wishing I could get lost in it. The sun sets behind my partially open curtains. Warmth peeks in. At the end of the bed, I hear my phone vibrate in my bag on the floor. I don't want to get up to see who it is. I roll over and fully submerge myself in the blankets. I close my eyes and try to see anything other than what happened today.

I wake up an hour or so later to a warm body by my side. *Callum*. Instantly, I feel safe. He slowly opens his sleepy eyes as I rest my head on the pillow toward him.

"I needed to be near you." His deep voice sounds so peaceful. I move my body closer to his. He releases a small chuckle of serenity.

"I'm sorry," I say.

"I never want you to be sorry, not for this." He's quick to respond but his voice remains calm.

"I just, I'm not tiny, I practice all the time, almost every day. I fight men bigger than Elliot. I don't just fight them, I win, Callum. But today, I wanted... I tried to-"

He grabs my face. "Don't, Scarlett." Tears fill his eyes. "You shouldn't have to train to fight off a man who wants to rape you." Hearing him say those words breaks down the wall I've been trying so hard to hide behind.

I quietly sob and he brings me closer. My salty tears land on his bare chest.

Sex is the last thing on my mind, but my body craves the connection with him.

"Callum—" I touch his torso.

His lips meet mine before I can finish, like a dance we've done a hundred times. Our bodies know their way to each other.

My hand moves down his to the top of his boxers. I can't stop myself.

"I need to feel you."

His hands trace my back, under my shirt. The hands that have killed for me run tenderly along my skin.

His hand lightly grips the base of my neck. He pulls back, and our lips part only for a moment.

"I've waited forever for you, Angel."

How can someone exposed to so much hate, love so delicately?

His other hand caresses the front of my pajama shorts. He must feel the wetness growing as he teases me. I do the same and firmly press my palm against the outside of his boxers. I feel how hard he is for me and moan.

He grips the top of my shorts and pulls them down. With my tank top still on, his head moves to my chest.

My nipples harden as his fingers brush the outside of my shirt. He opens his mouth and sucks on my nipple, through the shirt. The warmth of his saliva against the fabric of my shirt forces me to push myself against his cock and rub myself against him.

He grabs my hips with his hands and forces me onto my stomach. I can hear him pull his boxers down as he straddles me from behind. I lie under him with my closed legs tight together. I try to rub them against each other for any sense of relief, but it doesn't come.

He slides his left hand under my stomach and slightly lifts me. My ass rises. He holds me there as he enters me from behind, forcing himself deep into me. He hits a spot I didn't know existed. My clit burns for him to touch it. He slides in and out quickly, while his other hand comes down to my mid back, forcing my chest down.

"Fuck, Callum." I moan.

He lifts his hand from my back and finds my hand near my head. Our fingers intertwine and he slips our locked hands down the mattress to my clit. His hand guides mine to rub it back and forth.

"I'm almost there, Callum." I don't know if he can hear my muffled cry as he takes me to the edge. I can feel it building inside of me, I'm so close.

"Callum—"

"Don't move, Angel."

His cock grows harder as he drives into me with more force. I fall apart as the built-up tension releases from me like a wave. Callum moans and rests his head on my back. I sigh and my body goes limp.

He lies down beside me, his head resting on top of mine. I want to stay like this and forget. It isn't long before reality sinks in and I know that he probably has to leave soon.

"What did you do with the body?" I ask.

He hesitates.

"Callum, I don't want any more secrets, please." I know he wants to protect me, but I need to know.

"There's a place at The Society for things like this. He's been dealt with."

"But how did you get him out? Did Harrison help you? Are you going to get in trouble? Maybe if you tell them he was hurting me... I can tell them, so you won't get in trouble."

"I want you to really listen to what I'm about to tell you, Scarlett. These men, they don't care. They don't care about murder or rape or whatever crimes are committed. They are loyal to one thing and that is themselves. Never, under any circumstances, are you to trust any of them. And they aren't going to punish me because of who I am. My Father would never let me admit to killing Elliot, that's not an honour I'll ever have."

In this moment, I'm grateful. I still have so many questions about The Society, but I know this isn't the time to press. Callum has so many things happening at once—so much that he's done, for me. Although he's remained calm, I know he's falling apart. His ego won't let him show it.

We continue to lie together and pretend that this could be our reality.

Confrontational Fathers

Callum

We quietly lie in her bed, but things are different now. I have several missed calls from my dad and Leo, I know we don't have much time before I'll be expected at The Society. Time lingers as anticipation grows thicker.

I lean in and smell her shampoo. The sweet scent of lavender calms me. I take one last breath and kiss the top of her head. I need to get back to Harrison and make sure we fix this. I need to protect her.

I can tell by the way that she's breathing heavily that she finally fell asleep. Harrison took Elliot's body back to The Society so I could stay with Scarlett. She needed someone, and I had to be that person for her—the only person I know how to be. Harrison prepared Stirling to tell Sophia, and she knows to keep her distance for now. She's permitted to spend time with Scarlett tonight. With those two glued at the hip, I'm surprised I didn't see her over here sooner.

I carefully snake my arm out from under her head, trying not to wake her. I sit at the side of the bed for a moment, thinking about what's to come. I know The Society won't take what I've done lightly, and my final initiation is coming up. Before the Elliot issue occurred, Harrison asked me to help with a drop today. *I need to go.*

I pick my jeans up from the floor beside the bed, slip them on, and pull my phone out of my pocket.

1:10 a.m.

Harrison will be leaving soon. I text him so he knows I'm coming.

Callum: Your house or Society?

I slip my shirt on and open the window. Usually, I can make it through the house at this time of night without waking Jake, but tonight, I can't take that risk.

I grab onto the wooden lattice as I position my feet in its slots—muscle memory.

The front porch light turns on as I get to my car. *Fuck.*

I look up, Scarlett's bedroom window is dark. *Jake.*

He opens the door as I keep walking toward my car.

"Callum!" My feet stop in the middle of his lawn. I guess this is what it would feel like to get caught doing stupid shit as a teenager, I've never had the pleasure. I was always too calculated to get caught.

Jake walks off the porch and toward me. I don't say anything. As he approaches, I notice his heavy eyes and messy hair.

"I'm just going to come out and say it. My daughter is an adult, she's a smart girl, so I don't interfere. I know that she wouldn't stop dating you, even if I begged." He studies me. "Why don't you use the front door next time and come around dinner time? I'd like to get to know the person who takes up so much of my daughter's life."

"Sure." I nod. His eyes stay locked on mine for what feels like a long moment, before he turns away to return home.

An unfamiliar weight fills my chest as I walk to my car. *How can I kill someone without batting an eye, but conversing with Scarlett's dad made me so uneasy?*

I consider the father figures in my life. My father, grandfather, and the Highers—who have been in my life for as long as I can remember—don't have a parental bone in their bodies. Scarlett is so lucky to have a father that actually gives a damn about her.

I sit in the driver's seat, and my phone vibrates. *Speak of the devil.* Father's name appears on the screen. I hit accept and bring the phone to my ear.

"Where are you?" Immediate anger fills his tone.

Hasn't he learned? If he wants to know where someone is, he must keep tabs on them. This is what happens when everyone does things for you—you forget how to do them yourself.

"What the fuck did you do, Callum? It's like you're trying to get caught."

It's cute that he thinks I care about him being upset. *Fatherly love and all.*

"There was a problem, and I eliminated it." He won't see it that way.

"You *eliminated* the son of one of this town's most influential men. There will be consequences."

There are no consequences when you already live life in the depths of hell.

"We need to discuss this. When will you be back home?"

Home? More like solitary confinement.

"I'm doing a drop with Harrison. I'll be back in the morning."

"I'll be waiting, Callum."

He hates waiting, most powerful men do.

I hang up.

The car's engine idles for a few minutes before I pull off her street. I make my way to Harrison's house, across town. After his grandparents passed, him and Stirling took over their family's estate. The house is nothing like ours. It's warm and welcoming. Harrison's grandmother, Harriet, would always have fresh flowers in the house, picked daily from her second home—the outdoor garden. She was Harrison's icon, always so humble and sweet, with so much life left in her right until the end. She fought for what she believed in and had his grandfather wrapped around her finger. Harriet was a Nana to all of us, and Harrison still struggles to fill the void.

My mind drifts to Scarlett—the perfection in my life that I don't deserve.

I think about the first time I took her to the greenhouse. That day, I knew I could never let her go. But now we're in this mess. With all that is about to happen within The

Society, I can't help but wonder if she would be safer away from here, away from me. I struggle with the want to keep her close and the need to keep her safe.

The white house comes into view as I pull into the curved driveway.

Even with all the gardens out of season, a vase of fresh flowers sits on the foyer table when I walk in. Harrison's shoes thump against the old wood floor.

"I don't expect you to cover for me, say you weren't involved." I know The Society could probably figure out that Harrison helped me with Elliot, but I'll lie through my teeth for him.

"That's not your decision to make."

"It is when I'm the one responsible. You won't go down for this." Image is everything for his family, and if this ever gets out, I can't be responsible for their downfall.

He doesn't say anything. Instead, he walks past me, toward the door. He opens it and makes his way to my car. I follow him.

He grabs my pack of cigarettes and offers me one. We drive in silence, anticipating what's to come.

Better Left Unsaid

Scarlett

I pull into the parking lot, like I've done a thousand times. But today, it feels so wrong.

I grab my bag and stare at the main campus building, mourning the person I once was. I used to seek comfort here, now those feelings are long gone.

Slowly, I begin my walk down the path, toward the brick building. My feet feel heavier the closer I get. I didn't get an email about class being cancelled, so there must be a substitute for Elliot. *Who will it be?* While part of me is curious, the other part doesn't want to find out.

I try to ground myself and look around at things that I can identify. The trees are bare. The leaves have long fallen. The grass is still a bit damp from the morning air. The sun is trying to come out through the clouds. At this time of year, rain or snow can be expected.

I approach the door and a student in front of me holds it open. *I can't do this today.* I tightly clutch the strap of my bag and turn around, back toward the car, keeping my pace the same to avoid any attention.

I ease myself into the driver's seat and check my phone. If I call Callum, I know he'll come right away. *He's probably not far anyway.*

I don't want to worry Dad, and if I call him, I'd have to tell him what happened and I'm just not ready to.

I find Sophia's name and hit call.

"Hey Scar, how are you doing?" Her voice sounds calm and comforting. I wonder if she knows.

"I don't know. What are you up to? Do you want to do something?" I think that being around someone who isn't involved will help. Sophia knows what it's like.

"I'm free. Want to come here? We can have a couple of drinks then go for a dip in the hot tub."

"That sounds like just what I need. I can be there in ten? Do you need me to get anything on the way?"

"Oh no. We have everything here. See you soon. Love you!"

"Love you." I say back before I hang up.

Once, when we were younger, she told me you're always supposed to tell someone you love them before you say goodbye. I feel the need to say it to her now.

I find immediate comfort knowing that I'll spend tonight with Sophia. I pull out of the parking lot without looking into the rear-view mirror.

Sophia lives outside of town, in the same neighbourhood as Callum and Harrison. Her house is nothing like mine—it's not full of colour. Sophia's family doesn't eat most meals around the table, and they don't order takeout or watch movies on Saturday nights. Her house feels like it was created for the purpose of looking nice, not making memories.

I pull in, alongside the six-car garage, and text Sophia that I'm here. I don't like stepping inside without her.

The door opens. She pops her head out and waves for me to come in. I walk up the large granite steps to the two white pillars on each side of the front door.

"Hey," I say and wrap my arms around her neck. There's such warmth in her embrace.

"Come on in! Have you had lunch? I was just about to make something."

She shuts the door behind me.

That's the thing about best friends, they always know when something's going on. They might not know what, they can just tell by what you say—or by what you don't.

We walk through the foyer and into the kitchen. I throw my bag on one of the high bar stools around the extravagant marble kitchen island. Sophia goes to the fridge and grabs lettuce and meat with some condiments to make us sandwiches. We talk about school and how her classes are going—she loves to tell me all the drama. Sometimes her in-class debates get intense, and she says that there's a lot of competition to get the Professor's attention.

I've never had trouble getting a professor's attention. My good grades and love for the subjects always get me recognized. Personally, I hate it, but I guess that's something I won't have to worry about as much with Elliot gone. Once there's a new permanent professor, it won't be long before the year is over.

"Okay, now that we have some food, let's make a drink." Sophia says as she glances at the bar.

Drinking usually forces me to spill my guts, and I don't know if I'm ready for that yet.

We leave our plates on the island, and I follow her to the bar. It takes about two minutes for her to convince me when she starts to make margaritas. We make our way back to the kitchen with our drinks and sit down with our plates, just like we've been doing since middle school—but now, with alcohol.

"Thanks for lunch and having me over. I really needed this."

She takes a bite of her sandwich. "I know you did, I did too."

Her eyes meet mine, her look suggesting that she knows more than she's saying.

"Scar, you know that you can tell me anything," she says.

I don't know how much I can tell her—how much I'm ready to tell her.

"I know, it's just that so much has happened. So much has changed." I grab my drink and take a sip.

"How are things with Callum through all of this?"

"I don't know. Things are great but there's... There are some things that will never change. I guess... I just need to figure out if the good outweighs the bad."

She looks to me and smiles. "You love him." It's not a question.

"Yeah, I guess I do."

"Scarlett, that's huge!" She grabs my arm.

My face doesn't match her excitement.

"What's wrong?"

"There's so much, Soph."

I close my eyes to try and stop the tears, but I'm too late.

"Scarlett—" She moves her chair closer to mine. "I know."

A weight lifts off my shoulders, and I can finally breathe. A cry escapes me, followed by a laugh.

"Of course, you know. If Harrison knows something that means Stirling does, and you do too."

I'm not upset with her, but I am with Harrison and Stirling for telling her, making her also incriminated.

"Scarlett, you can talk to me about it."

"No, Soph, I can't! I can't talk about the fact that I was almost raped twice by my professor. I can't talk about the fact that Callum killed him, for me! I can't talk about it because if I think about it, everything becomes real. And it can't be real, Soph. Not yet."

"Okay, Scar. We don't have to talk about it, but I want you to know that when you are ready, I'm here."

I don't know what I've done to deserve such amazing people in my life. I don't know how to tell her how grateful I am for her, so instead, I have another sip of my drink, enjoying this moment before facing reality.

Time moves quickly after we eat and have a couple more drinks. It's just after 7 p.m. *I should check my phone to see if Callum texted me.*

Instead, we throw on our bathing suits, getting ready for the hot tub. We're met by the frigid air as we step out, onto the patio. With our drinks in hand, we head over and hop in. The warm water mixed with the cool air feels like another kind of therapy.

After a few hours of laughs and more drinks, we come back inside and change back into some comfy clothes. I belly flop onto Sophia's king size bed.

"What movie should we watch tonight?' She yells from the bathroom.

"A classic—maybe *Pretty in Pink* or *Sixteen Candles*?" I yell back. She doesn't answer.

"Or whatever you had in mind?... Soph?" She still doesn't answer. "You okay in there?" I get off the bed and walk to the bathroom door. I try the knob, but it's locked.

"Sophia?" My sweaty palms fight with the doorknob as I try to open it. "Sophia, this isn't funny!"

Just then, something grabs me by the waist, and everything goes black.

Panic

Callum

I need to make my way to The Society eventually, but I struggle with the idea, aware that scrutiny and punishment await. It's not that I can't handle it, but facing Father means I won't be able to see Scarlett for a while.

The streetlights guide the way to the mansion. Father has tried to call me four more times since our brief conversation earlier. I know that ignoring him will just provoke him more, but I'll deal with the consequences later. Right now, I need to talk to Leo and find out what's going on.

I look at the speedometer—I'm driving a hundred miles per hour in a sixty. Speed limit signs don't pertain to me, or anyone else in The Society. Sure, if we get caught, we're given a ticket, but it's always torn up shortly after.

Every time I pull into the driveway, I feel more distant from this place and these people. The Society is a duty, not an honour. Some would say it's the opposite, but I've felt this way since the day I began.

The lights are dim around the outside of the house. I walk through the long dark hall and up the staircase to the parlour. The scent of cigarette smoke floats down the corridor. Even though I haven't had one all day, the smell encourages me to wait. *I don't want to be like them.*

I only hear Leo's voice. He must be on the phone. As I turn into the room, Deluca and four other pledges stand there. Beside them is Victor Roberts, Sophia's dad. It's been a while since I've seen him here— they must be discussing some legal matters at hand.

"Gentlemen." I nod. Their eyes scan me like I'm not worthy— like they think they are better than me. Victor wears a smug smile. Behind me, Leo doesn't smile at all, his eyes are trying to communicate with me.

Deluca steps forward. "Callum, we warned you."

My eyes don't leave Leo's face. "I think I'd remember a warning," I respond.

"This isn't a joke, Callum." Leo answers. "I'm sorry."

His answer cuts me in half. There's only one thing that he would be sorry about. *No.* I don't answer. Instead, I pull my phone out and open her tracker. It's been disabled.

"Where is she!" I yell. Deluca steps back.

"She's safe, for now, Callum. You have your final initiation coming up and she's been a distraction. We're going to hold onto her until it's done."

"Where is she?" I step toward him, our faces barely apart. He doesn't move and his warm, liquor filled breath hits my face.

"You need to prove your loyalty to us, Callum. You've been far too sloppy lately."

The anger that I feel isn't rage, that's what I felt when I saw Elliot on top of her. This is pure fear.

I can't protect her if they have her. They will use her against me and make me choose. I know that they can break her, and that will fucking ruin me. Darkness washes over and clings to all my scattered emotions.

"If you hurt her, I'll kill every. Single. Person. You love."

It's not a threat, it's a fact. Deluca knows it's true, but I don't know if he cares enough about anyone to value their life. He doesn't know that messing with the one person who is everything to me will unleash a monster he's yet to see.

Before I leave the room, I glance at Leo one last time. *If I stay here any longer, I'm going to kill someone.* I don't have to say anything to him—he knows what they've done.

I walk down the hall and glance at a back room—where I found Emily. It's one of the places they hide anyone they bring here. I open it, and the room is dark and empty.

I check all the rooms in the upstairs and main levels of the house, but there's no sign of her. Finally, I go down to the basement. My area has been untouched. It doesn't look like anyone has been down here since Harrison and I brought Elliot in.

I walk over to the steel table and lean against it. *I need to find her. I swear to God if they've hurt her.* My thoughts spiral.

"Fuck!" I yell and throw the table across the room.

I can't be here anymore. I run upstairs and outside. All the other pledges have already left. I pull my phone out of my pocket and call the only person I know will help.

"Hey Callum, I'm just with some of the other guys can I—"

"They took her."

Silence. I don't need to tell him who, he already knows.

"I need your help."

"What do you need me to do?"

"Can you go look around campus? And around the houses of some of the Highers? Harrison, I can't lose her." My vision fogs.

"Okay. I'll let you know if I find anything." I hang up and get into my car.

I call her—there's no answer. I already knew there wasn't going to be anyone on the other side of the line. I listen to her voicemail.

"Hey, you've reached Scarlett. I missed your call but leave a message and I'll get back to you."

I replay it as I back out of the driveway.

"Hey, you've reached Scarlett. I missed your call but leave a message and I'll get back to you."

I call three more times just to hear her voice.

I drive down Main Street, unable to concentrate. I think about that first time I saw her, years ago, at the Burger Bar. I remember the way her hair fell to one side when she brushed it out of her eyes, and the way that she pursed and parted her lips when she concentrated on the book she was reading. It's fucking crazy how I fell for her the moment I saw her. I made her mine, and she still is mine—she always will be. *I need to fight for her harder now than ever.*

It wasn't long after the first time I saw her that I started fighting. God, I'd do anything to make someone bleed right now. Someone who deserves to pay, anyone but her. I call him instead.

"Hello, Callum."

"Did you do this?"

"You'll need to be more specific," Father responds. He's probably sitting in his office, sipping on a drink without a care in the world.

"Scarlett. Where is she?" I'm about to lose my fucking temper.

"She's safe, Callum… as long as you complete your initiation."

"You can listen to me now. I've played the part and became the person you've pushed me to become. I've fucking killed for you, and I've given up my life, for you. But to take *her*—you've gone too far."

His laugh fills my car. "You think that I'm proud of the person you are? You think anyone would choose to have *you* as their son? You've never been loyal to our family, and you've made that clear to everyone. You must be bribed to carry out your duties, and even then, you're sloppy. Look at the mess you've made. You want someone to blame? Look in the mirror, Callum."

His words give me the final push I need to let go.

"No, *Dad*. This will be on you."

I end the call and think about what he just said. I was supposed to keep Scarlett safe, but I knew she needed a night with Sophia. She needed some normal within this chaos, but it was a matter of time before they got to her.

I made the wrong decision and chose to let my feelings get in the way of her safety. That's something I'll never be able to forgive myself for.

I *need* to find her.

Eternity

Scarlett

The side of my head throbs and my hands are tied behind my back. My mouth aches from the gag that sits between my teeth. I try to call for help, but only muffled sounds escape.

They must've drugged me—I don't remember anything after I was grabbed. The side of my arm hurts. *Did they inject me with something?*

I look around for anything that looks familiar, nothing does. The grey walls around me make me feel like I'm in a windowless basement with stone cold floors. It reminds me of an old church choir room I used to get ready in before the Christmas Eve nativity pageant.

The air is thick. A light bulb glimmers above me, its dim yellow hue shines just bright enough to recognize my surroundings.

The last thing I remember was being in Sophia's room. *Oh gosh, Sophia!* They must have her too. I look around for any signs of life, but I'm the only one here.

"Sophia!" I try and scream through the cloth that silences me.

"Sophia!" I try again. I barely hear my own echo. "Hello! Hello!" I shuffle my feet around, trying to get them up and under me, but it doesn't work.

Okay, Scarlett. Think. Maybe Elliot's family found out about what happened, and they want me to pay. Maybe, if I explain what happened, I can get us out of this mess.

I hear footsteps in the distance. My heart picks up—I'm not sure if it's from fear or relief. I push myself back, trying to get to the wall, like it will protect me.

In the corner of the room, the door opens. A man flicks on a dull light and faces me. He steps into the room and stands there for a minute. He's no older than his mid-forties. He walks over to me.

"Where am I?" I demand.

"Such a feisty one." He smiles, exposing the gaps in the front of his mouth where his teeth are missing. A chill runs down my spine.

My ankle scrapes against the floor with my feet tied, as I try to back away from him, masking my fear with a blank stare.

He bends down and grabs a fist full of my hair, pulling at the roots as he brings my face toward his.

"It doesn't matter anyways because tonight, you'll be a part of something bigger, something more... eternal."

His words replay in my head as I try to make sense of them.

"Where am I?" I stare at him, his eyes surrounded by wrinkles.

"Your own personal hell." His half smile pokes out again. This isn't someone I would've expected to be associated with the Elliot family. His facial hair is overgrown, and his clothes are mismatched, like he just picked them out in the dark.

"Do you know the Elliot's?"

My question takes him by surprise. *He clearly isn't here for them.*

"My friend, the blonde one who I was with, is she okay?" *Please say yes.*

"She's off limits. Now shut up, I won't answer any more of your questions!"

"What do you mean—" His hand slaps my face—the sting makes my eyes water.

"I said shut up." *I think this is bigger than I thought.* I fight back tears harder than I ever have before. Although he has control over what happens next, I won't give him my tears—he will have to fight me damn hard for those.

He grabs my arms behind me and pulls me up. I cry out, the pain from the ropes makes it hard for me to get up while my hands and feet are tied. He drags me until I stand, the best I can.

He pushes me in front of him and down a corridor that leads to a set of stairs. A light shines at the end.

Something is about to get worse. At first, I thought maybe I could get out of this, but now, I think the chances are unlikely. My lip quivers thinking that these might be my final moments.

As we walk down the hall, I think about Dad, and how he'll be so lost without me, so broken. I thought I could fight back these tears, but the thought of Dad's broken heart forces me to let go of what little restraint I have left. *Who will help him if I'm dead? Who will love him and appreciate him.* Elliot wasn't worth this, he wasn't worth losing the people I love.

I think about Mom and how she's been absent for most of my life. She's too damn busy for her own family, but that was her choice. I can't be mad at her, not if those are my final thoughts of her. I wonder if she would miss me. *How do you miss someone you don't know?* Mom has become a stranger. I think about all the times we spent together when I was young, all the love we had before she took it all away.

Sophia will be upset, but she'll be okay. She has so many amazing people in her life to support her.

Finally, I think about Callum, the one who saw me when no one else did. The one who connects with every real part of me and accepts it. *No, I can't think about this. It's not going to happen.* I can tell whoever it is that Elliot tried to rape me. They'll understand—they have to.

We're almost at the bottom of the stairs, when he pushes me. My face hits the ground. I look around for a window, or anything I can try to fit through and escape.

He keeps walking as I struggle to get up. *Don't let him win.* My forehead rests on the ground—the strength in me is draining. The cold stone is stained with the blood from my nose.

One time at boxing, I didn't lift my hands up in time and I got punched in the face. I can hear Ricco's yelling, "Keep going, protect your face Scarlett". *Where is Ricco now that I'm losing the only fight I've ever trained for?* I can't give up, not like this.

I push up off the ground with my shoulder, move my legs underneath me, and slowly standing. He doesn't turn around as he walks in front of me. I taste the blood from my nose as it runs down my face.

Finally, I charge at him. Even though he's at least twice my size, I use my weight to shove him to the ground, and I do the only thing I know best. *I fight.*

He falls onto the ground and tries to get up. I kneel behind him, and with my arms still tied, I place my hands in front of his neck, pulling hard. I choke him. For a moment, it feels like I'm going to break my own fingers. The rope burns my arms as I use all my force. I wrap my knees around his back and attach myself to him.

He gasps for air and tries to pull my hands off. I tug harder and slightly lift my wrists. His flailing arms slow down. *Keep going.* Ricco's voice echoes in my head. I keep fighting.

Suddenly, an abrupt pair of hands pulls on the back of my shirt. I fall and stumble to get back up. I look back to see another man, around the same age but very well put together. He yanks he shirt hard, ripping it as I try and pull away from him.

"You're coming regardless, so stop fighting." He says calmly as he stands over me.

I look him in the eyes, and I lift my heavy feet. I kick him, shoving him back.

I flip onto my knees and stand, but he pushes me back down, already on top of me. Blood pours from my nose and enters my mouth. He's stronger and much leaner than the first man I encountered. This guy knows what he's doing and doesn't give in as easy. He fights like he kills for a living. I can't win this time.

He tugs on my hair, ripping it as he pulls me up the stairs. I try to place my feet under me while my hands pull at his. My scalp burns. At the top of the steps, he throws me on the ground, face up.

I slowly lift my head and spot white pillars in front of me, lining the room like an aisle. It looks like we're in a church that screams wealth and power. There's an altar at the front, but there are no chairs or pews. It's like a temple from a Greek mythology textbook.

A circle of men stands at the altar, their faces blocked by the shadows of their hoods. Tears and blood run down my face as I realize what's happening. This is what the man meant by eternity. It's a sacrifice.

I'm going to die.

Betrayal

Callum

I know where she is. I'm an idiot for not figuring it out sooner. You're only brought to the temple for one reason.

My car's engine roars as I press the pedal all the way to the ground. One slight movement would send me airborne. I tightly grip the steering wheel. *I can't lose her.*

I reach for the pack of sour gummies in the main console—my "just in case Scarlett needs them" stash. Running my fingers over the wrapper. *Anything to make me feel closer to her.* The rage builds, nothing can calm the fire inside me.

I slow down as the gravel from the driveway chips the sides of my car. I head past the mansion and toward the temple down the back road. Cars are lined up outside. I throw the car in park and jump out, slamming the door behind me as I run toward the temple.

The double doors creak as I open them. I see her at the altar, surrounded by The Highers. She looks to me—a sight that stops me in my tracks. Blood runs down her face, her eyes are wet, and she's gagged, but she still calls for me.

"Callum!" She cries.

I run as fast as I can toward her. No one stops me.

I drop to my knees, pull her gag down, then wrap my arms around her. I shield her from everyone around us.

"I'm here, Angel," I whisper in her ear as she sobs. I cradle her head between my hands and rest my forehead on hers. *This is the end. There is no way we can get out of this now.*

I stand in front of her and look at the six men on either side of us. Even though they try to conceal their identities, I know who they are—it's my job to know who they are. I know which one is Sophia's dad and which one is Harrison's. They've known me since childhood—the Highers, fathers, brothers, and sons. They decide who lives and who dies, and today, we're the ones that have to die.

"I was the one who fucked up, let her go. You can have me, but please, let her go."

They remain still and stare at me. "Let her go!" I yell. I need them to take me seriously.

"That won't be happening, Callum." Father walks out from behind Archer Alden, Harrison and Stirling's dad.

Of course, he's behind this. Of course, he wants this.

"You did this?" I point to Scarlett, she's still sobbing.

It all makes sense that he wanted to use her against me. To bait me. To control me. I don't matter to him—it all ends the same.

"I warned you, son. You chose not to listen." He stays calm and steps closer. He holds a pistol in his hand.

"You only have one option." He takes another step closer. "She's not in it, Callum." His dark eyes meet mine.

"NO! Please!" She yells behind me. "Callum! Please!" She cries.

"Callum, look what she's done to your life. Look at the lack of control you have when you're around her. You've become weak. Everything that you have worked for, everything that you want—it's yours tonight." He looks to Scarlett, then places the gun in my hand. He takes his place beside her.

"I'm sorry it had to be this way, Scarlett." He pats her shoulder. She shuts her sobbing eyes and shakes her head.

"Everything that you've wanted will be yours, Callum. After you complete your initiation here tonight, you can walk away from The Society, or you can join your brothers and eventually become a Higher. You can have all the freedom you've ever dreamed of. You can become whoever it is that you've been masking. All the lies can end tonight."

The gun feels heavy and cold, a feeling that usually brings me pleasure. I'll gladly kill those who deserve it, but her... she doesn't deserve any part of this. She deserves happiness, and love. She deserves *life*.

Father's words hang over my head— *you've become weak*.

But my life isn't for him, it's never been for him.

I stare at the gun in my hand and remember the person I've been the last twenty-four years. The man I've fought to become. *I'm not weak. I don't need her. We used each other, to pass time.* I can't do this for her. She was just another girl who I lured in to keep me busy.

I think about who The Society has pushed me to become—a man who would give up nothing for love. I look over at her. *I don't love her—I can't.*

Slowly I raise the gun, holding my hand steady. I point it at her head.

"I'm not the hero in your story Angel, I never was."

She tries to grab my legs, but I'm just far enough away that she can't reach me.

"Callum, please, I love you." She says quietly through her tears. "I know you love me too, Callum."

Her words burn my ears. Even in death, she clings to me.

I cock my head to the side. The heat of her fingertips lingers on my skin from where she traced it last. I push the memory down to a dark place I never want to feel again. I take a step forward.

I bring the barrel of the gun between her eyes.

Just then, I hear a high pitch scream behind me. I look behind Leo, who stands closest to the altar, and see Harrison with Vanessa in front of him.

"My baby!" She yells and runs toward Scarlett. Sophia's dad, Victor Roberts, grabs her. He pulls a gun out of his pants and holds it to her head.

Harrison stands beside me. I don't have to look at him to know that he was forced to bring her here, to watch her daughter die—some fucked up twist of fate. Vanessa's hair is a mess, it looks like she put up a fight or is still high.

I don't move. I know that if I remove the barrel, I won't be able to do it—I have to.

"Stop trying," Victor tells Vanessa behind me.

Scarlett shuts her eyes, unable to look at me. Her chest quivering as she waits for me to pull the trigger.

The gun clicks as I remove the safety. Fear and betrayal pour out of her eyes.

She's never looked so beautiful.

"I thought I couldn't live without you."

I pull the trigger.

Warm blood splatters on my face.

Vanessa's screams fill the room as my father's lifeless body drops to the ground.

"What the fuck did you just do, Callum!" One of The Highers yells.

Years of torture and emotional confinement slowly lift off my chest. *I killed my father.*

My ears ring and a heaviness builds in my head. I close my eyes, just when it feels like it might explode. *I killed my father.*

The one who was supposed to be there for me. The one who's blood runs through my veins, and the one who never taught me how to love. A sea of emotions overwhelm me.

I turn around and pull Scarlett up.

Just then, Harrison jumps beside me. His gun is already in his hand.

Chaos erupts as bullets and debris fly in the air.

Archer lowers his gun in disbelief. Deluca shoots at me but misses. Leo and Harrison point their guns at Deluca.

"Let him go," Leo says.

Victor points his gun at Scarlett then he brings his aim toward Vanessa. He slowly backs out of the temple with her, Archer, and a handful of others follow. Deluca and Leo stand there with their guns pointed at each other.

I turn around and drop to my knees, grabbing her wet face.

"I thought I couldn't live without you, but now I know, I can't. I can never be without you." She tries to pull away from me, but I grip harder. "I fucking love you, Scarlett. Just like I told you, until I die. You're mine, and I'm never letting you go." My heart races thinking that I almost lost her.

I bring her mouth to mine—the kiss is damp from her tears. For a moment, the rest of the room fades and it's just us. I get high from the ecstasy of her, she brings me back to life.

BANG.

I turn around to the sight of Harrison on the ground, clutching his leg.

Leo acts quickly and shoots Deluca in the shoulder.

"Fuck!" I hear Harrison scream from the ground beside me.

"It's okay man, I'm going to get you out of here."

"Go." I look up at Leo as he yells and nods his head.

I crouch and lift Harrison's arm over my shoulder. "We need to leave, now," I say to Scarlett. Still in shock, she doesn't process what I'm saying.

"Angel. We have to leave. *Now*. Get up." She slowly stands and follows me. I throw her my phone as I lead us all out the side door.

"Call Stirling to come get us. Tell him we'll be past the temple, down the back. He'll know what you mean."

"Your phone… it's locked." She stares down at it, moving slowly.

"0510, it's—"

"My birthday." She looks surprised that the man who just killed for her knows her birthday.

"Come on, this way."

We head behind the temple. I lead us down an abandoned road that used to be for the funeral director to bring the hearse in.

"Harrison," I lay Harrison down on the ground then I take off my belt, using it for a tourniquet on his leg. "Stirling will be here soon, just stay with us."

Harrison moans. "Don't worry about me, you idiot." I chuckle. *Only Harrison.*

Two minutes later, Stirling's car whips around the corner. He quickly jumps out when he sees Harrison on the ground.

"What the fuck happened!" He helps me pick Harrison up and we load him in the back seat.

Sophia's head pokes up from the passenger window. As soon as she spots Scarlett, she gets out and runs over to her. They cling to each other and cry, as Stirling and I stuff Harrison into the car.

"I'll explain it all later, right now we need to get somewhere with a first aid kit, preferably where no one can find us," I say to Stirling.

We all pile into the car. Before I open the passenger seat door, I look to The Society—a dynasty that's about to crumble.

And I'm going to be the one to destroy it.

Lake House

Scarlett

The car is warm. As we drive further from Millhaven, the metallic taste in my mouth gets stronger. I force down the saliva that builds. I watch as bare trees pass through the window.

I haven't been in Stirling's sports car since he picked me and Sophia up that night four years ago. Now, Harrison lays in the back with us—his head across Sophia's lap and his legs across me. His blood has stopped flowing onto the seat. I glance at the rip in his jeans, just above his knee that got shot. I try not to stare at the hole left by the bullet. *It's a clean shot, and the bullet doesn't look too deep.* My stomach turns.

Stirling places all his focus on the road. I feel bad for him, always pulled into things. My eyes are drawn to Callum, but I don't look at him. I close them and think of how the cold gun barrel felt against my head. I can't stop replaying the image.

He almost killed me and then told me he loves me.

I look at Sophia to force the thought out of my head. We've been driving for almost an hour, and she hasn't said much. She might be in as much shock as I am.

When we first got in the car, Sophia told me that she was tied up and taken in a car down a side road. She was then released to her dad. Originally, she thought that he would pay her ransom, but he was the one who helped organize everything. Sophia was only taken so they could get to me. She was never in harm's way—she's too important. She told me that she tried to call me, but I lost my phone when I was at her house.

"Dad." I whisper. I need to tell him that I'm okay. Except, he doesn't know about anything.

He doesn't know that I was kidnapped and almost killed. Or that Mom was there. Or that we're on the run from some of the most powerful men in the state.

We pull into a long driveway. The trees aren't well maintained, and I can't spot a house at the end. Brush covers the entire laneway. Once we get close enough, I see a small, quaint yellow house. It's not like ones in Millhaven. *We're in the country.*

The car pulls up toward the back deck and the sun glistens off the lake. We come to a stop, and my door opens. Callum holds it. As I slide out of the back seat, his eyes don't meet mine. Instead, he faces Harrison. Sophia gets out on the other side, then comes around to stand with me. Stirling steps out and helps Callum pull Harrison out of the car.

"What is this place?" Sophia asks.

"It was our grandmother's family cottage, no one in our family uses it. It's not up to their standards—as you can see." Stirling looks at the small yellow bungalow with its unkempt gardens.

"Grab the bag from the back." Stirling yells to me and Sophia.

We grab a leather duffle bag and follow the guys inside. Stirling walks around to the other side of the house and comes out the back door, letting us in.

"We don't spend much time here anymore." His eyes lock on the empty flower beds.

As we walk inside, dust fills the air. White bed sheets cover some of the furniture, and what's exposed looks like it hasn't been touched since the 70's. I glance at a couch with a mix of pastel colours and checkered patterns—it's almost comforting.

"I need to wash up, is there a bathroom?" I ask quietly.

"Just down the hall, last door on the right."

"I'll come?" Sophia asks. I nod in acceptance.

I lead us down an unlit hallway, until Sophia flicks the light on. We pass two other doors, both are shut. The last door is partially closed. I push it open and turn the light on. We both step into the bathroom, and Sophia shuts the door behind her. I grab a facecloth from a basket on top of the toilet and twist the tap on. It doesn't take long for the water to get hot. I step in front of the mirror and wipe blood off my face. My cheek stings as I run the warm cloth over it. I grimace.

"Does it hurt?" Sophia asks me with a quiet tone.

"A little."

I wash away all that has happened today, and all that I want to forget.

"I'm sorry." She adds.

"Sorry? For what?"

"I should've tried harder, I should've fought more..." She looks at the ground instead of me.

"Sophia, I don't blame you... You couldn't have stopped them. What happened wasn't your fault." I look to her. "It was mine."

"No, you don't get to do that." She grabs my arm. "You don't get to blame yourself. If you won't let me take any of the blame, you aren't allowed to either. You did all that you could. You tried, Scarlett. What Elliot did to you was his own damn fault. If you ask me, he got what he deserved. But you don't deserve any of it, you never did." She pulls me in for a well warranted hug.

Her warm embrace and strawberry scent comforts me, but it's not the comfort I crave. I hear mumblings as Callum and Stirling talk down the hall.

Sophia leaves, then brings back some clothes for me to change into. I assume they are Harrison or Stirling's clothes from when they were younger. I hold out the oversized dark green crewneck and black sweatpants.

I gather myself and walk out of the bathroom, toward the kitchen. Harrison lies across the table, partially sedated. By the empty whiskey bottle beside his head, I assume the alcohol is responsible. Callum uses a scalpel to try and retract the bullet out of his leg. His belt is still on acting as a torniquet to control the bleeding, he's focusing on the wound. Slowly his eyes drift onto me as I walk into the room. They barely meet before his attention is swiftly back on Harrison's leg.

"How's it going?" Sophia asks Callum.

"It didn't hit anything important, he'll be fine." His words are cold and calculated.

"Actually, it kind of fucking hurts." Harrison mumbles.

Sophia laughs and Stirling pats his brother's shoulder while he glances up at her. They share a look, one that feels private—like I wasn't supposed to notice. I turn away and my eyes can't help but land on Callum. He stays focused, but his jaw tightens. I know he can feel my eyes on him. I approach the patio's sliding door and look out at the view. The large lake curves, and I can't see its fullness. Before I slide the door open, I look to Stirling. He nods with approval.

Cool wind hits my face as I step onto the deck. It's still early winter, where the ground isn't covered in snow yet, but the grass is lined with a crystal sheen. As I look to the sky, the warm sun brushes against my cheeks. I step toward the railing and savour in the beautiful nature around me. Birds chirp and line the tops of some bare trees. I forgot that calm places like this exist. I've been so caught up in the chaos that I haven't stopped to appreciate what and who is around me.

A few minutes pass and I hear the sliding door open. Callum comes into my peripheral view as he props his hip against the railing beside me. He isn't looking at the view, he's looking at me.

There's so much I want to say, so much I should say, but I can't. He doesn't say anything. I finally work up the courage to look at him. The dark bags under his eyes don't take away from his beauty—they add to the image he tries so hard to protect.

"Callum, I don't know where to go from here—"

"No Scarlett." He calmly cuts me off. "Let me get it out, please. Just... just give me a minute."

The vulnerability in his voice makes me want to listen. He studies the water. Another moment of silence passes.

"I've never had anything good in my life. I hurt people. I don't know how many people I've killed—Elliot wasn't the first, and he won't be the last. And I'm not sorry about any of it. I keep replaying that moment when I walked into the room and saw what he did to you...what he took from you. I've never been so powered by rage and... and by love." His eyes meet mine and a single tear falls down my cheek.

"You have been the only good thing in my life, even when you've almost broken me. I've never wanted anyone to ruin me so gently. I can't live without you, Scarlett. But after tonight, if this is too much... you deserve so much more. I can't explain the agony I'm in when I see the pain in your eyes... after what I did...what I had to do. But Scarlett, you must know, I was never going to pull that trigger. I could never fucking do that. I'd kill myself before I ever hurt you. I killed my own father instead. But I needed the Highers to believe... I had to make it real, just for a moment. I went to the darkest place within me, but looking into your eyes is the only thing that brought me back." He plays with the ring on his index finger.

"I won't blame you if you don't want this, but know that you will always be mine, and I'll never let you go." He takes a step toward me. My breath hitches, just enough for him to notice.

"You have nestled yourself inside the darkest parts of me and made a home. You can never be set free."

He steps closer.

"I think you love my darkness."

He takes another step.

"I think you feel my darkness."

His lips part as he takes one final step.

"I think you crave the shadows within me."

I fight every emotion and every fiber in my body that wants me to pull away. I press my mouth against his. Our lips move in sync as he wraps his arms around me, and our bodies become one.

When he pulls me into his world, every fear and doubt slips away. I'm already so deep in it, I know I can't get out now. I belong here, in his arms. You can't reason with love, even when it might be wrong. If it is, *I don't ever want to be fucking right.*

His hands move up the back of my sweater. *I never want him to let go.* I tried to stay away from him, but that didn't do me any favours.

I pull my head back, away from him.

"I love you."

I stare into his eyes, begging to be let into his soul.

He rests his head on mine, just like he did right before he brought the gun to my head.

"I'll spend a lifetime proving how much I love you." His eyes remain closed.

I can't fight his darkness any longer—I want to drown in it.

Becoming the Fire

Callum

She looks at me like I'm a light, not darkness. It's been four days since I killed Father. Four days since I took the life of the person who created me. With the way he treated me my whole life, I've thought about killing him before. I've killed others for doing less. Still, I can't shake off the heaviness that lingers in my chest. *I did the right thing—it was him or me.* It was only a matter of time before the other Highers followed his lead. Everything could've ended differently. Now that I've done it, The Society won't see me as anyone else. My dangerous brand has been severely tarnished.

We're still at the cottage. Harriet used to hide here from her sons and always brought her grandchildren. She created a safe space for them here. That's exactly what it's proven to be.

The more time we spend here, the more it feels like we are hiding. I don't mind the escape, but in a way, it just builds on what's to come.

My mind flashes back to my father, lying on the ground, surrounded by his own blood. I can't help but wonder how my mom reacted when she found out. I wonder who told her and how they phrased it.

Mom tried to call me a few times, but I have nothing to say to her. She knows that her comfortable lifestyle will remain and not much will change in her day-to-day. I think about Vanessa and her reaction to the sight of Scarlett at the altar. Guilt eats away at me. One of the first things I need to do is make sure that Vanessa is safe. We haven't talked much about it, but with the way her mom looked, I think she needs our help now more than ever.

I lie in the small double bed, my arm under her head, supporting her like a pillow. I love how easily she sleeps, it almost makes me want to shut my eyes as well. But I can't, not when the monsters in my life are reality. I used to sleep to escape my demons, but they've since embroidered my soul. *Soon, I'll need to fight them.* She rolls over and clings to me, her warm hands on my chest.

My phone vibrates. I assume it's Mom again, or someone sending their condolences. I pick it up off the floor to see a missed call and a text message from Deluca, and a couple of messages from Leo.

> **Deluca:** You can only hide for so long, Callum. Come back and deal with the consequences before this goes too far.

He doesn't scare me.

His words replay in my head, *"before this goes too far."* I let out a deep exhale and open Leo's message. I haven't thanked him yet for letting us go at the temple. I know he's always been on my side, and he reinforced that when he shot Deluca.

Leo: We need to talk.

Leo: Call me.

Deluca can wait. I slowly pull my arm out from under Scarlett. I hate to leave her, but I don't want to wake her. I also don't want her to hear what Leo has to say, since I'm expecting the worst.

I crawl out of bed and pick my clothes up from the floor. I pull my dark Henley over my head, slide the deck door open, and step outside. The refreshing air welcomes me as I call Leo.

"Callum." He answers on the first ring.

"Leo." My tone matches his.

"Things are changing. We need to meet. I don't want to talk about this over the phone, I don't know who's listening or watching." He hesitates. "You should be careful too."

I've lived this life longer than anyone knows—hidden meetings and bugged phone lines aren't new to me.

"Where do you want to meet?" I ask.

"I'll send you the location," he says. I know he wants to keep details limited.

"Okay."

"I'll see you soon, Callum. Stay safe." There's a softness in his voice I've never heard before.

Before I walk to the kitchen, I turn to the sight of Scarlett through the sliding door, lying in bed. Stirling is already awake. He sits at the kitchen table and sips on a coffee. When he sees me by the balcony door, he gets up and lets me in.

"It was Leo."

He looks at me with hesitancy.

"Where's Harrison?" I ask him. Although I trust Leo, I can't see him alone. I will have to bring Harrison and Stirling.

"What is it?" Harrison's raspy voice asks from behind me.

I turn to look at him. His knee is healing well—the antibiotics we had in the bathroom cupboard paired with rest must have sped up the process. He's able to walk on his own again.

"Leo wants to meet with us." Stirling doesn't miss a beat.

"Can we trust him?"

"Absolutely, he is one of us, Harr." I answer without hesitancy. Harrison needs to trust him, especially now.

My phone buzzes with a text from Leo. I look at the location, and another text comes in.

Leo: 9pm. Tonight.

"He wants us to meet him at one of the old industrial warehouse buildings just on the outskirts of town. The one by the water, not far from the Burger Bar," I say.

We all look at each other.

"I'm not ready to fight, Callum. I'm not strong enough yet," Harrison pleas.

"There won't be a fight Harrison, not yet."

Silence fills the room.

"Who's fighting?" Scarlett's face pokes around the corner. Her hair is piled on top of her head in a bun, and she wears my boxers and an old t-shirt. If we weren't plotting against The Society right now, I'd take her back to the room and show her just how much pleasure pain can bring.

"No one is fighting." I roll my eyes at Harrison.

We spend the day around the cottage. There's more small talk than I'd like, followed by a few card games. Later, Sophia and Scarlett prepare dinner from what they find in the cupboard, while we pretend there's some normalcy in our routine. Just after we all clean the kitchen like a well-rehearsed dance, Harrison, Stirling, and I get ready to leave. Although I don't want to leave the girls alone, I can't take a chance by bringing Scarlett. I know she'll be safe out here, and we'll be watching them from our phones.

Scarlett walks me out to the car. I pull her close and inhale, taking in the scent of her. I know this goodbye is only temporary.

"I'll be back later." I kiss her forehead as Stirling gets in the driver's side and Harrison gets in the back.

"Don't do anything stupid Callum," she says. I give her a shit eating grin, she knows that I can't help it.

"Always, Angel." She holds onto my hand as I step toward the car. Our fingers linger for a moment before she lets go. Sophia's head pokes out from the front door and she waves at us. She walks out of the house and wraps her arm around Scarlett's waist.

I don't want to look back as Stirling shifts the car into drive, but I do anyway—*either I'm a masochist or I fucking love her too much*. I watch Scarlett get smaller and smaller as we drive away.

At ten minutes to nine, we arrive at the location that Leo sent. A dark SUV pulls into the lot across from us—it's Leo. I can tell he's not alone, but I can't make out who is with him through his tinted windows. As Leo climbs out, all four doors of his SUV open.

Leo and three other pledges walk over to us. Leading the group, Leo is the only Higher.

We form a circle and Leo steps forward. He greets us with a nod.

"Callum. Harrison. Stirling. I'm going to get right to it; we don't have much time." He looks at each of us and stops on me. "There's obvious uproar within The Society. Victor and Archer don't want to let this go. Victor wants you all dead, while Archer doesn't want to side against his sons—

rightfully so. But he won't just let you all go free. He's going to expect something. I don't know what that is yet, but it will be a high price."

He motions to the pledges. "We all want change. The Society isn't what it used to be, it's no longer a place where the powerful seek refuge. It's turned into something that doesn't align with how it started. I feel that together, we can shift things."

There's never been talk of an uprising. If one were to play out, it would be shut down immediately, with those involved silenced by the bullets through their heads. It sounds like Leo has been thinking about this for a while. He wants revenge. I can't help but wonder what The Society has done to Leo, or what they've taken from him.

"What do you need us to do?" I ask.

"We need to bring The Society down from the inside out. We need intel on all the drops, and we need to control the buyers. But be careful in who you trust. This stays between us." He's not wrong to be so hesitant with everyone. That's what The Society does, the rats will come to the surface quickly. We'll find out who we can trust.

"I have a few conditions." I speak up. Leo frowns.

"You're in no position to be naming requests, Callum."

"They aren't requests." I silence him. "Vanessa gets out, and I want her out now, not when things get settled. I need to take her to a rehab facility." It's the least I can do.

"That can be arranged." He waits for the next item.

"I don't want Scarlett involved at all. And if it comes down to me or her." I take a step toward him. "You always pick her."

"I know what you're asking, Callum. Are you sure?" He wants to make sure I'm ready to die for her, for love.

"There's no other option." My father's last words echo in my head. No, she is the *only* option.

"Well, I think we all know what we must do. We need all the information we can get. Everyone plays an important role. This isn't going to happen overnight, and we must remain patient and wait until every piece comes together," Leo says.

Stirling looks at Harrison, and Harrison turns back to me. Leo glances over at them, unsure what the future will bring. All eyes are on me.

"The Society will never change. If we can't tame the fire, we'll become it."

Grenade

Scarlett

A couple of weeks have passed since the incident. Stirling and Harrison returned home, and Stirling practically forced Sophia to stay with them for the first couple of nights. He can't trust Sophia's dad and wanted to keep a close eye on her for a few days.

After she planned the funeral, Callum's mom went out of town. It was beautiful. I've never seen so many flowers and tuxedos. Every influential person in town attended. I assume a lot of them were Society members.

Callum assured me that his mom wasn't overly upset and that his father's funeral was an act for the public eye. Regardless, I still feel bad for her. Life as she's known it is over, and a part of that is my fault. I'm not sure if she'll ever understand the extent of what happened—she wouldn't speak to me at the funeral. But by the look of it, her social status matters more than what happened to her husband.

Although so much has changed, I'm glad to be back in class. After a few rough days, it finally feels right again. I've craved my routine while trying to figure out a new normal. Dad hasn't been pushing me to talk, but he knows that something is different. He checks in to see if I'm okay more than usual. Callum told me that he invited him over for dinner. I don't know if his actions have any ulterior motives. I don't want to stress about that as I begin my thesis. I finally decided to pursue my master's. It seems right—I don't just want to live, I want to learn from all that's happened.

I'm supposed to meet Callum at the greenhouse tonight. Twice a week, we meet there to feel at peace. Although, we usually end up having sex. Selfishly, I love it. It's a place we both feel at peace. Callum has lots going on with The Society.

Since we returned home from the cottage, I've tried to contact Mom a few times, but she hasn't answered my calls or texts. I understand that she needs space, but I have so many questions for her. I also just want to make sure that she is okay. She didn't look well when I saw her in the temple.

Since she won't answer me, I need to find the answers on my own. I drive by the river. It's funny, all this time she's lived a ten-minute drive away from Dad's, yet I hardly saw her. *What did I do to deserve this treatment from her? What kind of mother doesn't stop by to see their daughter?*

It's dusk. As I move through town, the streetlights begin to flicker on. The little creek that flows through this part of town isn't lined with huge houses. All of the rich and powerful people live on the top of the hill, known as Millhaven Estates. They look down from their metaphorical castles at all us peasants—the ones just trying to get by.

I turn onto the road where mom's house is. I can tell from the end of the driveway that she hasn't been maintaining the property. The grass is almost knee height, and her flower bushes are all overgrown. When I was a child, she spent lots of time in the garden, planting weird seeds she found or just weeding. She cared about her plants. There are so many pieces to Mom's puzzle that I have yet to uncover.

Her 1995 Lincoln Aviator is parked in the driveway. Dad restored it nearly ten years ago, right before she left. She wanted that SUV so bad, and Dad searched for forever to find the right one. It's just another piece of him she'll always carry. I get out of my car and walk over to the door of her tiny bungalow. I try it but it's locked.

"Mom?" I call out. There's no answer.

"Mom!" I yell again, a little louder this time.

I pull my keys out from my pocket, and find the one to her house. I unlock the bright teal door.

As I push it open, I can tell she's not here. It's too quiet. Mom always has the TV on or music playing in the background. She never sits in silence.

"Mom, I'm here," I say just in case. The stillness of the house speaks for itself.

I walk over to the kitchen, passing my baby picture on a table in the living room, and open the fridge door. A terrible smell escapes it. *How long has she been gone?*

I shut the fridge and walk over to the living room, tracing my finger along the dust covered coffee table. I walk across the shag carpet to her bedroom. Her once cozy abode feels deserted, but nodes of her orange and vanilla scent remain. I spot her perfume on the dresser, pick it up, and bring it to my nose. I hear her laugh in my head. A distant memory.

I return the glass bottle to the dustless circle on her dresser and walk over to the closet. The door sticks when I try to open it. I give it another good tug, and it comes loose, making a loud creak as I prop it all the way open. There are at least six boxes in here. Some of them are labelled, and I read the sides of them.

Scarlett
Jake
unlabelled
unlabelled
DO NOT OPEN
Unlabelled

My eyes move back on the *DO NOT OPEN* box. I pull the second last box out from the bottom of the stack and hope that the rest don't fall on me.

As I open the box, I prepare myself for the worst. It's half empty, filled only with another small box, some pictures, receipts, and notes.

I pull the pictures out and look at them. They look about ten years old, back when Mom was in her silver jewelry phase. She wears silver hoops in the photo, even though she has the perfect skin tone for gold. She always referred to this phase in her life as "when things changed."

The next picture is of her on a man's lap. I recognize him—Archer Alden.

I can't stop looking through the stack of pictures. In most of them, she is fully naked, captured giving different men lap dances. She never looks at the camera, almost like she didn't know these were being taken. I go over our family's timeline in my head— she was still with Dad at that point. Her silver phase was almost a year before she left.

A handwritten receipt from a hotel falls out from the bunch of pictures. It's from a place in Boston. *Why was she going there?*

More receipts fall onto my lap—from phone bills with unknown numbers to restaurant bills from Boston. I think back to the moment I've tried so hard to erase. When Mom left, she didn't just leave us gradually, she left like a grenade. She took all of her things and never came back, with no care in the world about who she hurt. She pulled the safety pin out before the final explosion. Finally, I open the small box and spot mom's handwriting.

I'm not happy with the person I've become. I walked away from my family and I'm so disgusted with myself, I'd rather stay high then remember. My precious baby. My heart breaks every moment I'm not with her, but I have no other choice. I didn't give them up for money, I did it so they wouldn't be brought down by what I've done. They'll never understand, and I'll never forgive myself.

What is she talking about? I pull out the next letter to try and make sense of it all.

I saw Scarlett today. I can tell by the way she looks at me that she's humiliated by who I've become. She's the only good thing in my life, and I'd give everything up just to spend ten minutes in her presence. Instead, I weigh her down. I know she'll never understand that I've done all of this for her, so that she can have a future. I can't tell Jake. Every time he looks at me, it's like he's erased all the memories we've made. He'll always be the only man I'll ever love. I hope one day he can find out that once they took those pictures and used them to blackmail me, they had my life in their hands.

Tears fall and blotch the paper. *She suffered in silence.*

I'm so lonely. I miss my daughter, I miss my husband. I miss my family. Sometimes I drive by their house just to mourn the loss of my old life. These people don't care about me, they just use me until they're tired and then it starts all over again. Scarlett never returns my calls, and I don't blame her. Sometimes, I call just to hear the sound of her voicemail. My sweet girl, I'm so proud of her. I wish I could just end it all. No one will miss me. I'm just someone who used to be loved. I've tried and just got punished. They'll never let me succeed. They own me.

She didn't choose to leave us, she was forced. She traded herself for our freedom, and for that, The Society blackmailed her with photos from a job she never wanted to fulfill. Dad never knew what she was doing for extra money, for our family. What started off as her stripping for extra money, turned into her being manipulated by The Society. They used her as a pawn in their game. She was broken before she was given the chance to fight back.

I place the letters close to my chest. "You don't have to fight anymore. I'll fight for you." I whisper and regret every time I ever judged her—my amazing mother.

Quietly Suffocating

Scarlett

I grab a couple of the letters, tuck them into my back pant pocket, and leave Mom's house. I start the car and sit there for a moment. My face falls in my hands and I cry. I cry for Mom. I cry for Dad. I cry for myself and all that's been taken away from us because of The Society.

As I wipe the tears away, I pull out my phone and call the only person who will understand. Someone who has been controlled by The Society his entire life.

"Callum..." I don't know if I'm ready to tell him.

"What is it? Where are you, Scarlett?" There's panic in his voice.

"No, I'm safe. I just— I just... I'm at my mom's. I went through some of her things and Callum, it's so much worse than I ever expected." Tears return as I lean back against the headrest.

"I'll be there in five minutes."

"No, you don't have to. I know you have a meeting and class today. I just wanted to tell you." He's the first person I want to turn to when things go wrong.

"I'm going to go to the gym anyways and see Ricco. I bet that old man misses me."

"Ha, yeah, you're not only his best fighter, you're also his top client." He teases.

"Hey, other people go there!"

"Angel, I've seen him leave others mid-training just to help you. The guy relies on you."

I smile. "Thank you." It was the first time Callum comforted me with humour.

"I'll see you later. Call if you need me before tonight."

"I might call just to talk to this sweet side of you again." He laughs.

"Oh, Scarlett." He adds. I wait for him to continue.

"Check your glove box," he says and hangs up. I open it to find a manila folder with my last name on it. Inside, I see the same receipts and pictures of Mom, along with Elliot's name on a sticky note. My name is written beside his, with details from the night I was almost raped. *This must be The Society's property. Callum must've taken it for me.* I smile, thinking of the man who'd do anything to protect me, and the answers I finally have.

I crave a round with Ricco. It's the one thing that makes me forget. I turn and make sure that my gym bag is in the back seat. Thankfully, it is.

I drive to the gym. Once I step inside, the familiar lemon scent greets me. I look around for Ricco and spot him in the ring.

I wave to him as I head to my locker. I open it and see the pictures. My hand runs over them like I've done a hundred times, but this time I feel guilty. I started boxing when Mom left. Dad said I needed to put my anger to good use and pushed me toward Ricco. He dropped me off one day and said, "I'll pick you up in an hour." It feels like just yesterday, but so many things have changed. So many things that will never be the same.

Over the years, I've changed. I don't fight against myself anymore. Now, all my demons are at the surface, and I know what I need to do.

I shut the locker door and carry my gloves over to the ring. I lean against it as Ricco finishes with the younger kid he's training.

"Thought you were a goner." He looks to me.

"Are you kidding me? You could never get rid of me."

He smiles from ear to ear, knowing that's the truth.

I watch him train the boy. He looks troubled, with tattered clothes and holes in the bottom of his sneakers. Once they finish, Ricco walks over and ruffles his hair.

"Tomorrows another day, kid. Don't beat yourself up," he says. The boy climbs out of the ring with his shoulders down and his face flat, defeated.

I jump into the centre of the ring and slip my sparring gloves on. Ricco throws his hands up and I bounce from side to side. It's as if I haven't missed a day.

After I take a few jabs, I stop and look at him.

"I don't tell you enough, but you're amazing you know?"

"Oh, shut up. Quit trying to throw me off." He looks off into the gym.

"I'm serious. You save us— kids like him... kids like me. You give us a safe haven when we need it most."

Tears gather in his eyes as he sniffles and shakes his head.

"Don't go soft on me now." He punches his fist together. "Come on, let's go."

I laugh and throw him another punch. It's exactly what I needed.

When we finish our round, I grab my bag, change, and wave to Ricco before I leave.

"Don't wait so long between sessions next time." He yells.

"I missed you too, old man." I push the door open and walk toward my car. I pull my phone out and see a text from Callum.

Callum: 437 University Ave, Boston.

I type the address into my maps. "Boston Medical Rehabilitation Facility." *Rehab? Why did he send me this?*

I get in the car and look at my phone again... This isn't what I think it is? *No.*

He got her out.

I follow the map as I start my drive into the city.

I've never enjoyed Boston much. I don't go to the city often, and when I do, I'm always reminded of why I don't— the noise, the chaos. Adrenaline pumps through my veins.

What will I say to her once I'm there? How do I tell her that I'm sorry for everything I've done? I want her to know that we can get through all of this, together.

I want to call Callum and thank him, but I have to get there first.

As I approach the large building, I pull into the parking lot and prepare myself. I sigh before I get out of the car—*it's now or never.*

I walk through the front glass door. The foyer is lined by a wall of windows, and the entire building is surrounded by tons of gardens and stone paths. I feel like I'm on a movie set. I step up to the lady that sits at the reception desk.

"Hello Miss, how can I help you?" The roots of her hair are grey, and wrinkles trace her forehead. Her glasses sit at the edge of her nose—I have an urge to reach over the counter and push them up.

"Vanessa Voss. I'm her, I'm her, um, daughter."

"Just one moment." She looks at her computer screen and clicks her mouse.

"She's in room 203. Up the elevator and then second door on your left."

"Okay, thank you." I smile.

"Let us know if you need anything else."

Jeez, the people here sure are nice. How can mom afford this place.

I go up the elevator and stand outside the second door on the left. I stare at it, unable to bring my hand up to knock. I feel like a disappointment.

Just then, the door opens, and woman in a crop top and baggy black jeans walks out.

"Oh sorry, I was just leaving." She looks me up and down with a smile. "And you are?"

"Her daughter." I purse my lips. "And *you* are?"

"Her sponsor, Lexi."

Lexi's pixie cut hair is bright red—clearly it's not natural. She has a piercing through her eyebrow and isn't the typical person I'd envision as Mom's new best friend. I enter the room and shut the door behind me.

"That was awkward." I mumble under my breath.

I walk further into the room and spot Mom, sitting in a chair by the window.

"Mom?" I call out to her softly.

She slowly turns her head. Her face is pale, and her eyes are red, like she's been crying. Still in her pajamas, her golden hair needs a comb.

"Scarlett." She uses a tone I've never heard, it's not happiness or excitement or sadness—it's just calm.

"Hi Mom." I walk over to the window, not sure whether to hug her or cry.

"How are you, Sweetie?" She quietly asks.

"I'm okay. How are you? I'm so glad you're here." I reach for her hand. It's probably the most affection I've shown her in years.

"I'm glad too." She forces a smile and bites her lip, trying not to cry.

I don't know where to start, so I just begin.

"Mom, I went to your house. I found the box. I know everything." I can't look away from her. I owe her that.

"You had no right Scarlett." She remains still.

"No right? No Mom, *you* had no right. Do you know how many times I fell asleep crying? How many times I thought you didn't love me? How many times I thought it was my fault? I hated you for that. I... I was awful. All while you were quietly suffocating." She keeps biting her lip, but her tears fall.

"Scarlett, I couldn't tell you. You were so young, you had so much life ahead of you. Look where you got. I wouldn't change my decision... because it got you where you are today."

The person I've cried for, the person I've needed the last ten years, is finally here.

"I'm.. I'm.. so sorry, Mom."

"Honey, it was never your fault." She places her other hand on top of mine.

"We should've known that you'd never leave us unless you had to." I pause. "Dad? Does he—"

"No. I haven't told him... you should though." She looks out the window. "Your dad gave up on me a long time ago."

"He's never given up on you Mom, he never will." She faces me with a warm smile. It's one I haven't seen in a long time.

"I'm so mad at them Mom, they took so much from us. So many years and missed memories." My tears match hers.

"We can't look back honey." She brushes the side of my cheek with her thumb. Her fingers are soft. She blinks through tears. "Thank Callum for me when you get back. He comes with lots of baggage Scarlett, but he loves you. I'd love to hear what your dad thinks of him?"

"Thank him?" I don't understand.

"He got me here. He bargained with Leo and got me out. It must not have been easy. He found this place and brought me here. He's paying for it all. I didn't want to accept, but he insisted."

My heart skips a beat. *Callum fucking Mercer.*

"I love him, Mom."

"And what's a little carry-on luggage hmm? Who am I to judge. He saved my baby girl after all." I smile as she laughs.

"Yes, I guess he did."

"We're going to be okay, Honey." For the first time in a long time, I believe her.

"So, the silver phase? That's when it all, um, started?"

She looks down at her hands and then back at me. "There's so much that I'm ashamed of, but I'll tell you anything you want to know."

"Archer Alder." The life from her eyes drains at the mention of his name.

"Not that. I'm not ready for that, Scarlett."

I wrap my arms around her, bringing us both the comfort we've needed all along.

"I'm so sorry Mom. You don't have to face any of this alone anymore. I'm here now."

And just like that, after years of trauma and trials, we talk like two teenagers who are getting to know each other.

For so long, I've tried to fill the void with so many other things like boxing and school, but at the end of the day, I needed my mom. And finally, I have her.

Keep Your Enemies Closer

Callum

Angel: *Thank you.*

I tuck my phone back into my pocket and picture her with her mom. I think of all the moments that were taken from them, and all the time they have to make up for.

It was always my plan to set Vanessa free. Things just fell into place now instead of later. I'm glad that Scarlett has her back in her life. While I don't understand the depths of their relationship, I'll try—for her.

I have to meet with Leo at The Society today. Their downfall must come from within, but we aren't in a hurry to do so. The Society has killed my family and attempted to bring me down in the process. I need my well thought out revenge, and I'm in it for the long haul, not a quick defeat.

I haven't fought in a couple weeks, and I'm craving one now more than ever. I need it to tame the darkness. I pull a cigarette out from my pocket and walk into the place I vow to take down. It's the first time I've been back here since that night.

Everything is measured by that day now—the five of us talk about things before that day or after. Nothing else matters. I light the cigarette and walk into the mansion.

Usually, smoking inside is limited to the parlour, but they're about to see an unhinged side of me they've never thought they'd experience.

I don't forgive, and I don't forget. Leo knows my terms.

The once beautifully aged wood floor now looks decrepit and worn. The curtains that hang around the windows seem colourless and dull. They were once a luxurious accessory, but now they are forgotten.

I climb the stairs, ready to face whatever consequences await me. I can't rule out the possibility of the other Highers wanting me dead. I'm not just a threat. I'm a ticking time bomb. The voices down the hall tell me that Leo isn't alone. I don't hear Deluca's voice, but he could be in there as well. I roll my neck as I get closer to the door frame.

As I walk into the parlour, everyone stops talking. I see Leo, Deluca, Archer, Victor, Chase, and five pledges who recently completed their initiations.

Victor steps forward. "Ah, just the man we were talking about." His voice sounds sarcastic.

My eyes shift to Leo, he doesn't nod in reassurance like the others do. Instead, he stares right at me. *Something is wrong.* My shoulders tense as my guard goes up instantly, but I don't reach for the gun in the back of my pants concealed by my belt. I want to see how this plays out first.

Victor demands my attention by clearing his throat. He adjusts his cuff links and gives me an ominous look.

"Things change now. There's a specific hierarchy within The Society, and it will be followed."

Well, I didn't expect this. Victor Roberts, District Attorney for the city of Boston, is the new silent leader of The Society.

"We've let too many emotions interfere with legacy. This ends now." His stern voice comes naturally.

"Scarlett is off limits, not because of the shit show you created, but because she's an extension of my... family. If I hear of any more women being targeted, I will not hesitate to take matters into my own hands. And *you*."

He takes a step toward me.

"One wrong move and you're done. No more killing aimlessly. You do what we say, when we say it. You're on probation, Mercer. The only reason you're still here is because you can't be trusted."

Keep your friends close.

He left out the part where no one else could do what I do. No one else has such high stakes, and I'll be damned if he thinks I trust him in a world where Scarlett exists. *Extended family... not if I can help it.*

Leo briefly closes his eyes. He knows that Victor is saying all the right things to push me close to the edge.

I have to warn Harrison and Stirling of what's to come. More is at stake now. We need this uprising more than ever. With someone as power hungry as Victor leading the other venomous men, I worry that we might have to eliminate The Society for good.

"You don't need to worry about Callum. I'll keep a close eye on him." Leo's words seem like a distraction.

"I don't need a babysitter." I spit through my teeth.

"No, you need a leash, but that wouldn't be humane now, would it?" Victor's words cause a physical reaction, my hands close at my sides and my back straightens.

A tight hand grips my shoulder. I turn and see Harrison. Through his eyes, he tells me to hold it together.

"I can't stay all day. We'll set up an official meeting for next week. In the meantime, there's a new drop site for the East end. I'll text you the details." Victor looks at Harrison as he walks out of the room. Deluca, Archer, and Chase follow him.

The atmosphere shifts as soon as they leave the room. A few other pledges walk out, while Leo makes his way toward the window to watch Victor drive off.

"Well, that was unexpected." Stirling says as he comes in and shuts the door behind him. I can tell that this is going to be hard for him, given his complicated relationship status with Sophia. While they aren't together, his eyes don't land on anyone else. She's the only one he sees.

"I was going to warn you, but I didn't have time, he wanted to talk about the new drop sites before." Leo speaks up.

"It's fine." My words are sharp.

"We just need to shift our plan a bit. It might take longer, but we can still demand change," Harrison says.

"We need to be strategic, being on the wrong side of the DA could ruin all of us." Leo's always the logical one.

"I don't know if taking it over is the right move anymore, we may need to dissolve it," I say.

"But that could mean the end of everyone." Stirling adds with confusion.

"Not if we do it right. We don't act until we have everything that we need." I look at Harrison then back at Stirling. "You're going to have to pick. Your blood or your brother's."

They know what this means. Their dad can't be trusted. He's been in the game for too long and has relied on The Society for over twenty years. He rose to the top beside my father and Victor. He won't betray them now.

I look down at my watch. *I should go meet Scarlett.*

"Keep me posted with any updates or new information. We're just getting started, it doesn't all need to be discussed tonight." I turn away and walk out, past my chosen family.

I drive to the greenhouse by campus—the only place I feel at ease. I walk into the musty shed and feel the closest thing to home. The sweet smell of roses reminds me of all that I have to live for.

The Society does not control me. Only one person can, and she's five foot six and relies on sour gummies to calm her down. She also packs a mean right hook. *My Angel.*

Epilogue

Scarlett

I can't remember a time where I've felt so at peace with my life. It's winter break, and Sophia and I decided to go away for the weekend. We didn't want to go too far, so we opted for Harrison and Stirling's cottage. Naturally, the boys followed us here. It's become the place where the five of us go when we need time away from reality. The bond that I've formed with Harrison and Stirling feels like I've gained the brothers I've always wanted.

They say that the people who you surround yourself with become a reflection of yourself. I'm not naive to the fact that the five of us aren't perfect, but we sure as hell are strong.

The cool breeze pushes through the sliding door, masking the tension that remains under my surface. The only thing we know how to do is carry on. The smell of Italian spices comes from the stove. When we're here, we always take turns cooking dinner. Tonight, Sophia is cooking shrimp stir-fry.

The Aldens and my very own Mr. Mercer are amazing cooks. They made pasta last night, and even though I've never been to Italy, I would plead that it was some of the best pasta ever made.

Tonight, they are going to teach me to play the card game 'Euchre'. Apparently, it's not hard once you figure it out, but I'll be the judge of that.

Even though we all try to unwind, I can tell that the guys are still tense. It's no secret that they are plotting something within The Society. Callum hasn't told me all of it, but I know that there's been a shift and they are planning to change it. He says the less I know the better. I can tell by the way that he acts and talks about it that the stakes are high. I can't imagine how hard everything is on him, and I'd wait forever trying to understand.

As I chop veggies, hands snake around my waist from behind.

"Um, she's working!" Sophia yells at Callum and points her knife at him.

"Alright, alright, I'm just saying hi." He puts his hands up and backs away.

"Jeez, the guy can't leave you alone for ten minutes."

Dinner was amazing, as usual. The guys are on dish duty while I go over to the wine rack in the pantry and grab another bottle of wine. Harrison and Callum won't have more than a glass with us, but Stirling is always up to split a bottle.

Stirling puts away the last of the dishes while Harrison and Callum hang up the dish towels, then walk outside to the back deck.

"Everything okay?" I ask Stirling.

"Yeah, just Society stuff." He replies.

It seems like more than that.

"Have you seen Sophia?" He asks as he looks down the hall.

"Yeah, I think she just went to change."

He follows her around like a lost puppy most days, but lately something has been different between them—something more real. I hope she knows she can always talk to me about it.

I go to one of the guest rooms Callum and I are staying in and throw a sweater on. I look out the sliding door. Callum's back faces me while Harrison leans against the railing.

It looks like they've stopped talking, so I open the door and go outside.

"What are you guys doing out here? It's freezing!" I rub the sides of my arms and cross them.

Callum smiles at me like I'm the only thing that matters.

"Hey, you." I say and walk over to him. He wraps his arms around me and the noise in my mind fades.

"I've been wanting to talk to you." His voice shifts.

"Oh?" I can't help but worry.

"There's been a change within The Society, something we didn't see coming." His face scrunches, almost like he's in pain. "Victor Roberts is the new silent leader."

I gasp. "What does that mean?"

He looks down at me. "It means that your safety is guaranteed and that's all that matters." His jaw stiffens.

I know there's more that he isn't saying.

"Callum, what does that mean for you?" I watch his face for any reaction.

"It means that we're going to have to change the plan. We're going to be closely watched now."

"Oh." Their original plan was to bring The Society down from the inside and change the direction it's headed. His face remains stoic.

"Callum, what aren't you telling me?"

"It means that they own me, Angel. It means that I have to play by their rules, for now."

I rub his arm. Callum can't be tamed, but he will suffer to make things work. He's not only doing this for himself, he's doing it for everyone that they've hurt. All the women that have been abused, all the lives that they've taken. I grab his hand in mine, and we walk back inside. Everyone sits at the table. Callum's words replay in my head.

He's lived through the trenches of hell, and now he needs to go against everything he's been trying so hard to change. Callum needs me now more than ever, and I'm not going anywhere.

Although we've already survived a war, something worse is coming, I can feel it.

I look to Sophia, who looks over her shoulder at Stirling, he's already lost in her eyes.

The darkest battles are always fought in the shadows... and some shadows never fade.

The End.

About the Author

Cassy Vincent writes dark, emotional romances where obsession, secrets, and slow-burn tension collide. Her stories dive into the shadows of love, where it's messy, dangerous, and worth everything. When she isn't plotting morally grey heroes, she's hanging out with her partner and two daughters, walking her dog, or sneaking in one more chapter of her favourite book.

Made in United States
North Haven, CT
07 October 2025